Written in Stone

A.J. Cadell Mystery 1

Diane Bator

Escape With a Writer Publishing

Written in Stone: A.J. Cadell Mystery Book 1

Print ISBN: 978-1-7383328-0-9

Copyright © Diane Bator, 2024

Published by Escape With a Writer Publishing

303-69 Gateway Drive, Airdrie, Alberta, T4B 4H7

There are so many people I would like to thank you have supported me on my journey.

Headwaters Writers' Guild in Orangeville, Ontario for their encouragement to send my book babies into the world.

Joy George and the late Dawn Dowdle, for starting my on my publishing path.

Jude Pittman, BWL Publishing, for taking a chance on me.

Gemma Halliday, GH Publishing, for giving my Gilda series life.

WCYR, Pam Bustin & the Monday Muses, Sisters in Crime Toronto, Crime Writers of Canada, and the Next Chapter Group. I can't even describe all I've learned from all of you!

Nancy M. Bell, Victoria Chatham, & Astrid Theilgaard – here's to many more lunches! Thank you for the friendship and laughs!

Marilyn Kleiber and M.J. Moores for our monthly sessions. You've both been fountains of information and help!

Mickey Mikkelson for the ongoing dedication and understanding.

Huge thank you to my amazing Beta readers for this book who all went above and beyond: Sonja Briggs, Victoria Chatham, Kathleen Kalb, Winona Kent, Maggie Kirton,

Marilyn Kleiber, Katie O'Connor & Angela Van Breeman. Talented writers, editors, and fabulous friends! I wish you all great success with your books.

Darryl & Kathy for road trips, long talks, and never ending support and encouragement.

My mom, Trudy, for life and love.

Matt, Will & Athena – You are my heart and soul! Love you forever and always!

I know I've forgotten some but please know you are loved and cherished for being a part of my life!

Contents

Chapter One

S weat trickled down my spine as the phone rang twice before I started to chant, "Pick up. Come on, Roxie. Pick up."

I shivered as I paced in front of my bedroom window. Three more rings. After two more, I whispered, "I know you're home, Roxie, and Paul's out of town, so pick up."

"What do you want, Alison?" my sister snapped after the eighth ring.

"I had another nightmare."

"It's two in the morning and I'm trying to sleep. Go wake up your roommate."

I sat on the edge of my double bed. "Please, Roxie, I just need to—"

"Where's your journal? The one the therapist told you to keep," she said. "Open it to the back cover. Then I want you to write down the same thing I told you the last time you called in the middle of the night."

"That was months ago." I reached into my nightstand then sat back against my headboard and clutched the plain black journal to my chest with no intention of writing a single word. I knew exactly what she was about to say.

"You and Dad were in a car accident when you were little," she started as I lip-synced her word for word. "Dad died. You suffered a brain injury. That's why you have headaches and can't remember things. Your brain makes up stories that give you nightmares, then you get confused. Heaven knows how you can keep your thoughts straight to write books."

I flipped open my journal to a sketch I'd drawn of a large house and a fire. Not once had I ever drawn a car. For some reason, the truth felt so wrong.

"You wrote down all those dreams and stories in your journal, remember?" she asked. "If it weren't for those journals, you would never have written your first novel."

Although my room was semi-dark, my gaze darted to where the poster of my first book cover, *Kiss of Velvet*, hung on the wall. A gift from my roommate Emily when I launched my romance novel in a local bookstore run by one of her friends.

"Did you write it down?" My sister's question jarred me back to the present.

The sound of her voice was what calmed me, not the story. "Yes."

Roxie groaned before she whispered, "Alison, you can't keep calling me in the middle of the night, it drives me crazy. I can't keep doing this."

"I know."

She hesitated. "Why don't you call Mom?"

"You know why. She won't answer."

"What about Emily?"

"She wears headphones to bed, so she can't hear me or the neighbors."

My sister hesitated then chuckled. "I think I'll start doing the same thing."

"I wish you wouldn't." I blew out a breath and deflated over my journal. "I'm sorry, Roxie. It's just that I haven't had any nightmares in months, and I don't know why—"

When she cut me off, her voice softened. "It's okay. Get some sleep, Alison. I'll drop by the candy store tomorrow. Maybe we can go for lunch. Since you're my Maid of Honor, I need your help to pick invitations and a theme for my wedding."

"Why doesn't Paul help?"

Roxie chuckled. "Aside from being away with his buddies? He's hopeless. He says he likes whichever ones I like, which is great but not all that constructive when I have no idea what I like."

"Why don't you ask Mom?" I regretted the question as soon as it left my mouth.

"Don't be absurd. You know what her tastes are like."

"Over the top and expensive."

She yawned then said, "You know it. Now that you're feeling better, we both need to get some sleep. I'll call Mom in the morning. Maybe we can meet for dinner tomorrow instead of lunch."

"That sounds nice. Goodnight, Rox. Thank you for not hanging up on me."

I plugged my phone into the charger before I reached for the odd little rock I'd carried around since I was a kid. Although I had no idea where it came from, someone took the time to carve a deep, crude pineapple with spiky leaves into one side. The rock became my worry stone over the years. It wasn't so much the pineapple that comforted me as the feeling of the rough lines beneath my fingers and the distraction of wondering who put so much work into creating it.

Instinct told me it was important, but that didn't explain my almost obsessive attachment to it.

***

"You had another nightmare?" Emily Nelson, my roommate and best friend since second grade, asked on her way out of the bathroom the next morning. Her elbow-length black hair dripped water onto the thin carpet. "Why didn't you try to wake me?"

I wrapped my arms around my stomach. "I called Roxie. She wasn't happy, but she offered to call Mom to arrange dinner tonight."

Emily stopped and frowned. "Uh-oh. What does she want this time?"

"Roxie?" I asked. "Help with her wedding invitations."

"Nah. I know your sister. She's after something otherwise she'd have dinner with your mom and leave you out. I'll bet you ten bucks she needs to ask your mom for money and wants you to back her up."

As I hopped into the shower, I had to agree. My sister—despite my late-night phone calls—rarely did something for nothing. Every time I called for help, there was a price tag.

Barton's Candies was busy that day. I ran off my feet restocking jujubes and jellybeans while avoiding my boss who always seemed to find "just one more thing" for me to do. I was surprised to see no sign of Roxie by the end of my shift at six o'clock.

With a sigh of relief, I wandered the twelve blocks home. That was when Roxie began to text me every five minutes to say she would pick me up at six-thirty and I'd better not be late since we were meeting Mom at the restaurant at exactly at six-forty-five. Knowing my mom, even if we were a minute early, we'd still be late. Ingrid Tracey-Cadell had no threshold for tardiness in either her clients or her kids.

"Good timing," Emily said as she glanced up from her laptop. "I'm trying to come up with a good name for my new blog. Which do you like better 'For Goodness Sake' or 'Zest for Goodness'?"

Not only was she a wonderful cook, but she was trying to build a reputation as a food blogger. Sharing videos of her creating amazing food would win over hearts and stomachs.

"How about 'Emily's Good Eats in Toronto'? You are a food critic, aren't you?"

"That was awfully hasty. Give it a little thought, will you?"

I glanced down at my dusty, gray cargo pants and pink uniform shirt. "I have to change. I'll never hear the end of it if I showed up for dinner dressed like this."

"Lucky you. Where are you going?"

"Figaro's."

Emily batted her fake eyelashes. "Oh, yummy. Try the seafood risotto and wear that blue dress you got when you broke up with Cory last time."

"You make it sound like we break up once a week."

"Well, you do," she said.

I blew out a long breath. "My mom will hate that dress. I got it at that clearance place."

"Yeah, but it's sexy and makes your eyes pop. Besides, you work in Barton's Candy store and have no money, what does she expect? Once your romance novels become best-sellers, you can shop where she shops."

I shook my head. "Not a chance. Those places are so pretentious."

Emily tapped her pen on the table. "Why didn't you wake me up to talk last night?"

"I needed to hear my sister's voice. She recited the same thing she always does. Accident, brain damage, blah, blah, blah." I paused. "What I don't understand is if I have brain damage, why do I feel as normal as everyone else?"

She shrugged. "Maybe you were some super genius before the crash and now you're just as lame as the rest of us mere mortals."

I chuckled, wandering to my room to change. I pulled on the blue dress then, as an afterthought, stuck my pineapple-etched rock it in my purse. In case things got a little iffy with my mother and I needed comfort.

My phone chimed as I reached for my coat. "Roxie's downstairs. I'll see you later, Em."

Emily pulled a foil pan from the oven. The divine smell of her delicious butter chicken was enough to change my mind on most days. "Don't have dessert though. I'm making a cheesecake to celebrate."

I pulled my boots on with half a mind to stay home. "Celebrate what?"

"It's Wednesday," she said. "Oh, and my new blog you forgot about already. I'll pack some butter chicken and rice for your lunch tomorrow. Make sure to brag to your coworkers about your roommate who's an amazing chef."

After she set the pan on the table, I caught a whiff and sighed. "I already do brag and they're super jealous. Maybe I can convince Roxie to let you cater her wedding."

"Why not? Me and my three pots and two pans. Piece of cake. What I wouldn't give for a big, beautiful kitchen."

"Maybe one day," I told her as I left. Rather than taking the stairs, I decided to burn off some energy by taking the stairs. By the time I got to my sister's car, she scowled as she tapped the steering wheel with the tips of her long purple nails that glittered under the streetlights.

"Feeling better today?" she asked.

"For the most part." I closed the passenger door of her Passat and buckled my seatbelt.

"That's good," she said. "Do me a favor and don't bring up my wedding tonight. Mom's been trying to take over. That folder beside you has some sample invitations she got from one of her suppliers. That's what I need your help with."

"She is an actual wedding planner, you know. Trying to keep her out is pointless. She's bound to dig her talons in sooner or later." I reached for the white folder wedged between my seat and the gear shift, then used the light from my phone to check them out.

Roxie sighed as she drove. "Yeah, I know. The problem is she refuses to do it for free, or even at cost. I'm just another client."

I grimaced. "So much for you being her favorite."

The invitations ranged from gold and silver matte embossed with black or white to plain white cards with a ghastly shade of green. I cringed and asked, "Green?"

"Don't start. It's not even a nice green. It looks like baby vomit."

One invitation caught my eye. Simple white satin paper with black lettering. "This is pretty. The satin paper would go better with the fancy writing, not the block lettering."

"That's great," Roxie said. "I can make those at home for a quarter of the price. Told you I needed your help. You're the artist in the family."

"Writer. I can't draw." No one knew, or needed to know, about the child-like sketches in my journal.

"Writer. When's your next book coming out, by the way? I need a distraction."

"As soon as I write it." I gazed out the window. White capped waves danced in Lake Ontario. While a swim was out of the question, I loved to take walks along the shoreline after dinner. Just not in winter wearing a dress and heels.

Mom—aka the elegant and emotionally challenged wedding planner Ingrid Tracey-Cadell—was already seated at a table near a floor-to-ceiling window overlooking the Toronto Harbor with a martini in one hand. Her long legs were crossed at the ankle near her chair. When she saw us, she stood to greet my sister and then turned to me.

"Alison, you look nice." Mom hugged me then kissed my cheek. "Your sister said you had another nightmare. Have you been taking your medications?"

I bowed my head and muttered. "Yes, I have. Thanks, Rox, all bets are off."

"It's stress," she insisted. "You need a better job. One that pays well."

My sister growled. "Mom."

Our mother took a sip of her drink as we sat. "What? It's not exactly a secret Alison has issues. Did you call your doctor?"

"I had to work today. We'll be getting busier with the holiday season coming."

My mom wagged her finger. "It's only the end of October. Doctor Agrandie may need to increase your medications. I'll call him in the morning since you can't be bothered."

I reached for my water. "I just saw him a month ago. He cut my dose back to see how I'd react. So far, I've been fine."

She patted my hand. "Not if you're having nightmares."

"Only a couple."

"You need to be honest with the man," Mom said. "If you don't tell him the truth, he'll cut you off your medication completely and then where will you be?"

My eyes welled. My sister could step in any time now.

Roxie piped up as if reading my mind. "I asked you both to come because I have something to tell you. Paul and I want to have kids."

"Of course you do." Mom's smile stiffened like someone hit her with a blast of spray starch. "Once your career is established and your fiancé has a real job, you should buy a beautiful home in a neighborhood with high-ranking schools. Two kids would be perfect."

"I meant right after the wedding."

Despite my medication, I itched to order the largest glass of wine the restaurant offered.

Mom's penciled eyebrows rose before she took a gulp of her martini. The calm before the storm. "Is that a wise idea? You have your new career to think about and Paul's still looking for the perfect job. Both of your careers are far from stable."

Roxie's jaw tightened as she met my gaze. I wished she'd given me the heads up rather than made me look at invitations.

"It's better than waiting until I'm in my forties, then never being able to give you grandkids," she said, earning a twitch of Mom's cheek. "What I need from you is Dad's medical history."

Mom's face hardened. Her cheeks paled before her next gulp. Finally, she asked, "Why?"

Roxie toyed with her fork. "In case there's any heart disease, diabetes, or that sort of thing on his side of the family."

"Then you'll have to ask him," she told us, tossing back the rest of her drink.

We both stared as if Ingrid Tracey-Cadell, the woman we'd called Mom our entire lives, had completely lost her mind before Roxie and I said, "What?"

She sucked back some invisible remains in her glass before she flagged down our server. "Ask him yourself."

"I can't ask him. He's dead," Roxie said. "At least that's what you've told us for the past twenty years. Were you lying?"

"Did you abduct us?" I asked.

Mom huffed and rolled her eyes. When the server arrived, she ordered a double martini, dry with two olives. Roxie ordered a large glass of wine. I compromised and asked for a white wine spritzer.

After a long couple of minutes, and an off-limits warm bun with butter, our mom pursed her lips. Finally, she spoke the words that made my entire life feel like a lie. "Perry Beyer is alive and a deadbeat. Last I heard he was still a smokejumper somewhere up north."

I clutched my water glass with both hands like a life preserver as my heart raced. I'd drawn so many pictures of fires in my journal that she said was because of the car accident. I gazed at the faint ripples that rose from the backs of my hands and up my wrists. Second degree burns from trying to escape the car.

"What's a smokejumper?" Roxie reached for her wine the instant the server placed it on the table.

"He jumps out of airplanes to fight fires." My words seemed to come from across the room.

Mom flinched then cleared her throat. "Exactly."

"Why haven't you ever told us before?" I asked, hands shaking so badly I placed them under my thighs before I spilled my water. "You told everyone Dad and I were in a car accident. Were we?"

She fluttered her eyelashes. Was it possible she was tearing up? "Alison, I had to protect you after everything that happened."

My heart raced and my breath came in short gasps. "So, you lied to the doctor and to me?"

"You don't understand—"

Coming to dinner was a mistake. I should have stayed home to help Emily with her blog, eat butter chicken, and drink sparkling water. My ears rang as I made my escape to the washroom and shook one of my anxiety pills into my hand.

Roxie burst into the bathroom, keeping a safe distance while I ran cold water into my hand to wash the pill down. "I'm sorry, Ali. I had no idea,"

Splashing my face would only ruin the small bit of makeup I'd worn. Like my mom needed something else to complain about. "Did she send you in here to drag me back?"

"She has a fresh martini. I took advantage of the distraction."

"I should've ordered a bottle of wine."

"You don't want to do that. Booze messes with your meds and you can't sleep, remember?" Roxie leaned against the counter. "I'll trade you drinks since I have to drive. Believe me, I'll polish off a bottle for both of us when I get home. You didn't tell me the doctor was weaning you off some of your meds. That's good news, right?"

I let the faucet's sensor turn off the water while I stared at my reflection in the mirror. "Yeah, we should celebrate. Except that after tonight I'll have to double my dose again. I'm having more nightmares than ever. Maybe Mom's right."

"What if she's wrong, Ali?"

"What do you mean?"

"For what it's worth, I didn't know Dad was alive either. What if those nightmares are your brain's way of telling you the truth about what happened?"

My eyes grew wide as I faced her. "What do you mean?"

The washroom door opened and a heavy-set woman wearing a basic black dress and a long string of pearls strolled inside. She ignored us as she sequestered herself in a stall.

Roxie leaned closer as she lowered her voice. "What if you don't really need those pills and the doctor's only trying to help?"

"Then why would I be taking them?"

She hesitated before blurting out, "To keep you from remembering. To keep you numb and under Mom's control."

I shook my head. "Then why aren't you on medication?"

Roxie's eyes watered. "Because I wasn't there. I don't know what happened, just that you were in the hospital covered in bandages with..." She paused for a deep breath. "Ali, Mom's kept so many secrets from us that I don't even know if she knows the truth anymore. Maybe you and I need to find him."

"Who?"

"Dad. We both need answers, especially you."

I closed my eyes to keep in my own tears. "What makes you think he wants to be found?"

"We won't know until we find him, right?"

I gazed up at the ceiling. "First, we have to get through dinner. She won't be in the mood for conversation now."

"This was my fault, Ali," my sister said. "I'll take one for the team and ask her advice about my wedding."

"I so wish I could have a stiff drink right now."

She hugged me. "Don't do it. I'll text you later and tell you how weird it feels when the room spins."

Wedding talk seemed to magically erase our earlier conversation. When we sent Mom home in a cab an hour later, she was more sheets to the wind than I could count, which concerned me. Roxie and I had both seen her drink before, but not like that. I bet my sister ten dollars our mom regretted ever opening her mouth about him.

"No bet," she said. "We're in agreement on that one."

During the drive home, Mom's revelation about Perry Beyer occupied every corner of my mind.

While I helped Emily polish off half the pumpkin cheesecake, I filled her in on what little I knew. After she took our plates to the kitchen, I sat on the couch with my laptop to search for my father online. I found several Perry Beyers. Obituaries, social media sites, and images. Not ready to sift through any of them, I slammed my laptop shut and took a deep breath.

"Can I take advantage of your writer's brain to help get my first blog post ready?" Emily asked. "I have pictures, links, and buckets of enthusiasm, but can't string three words together."

"You're a journalist. What's wrong with your writer brain?"

"It's stressing out and gone into hibernation mode," she said. "After three glasses of wine, my brain is pretty much embalmed."

I sat next to her with a laugh. "I'd say that was a bad life choice."

She giggled, leaning against me. "I am an amazing journalist, Ali. If you want, I can use my resources to help you find your father. Once I'm sober, I mean. Hopefully, he can tell you what happened."

"Let's get this blog finished, so we can go to sleep."

"Maybe you'd better type," she said. "I have two left index fingers. I also have a feeling I'll end up writing about pickled brains, which is not as appetizing as Butter Chicken."

Two hours later, I fell asleep with the pineapple rock in my hand. The nightmare I woke from that night took on a whole new meaning. Instead of calling anyone for moral support, I sat in bed for over an hour to sketch and make notes about what I saw.

Fire. A child. A horse. The sensation of falling.

None of the images made sense. I always dreamed about fire, but I didn't remember being around horses. Of course, I didn't remember being a child.

Chapter Two

"The million-dollar question is are you going to help me find him or not?" Roxie asked over the display case two days later. Her long, dark curls were damp with Toronto mist. The day before, she was too hung over to crawl out of bed.

"I don't even know where to start."

"Come on, Ali," she said. "How hard can it be to find a man?"

A middle-aged woman shopping nearby raised her eyebrows. "You'd be surprised."

Roxie and I laughed as she walked away.

"How do you expect me to find a man as elusive as Perry Beyer?" I asked, folding my arms across my stomach. "Depending on what happened, he could have changed his name, had plastic surgery, or left the country."

My sister scowled at me over the glass display case filled with hand-made chocolates. "You're a writer. Don't you live for doing research?"

"I'm a romance novelist, Roxie. All that's required is daydreaming and not much research. So far."

"Aren't the skills all the same no matter what genre you write?" she asked. "You still need to find things to write about."

"That doesn't mean I know how to find someone who doesn't want to be found. I'm not a detective," I told her, running a hand over my tied back hair. When I reached the odd series of bumps and scars that came from the accident. I closed my eyes. Had Mom lied about them, too?

Neither of us had heard from our father in twenty years. My queries over the past two days had ended in dead ends in the wilds of British Columbia, more specifically near Mount St. Patrick on Vancouver Island. I'd abandoned my search in frustration.

"Are you in line, dear?" An elderly woman tapped Roxie's arm.

"No, sorry. We're just... I need to get back to work."

The woman placed a book on top of a box of chocolate truffles and smiled at me. "Good afternoon, my dear."

I stepped closer to the cash register returning her smile with one of my own and asked, "Did you find everything you were looking for today?"

"That depends. Are you A.J. Cadell?"

Roxie raised her eyebrows. "The romance writer? Yes, she is."

My breath caught in my throat. No one ever called me A.J. except my readers. "Yes, I am."

"Splendid. Then, yes, I did." She peered out from between a white fedora and a lacy white scarf. Way overdressed for Toronto's mild October weather. "Would you sign my book please, Miss Cadell?"

Moment of Weakness. My second novel had come out a month ago. While I'd received great feedback, reporters weren't exactly hounding me for interviews. Well, there was that one. I shuddered.

Roxie gave a finger wave. "Call you later."

The woman watched her leave before she said, "Your sister Roxie is very pretty."

I gasped. The blue-eyed woman suddenly made me wary. "How do you know my sister's name?"

"You and I have two things in common, Miss Cadell. We're suckers for a good romance and we both do our homework."

My heart raced as I reached for a pen. Was I famous enough to have a stalker? "Who shall I make it out to?"

She pushed her scarf away from her bright pink lips. "Just sign your name. It's a gift for someone special."

I signed the front page with a flourish. "You just made my day. Thank you."

"Oh, no, dear. Thank you. You have no idea what this means to me." Her eyes, the color of blue-raspberry cotton candy, lit up. "I imagine you get hounded for autographs every day."

"Not exactly," I admitted, ringing in her order. "Everyone here is an actor, a singer, or a writer. We're all hungry for sugar and a paycheck."

She chuckled. "I see. That's a shame. I'll bet that if you set up a table with your books and some cute bookmarks and candy hearts, you would sell out in no time. Chocolate and romance novels do go hand in hand."

"I'm not sure they're a Christmas kind of thing."

"Oh, they're all the rage at any time of year," she said. "You're a pretty girl. You must have a dozen gentleman callers who help you write such delicious books."

Gentleman callers? I grinned as I handed her the autographed copy of my novel. Romantic daydreams were my specialty. Romance in reality, not so much.

"Excuse me, Miss Cadell," Loribeth, my boss, stood two feet away. "I need you to take care of paying customers, please."

"She is paying." I bagged her candy and the book, then winced an apology.

The woman winked. "It was a pleasure to meet you. I'm sure we'll see each other again one day."

Once the afternoon crowd died down, Loribeth pulled me aside. "Look, I don't say anything when you take days off to do publicity stuff, but you need to focus more on our customers and less on your writing."

"But I—"

"It's less than two months until Christmas. I need everyone at their best. If you'd rather write than work, maybe you should quit." She held up a hand. "But not until after Christmas. You're my hardest worker and I need you here for the holidays."

In the past two years, I'd taken one day off for an interview and one more when I had the stomach flu. Loribeth made it sound like I missed shifts constantly. Between Halloween and Christmas, my days at the candy store would be non-stop and I was counting on the extra money to do some extra marketing for my books.

Any writing I did manage to squeeze in was inspired by customers. For example, the handsome man who brought a bouquet of chocolate roses. The young woman who bought candy canes and chocolate bars to create Santa sleighs she saw on Pinterest that she planned to make for guests at the homeless shelter. Is that where she would find romance? What if the two ran into each other?

I couldn't help but daydream, and blog when I remembered, that one day I could give up my dead-end job to write full-time and still pay the bills. I envied authors who earned a living doing what they loved. My mom and Cory, my ex-boyfriend, wanted me to be more practical. Since our last on-again had careened into a spectacular fight and a fortune in Rocky Road ice cream, I no longer cared what Cory thought. For now, I would keep my day job in case my books didn't sell. That fear kept me elbow deep in jujubes and jawbreakers.

"Hey, Miss Up-and-Comer." My roommate strode into the candy store waving a rain-speckled copy of the Toronto Star. "Have you seen this?"

"Oh no. Emily, put that away before Loribeth sees it. That reporter sure was awful, even after I bought him some expensive soy latte coffee thing and a gluten-free muffin."

Emily lowered the newspaper to her side as she shook her head. "Bah humbug. That woman would kiss your feet if she knew what a big deal you are."

"I'm not a big deal." My face burned.

"You made the Arts and Entertainment column in the Toronto Star, Ali," she gushed. "That makes you a pretty big deal."

Loribeth appeared next to me and snorted. "If you're not here to buy something, step aside for paying customers."

"What makes you think I won't buy anything?" My roommate raised a freshly waxed eyebrow before she grabbed a package of candy off a nearby shelf. "I'll take one of these."

"You hate those," I reminded her. "They taste like soap."

"Then help me find something I like. That is your job, right?" Emily winked.

Loribeth rolled her eyes, then turned to help another customer.

I reached for a package of red licorice and some chocolate-covered peanuts. "Anything else, customer who is always right?"

"Toss in a bag of those yummy Christmas jellybeans you hoard behind the counter." Emily chuckled. "You know, I should write a critique of this place for my blog."

"Do me a favor and wait until I find another job first." I added a bag of red, green, and white jellybeans. "That'll be twenty dollars and fifty cents, please."

Emily huffed. "That's outrageous. I'm buying candy, not financing a car."

"Then go somewhere else," Loribeth said over her shoulder. "Anywhere else."

"Great customer service you have here," my roommate grumbled.

"I'll see you later, Em."

My roommate handed me cash for the candy, then tucked the newspaper beneath her arm. "I'll whip up your favorite dinner to celebrate."

"Celebrate what? Me nearly getting fired three times today?"

Emily waved the newspaper once more as she widened her black-rimmed eyes. "One of these days, you'll be able to quit working here and do what real writers do."

"Starve?" My boss smirked.

My curly ponytail slapped my cheek as I shook my head and said in a stage whisper, "I think she means write."

"I suggest you get back to work before you need to look for another job. On the upside, you'd have more time to write and sign autographs."

"As if anybody wants them," I sighed.

Once Loribeth walked away, Emily groaned. "Look, I know you thought that reporter was a clown, but he did a nice job. The story will give you some great publicity and hopefully sell more books. All you need is to share the link all over social media and brag."

My face burned at the recollection of a harried interview in a crowded coffee shop. "The guy didn't bring a pen or phone, so heaven knows what he wrote about me. I'll check it out when I get home."

"Don't worry, Ali," she said, sticking her candy in her tote bag. "You'll show her."

"Yeah. If she doesn't fire me first. I'm closing tonight. I'll be done at nine."

"And I will have Seafood Lasagna and a glass of sparkling water to cheer you up." Emily grinned. "Then we can upload my food photos and talk about plans for Christmas. Or brainstorm your next awesome book, whichever you prefer."

As my roommate breezed out of the shop, I closed my eyes. Christmas meant appeasing my mom as she ranted about my lack of a career since writing didn't count, a boyfriend, or any sort of life... Last year, I'd spent Christmas Day listening to my mom and stepdad argue while my sister shopped online for a new wardrobe for her job at a huge corporation. Her fiancé ate junk food and watched football.

"Bah humbug," I muttered, not caring who heard.

Across the store, I spotted the woman with the white fedora hovering near the exit. Her eyes shone as she watched me. Did she want something more? For me to speak to her book club or knitting group?

I blew out a breath as my thoughts refocused on her being a stalker. From blissful high to humiliating low in ten seconds. A new record. Even for me. Hands shaking, I excused myself to take my anxiety medication.

By the time my shift ended, my feet ached and my mood felt trampled by a dozen elephants. I left the candy store to start the twelve-block walk home as a light rain began to fall. I gazed at the leaden gray sky, then began to shuffle through the bone-chilling drizzle.

My shoulders sagged. The only bright spot was that Emily had made the newspaper article sound positive and was making seafood lasagna for dinner. Maybe I should have a small spritzer before I read it. Just in case she exaggerated.

"Miss Cadell?" a man called out behind me.

My stomach did a quick somersault as I turned around slowly. I faced an older man, mid-sixties maybe, who had a slight accent. English? Australian? Whatever it was, he sounded like someone's butler. "Yes."

"Are you A.J. Cadell?" The shoulders of his dark trench coat and his fedora sparkled with raindrops as he approached me.

"I am." My heart beat a little faster, not sure what to expect. Was this an *It's a Wonderful Life* moment where he offered me a better future, or something more sinister?

"Miss Cadell, I am Robert Foster."

"If you want an autograph, I don't have a pen or a book handy." I gave a nervous laugh. "And if you want peppermints, the shop is closed until nine o'clock tomorrow morning."

"I am aware of that from the sign." He gave a little bow then touched his gray moustache. "In truth, Miss Cadell, I represent someone who would like to make you a special offer."

"Look, I don't know what it is you think I'll do, Mr. Foster, but I'm not that kind of girl."

"I'm glad to hear that," he said. "I assure you it's not that kind of offer."

When Foster reached into his trench coat, I flinched. My breath caught in my throat until he withdrew a glittering white envelope that reminded me of one of Roxie's wedding invitation samples. "I was instructed to give you this, then await your reply."

"What is it?"

The lines around his eyes softened when he replied, "My client's offer."

"Who exactly is your client?"

"I am not at liberty to say."

Curse client-whatever confidentiality. A chill ran through me as I reached for the envelope. "Do I get to think things over, or do you need an answer this second?"

He shook his head. "There is a grace period. You have until six o'clock tomorrow evening to make your decision. If I do not hear from you by then, I shall assume you are not interested and inform my client thusly."

"Can you at least give me a teensy clue?" I examined the envelope and saw it was embossed with a gold thistle on the flap. I began to open it, but when he didn't respond, I glanced up.

Robert Foster was gone. A swirl of raindrops danced in his place. My smile faded. He was fast for an old guy. As the rain grew heavier, I jammed the envelope into my purse to keep it from getting soaked and practically ran the entire twelve blocks home.

"Emily!" I shouted before I'd even opened the front door of our fifteen-story building. With no patience to wait for the elevator, I ran, then half-dragged myself, up the stairs to the tenth floor. For someone who walked a lot, I was badly out of shape.

Once I'd entered our two-bedroom apartment and closed the door behind me, I leaned against it to catch my breath. "Em, you won't believe what happened."

"Loribeth finally fired you."

"No."

My roommate glanced up from placing two plates on the table we found in the alley and repainted a soft teal. "You finally beat some snooty businessman out of a cab after work."

"Ha, ha." I peeled off my gloves and coat. "Ran the whole way."

She raised her eyebrows. "Now that I don't believe. Who was chasing you?"

"Funny."

"Did you finally meet the man of your dreams?"

"What? No. As if." I dropped my things on the sagging couch.

She shrugged. "I give up. You said I wouldn't believe it. Those were the most unbelievable things I could think of."

I tugged the envelope from my purse. "Trust me. This is even crazier."

"An envelope? You're right. That's completely insane. Is it from a secret admirer?"

"When I left the shop tonight, some old guy handed me this. He said it contains an offer." I sat at the table.

Emily half turned as she opened the oven. "Did you call the police?"

"Not that kind of offer. It could be a prank for all I know, but he disappeared so fast it made me curious." I used a butter knife to open the envelope then paused for a deep breath.

"What is it?" she asked.

Inside was a simple white notecard embossed with the same gold thistle. The name Thistlewood Manor was stamped below it in gold script. The card was an invitation to become Writer-in-Residence for a month. No fine print. The only details stated all my expenses would be paid and my only obligation was doing three workshops and a reading at the local library. I was both impressed and wary all at once. Didn't writers have to apply for those things?

"Ooh, that's fancy. What's it say?" Across the kitchen, Emily took a foil pan and packet out of the oven and set them on the table.

I silently read the card three more times.

"Alison?" she asked, waving a hand in front of my face. "What is it?"

"Whoever this Foster guy represents wants me to go to somewhere called Thistlewood Manor to be Writer-in-Residence. All expenses paid."

"What do they want you to do?"

"A reading, teach a few workshops, evaluate a few manuscripts, and participate in other library activities. The rest of the time, I can work on my own project."

My roommate snatched the card from my hand. "Get out! Ali, you've dreamed of this since we were kids. Who's it from?"

"The guy wouldn't tell me and there's no name on the card." Stomach growling, I opened the hot foil packet with my fingertips and pulled out a thick slice of homemade garlic bread. I took a bite, then fanned my mouth.

"What are you going to do?"

"Faint."

"I meant after that."

I wiped my fingers then tucked the card back into the envelope. "Find out why would someone make a nobody like me this kind of offer? It doesn't make sense."

Emily lunged toward the cupboard then slapped the newspaper onto the table in front of me. "You're not a nobody. Someone is giving you a chance to live your dreams, and I'll bet it's because of this article. The guy even quoted you saying how hard it was to write full-time when you're trying to earn a living. Face it, Ali, you'd be crazy to pass this up."

"The reporter said that? Wow, I thought he was just checking out the barista the whole time. I guess he was listening."

"Read the article."

I tore off a piece of garlic bread not sure what to do first. Read the story, research Thistlewood Manor, or eat. My stomach was winning, but I pulled out my phone to do a quick search. "Except that article just came out today. From the looks of this invitation, someone planned this a while ago."

"That means someone has a reason for wanting you to be their Writer-in-Residence. All the more reason for you to jump at the offer. Dig in while the food's hot, then we can hit the computer and check this place out."

While Emily scooped seafood lasagna onto my plate, I gazed around the apartment we'd shared for the past three years. "I can't leave you stuck, Em. You can't afford this place on your own any more than I can."

"It's only a month. You're not leaving forever," she said, then paused. "Are you?"

I tapped the notecard. "I should call Cory. He's more practical about these things."

"Forget it, he's closed minded which is why you broke up seven times, remember?"

"You're right."

Emily opened a bottle of wine. "Your heart is set on writing, Ali. Cory would try to talk you out of going."

"I should call Roxie."

"Be honest. If you didn't think you had to worry what anyone else thought, which you don't, what would you do?" She poured us each a wine spritzer, mine light on the wine.

"I don't know." My heart raced as I bordered on an anxiety attack.

"Breathe, Ali."

"I am breathing."

"No, you're hyperventilating." Emily handed me a paper bag kept for emergencies. "Let's try this another way. What if this same situation happened to the main character in your books? What would she do?"

She had me there. I set the bag aside and took a deep breath. "She'd accept the mysterious offer, go on an epic adventure, and meet the man of her dreams or else I wouldn't have much of a romance novel."

"Exactly. Then why not create a great story for you instead of some random character? What do you have to lose?"

"You. Roxie." I took a bite of lasagna. "Cory."

She jabbed a finger toward me. "I never want to hear his name again. I can still see the last layer of Rocky Road rippling on my butt. With both of you gone, I could finally lose the ice cream and cookie dough weight before Christmas."

"True enough." I sipped my spritzer. "My sister won't be happy. Not with her wedding coming. She wants me to search for our father."

"Roxie is a frustrated corporate office worker with an out-of-work fiancé. I'll bet she'd jump at an offer like this if it meant taking pictures for National Geographic or something. She's always dreamed of being a photographer but can't stand up for herself with her fiancé or your mom."

"She'd never dare. But she does know me better than anyone, except you."

"Even better than you know yourself?" Emily raised her eyebrows as she reached for her wine. "How could Roxie and I know you better than you do? What I do know is that you worry too much about what everyone else thinks."

"Ouch." I poked at my lasagna. "Would you accept the offer if you were me?"

She nodded so hard I swore she'd get whiplash. "Girl, I'd go instead of you. Who knows, you might meet Mr. Right while you're cavorting through the halls of Thistlewood Manor."

"Cavorting?" I ate a shrimp. "If this involves cavorting, it's already a bad idea. With my luck, this place is in some remote part of the country kilometers from civilization where I'll probably run into Bigfoot."

"At least you'd have something to write home about," she said. "Besides, Bigfoot's probably single. What's wrong?"

"How can I leave my job to run off somewhere for a month just to write a book?" I asked.

"You want me to go instead?"

"No."

"Then tell Loribeth you quit. Throw your pink apron on the counter. Pack your bags and go."

I re-read the notecard. "I've never been outside of Toronto in my entire life. I don't even know where I'm going."

Emily tore off a piece of garlic bread. "Eat. After dinner, we can consult the almighty Google and find out."

While we ate, I ticked off a list of all the reasons why accepting the offer was a horrible idea. Finally, I mopped the last of the sauce on my plate with a piece of garlic bread and realized I'd stalled long enough. "What if this place is on the other side of the country? What will I do without you for moral support?"

"Call. Text. E-mail. Video chat," my roommate said. "Come on, Ali. You're twenty-five years old with your entire life ahead of you. This is the exact opportunity you've always dreamed of, so don't you dare chicken out. Call the guy and accept the offer before we have dessert. I made trifle."

"I will totally miss your cooking." I blew out a breath.

Emily barely finished chewing before she ran across the room for her laptop. "At least we have the name of the place."

I scooped trifle into fancy dessert bowls we'd found at the nearby dollar store while my roommate typed. My stomach churned in anticipation. I hoped I wouldn't throw up my lasagna.

"All that comes up is a Thistlewood Manor Bed and Breakfast along the Strait of Georgia. Look at this place, will you? The place looks like something a rich lumberjack would build. Huge logs, lots of windows, beach front property. It's stunning."

"Where is it?" I asked.

"Cedar Grove, British Columbia on Vancouver Island. Whoa. That's definitely across the country."

My pulse quickened. The same town where my search for my father had stalled. It could be a coincidence, but what if this Foster guy's mystery client was Perry Beyer who was trying to find his missing family?

"I hate to break it to you, but there have been Big Foot sightings on the island."

"I can't do this." I sat and stared at my trifle.

Emily sipped her wine. "Don't you dare tell me you plan to sleep on it. I couldn't stand the suspense."

"There's a lot to think about."

"Don't think. Just go for it. Ali, this is exactly what you need to inspire your new book. An adventure."

I gazed at the images of the small town on her computer. After two days of searching for traces of my father, I felt like I'd been to Cedar Grove before. "Will you visit me?"

Emily winked. "You'll be gone and home before I can get a week off. Although, a place like that's bound to have handsome, single guys. My soulmate might be one of them since he doesn't seem to be in Toronto. Not where we hang out anyway."

I fought off a wave of dizziness. "I need to think. I'll call Mr. Foster in the morning."

"You should call him now before you talk yourself out of going."

"Either way I'm not going to get much sleep. Vancouver Island is a world away. What'll I tell my sister?" I wiped my clammy hands on my pantlegs.

Emily frowned. "Don't tell her anything. Better yet, tell her you found a rich boyfriend on some dating site and you're flying across the country to meet him."

"Yeah, that'll go over well."

"So, take her with you," Emily said. "Better yet, take me. Honestly, I'd worry more about what you're going to tell your mother."

My lasagna sank in my stomach. "Maybe sleeping on that one is a good option."

As I got ready for bed, I opened Mabel, my laptop, that I'd named after my favorite English teacher who'd encouraged me to write. Much to my mother's chagrin. I still couldn't remember Perry Beyer, nor had I found proof he was dead or alive.

I gazed at a couple photos I'd found of him fighting fires then typed in the information from Thistlewood. Cedar Grove, British Columbia had come up in my search. Having someone who wanted to pay the expenses for me to go there seemed like one more sign. I closed Mabel.

What was I thinking?

Agitated, I pulled the black velvet pouch out of my bedside table and shook the smooth gray stone inside onto my palm. Although I couldn't remember where it came from, it comforted me when I was stressed. Like a worry stone. Good thing the lines were deep, and I hadn't worn them off by now.

The entire night I tossed and turned just as Emily predicted. One minute I wished I'd already accepted the offer, then I'd change my mind out of fear. It was like changing outfits before a first date. If I went to Vancouver Island, I'd have time to write and try to find Perry Beyer. If I stayed in Toronto, I'd need a new dead-end job before I lost my mind.

My stomach churned until a noise awoke me.

Emily stood next to my bed wearing her fluffy pink bathrobe. Her dark hair was rumpled, and her eyes were narrow slits. She handed me the card. "Either you call that guy right now, or I will."

It was barely six o'clock when I set the pineapple stone on the night table. I'd squeezed it so tight the design was imprinted on my palm. Brushing the hair out of my eyes, I reached for my phone and said, "Glad to know I'm not the only one who's excited."

Emily sat on the end of my bed gnawing her thumb. She hadn't bothered with her slippers. "Excited, nothing. I'm terrified you'll leave for good. Then I'd have to move to the Island."

My heart raced as I dialed. When Robert Foster's phone rang three times, I worried I should've waited an hour or two.

"Miss Cadell, I presume?" he asked, probably already showered, dressed, and ready to face the day. I pictured his elegant attire, white mustache, and the trace of a grin on his weathered face.

"What are you, psychic?"

He chuckled. "I knew you would call. I hope you plan to accept my client's offer."

"Yes. I will accept your client's offer," I spoke the words to seal my fate. What a dramatic thought that was. Right up there with an elderly lady in a white fedora stalking me. "I'll need some details though. Like when I leave, what I have to do, do I need to sign an agreement of some kind?"

Emily bounced on the end of the bed clapping while she stifled a squeal.

When the phone hummed in my ear, I moved it away and stared. "Are you kidding me?"

"What did he say?" She inched closer.

"He hung up."

"That's not a good start."

"Tell me about it." I tried to call back twice, but Foster was probably already on the phone with his client. It wasn't until I was in the shower before I realized this was the first night all week that I hadn't had a nightmare. Of course, I hadn't slept much either.

Emily and I lingered over breakfast before rushing off to work. I left the card on my nightstand and managed to convince myself the life changing decision was a wine and seafood-induced dream. Nothing more. There was no trip to British Columbia. No mysterious benefactor. No wish come true. It was all a hoax. It had to be.

Until Robert Foster appeared in the candy store at high noon.

"Can I help you?" I asked, struggling to breathe.

He handed me a large yellow envelope. "All of your answers are in here, Miss Cadell. As well as your plane ticket."

"My plane ticket?" My heart beat so fast I grew lightheaded.

"Plane ticket? What's going on?" Loribeth leaned over my shoulder. "Is this your grandpa?"

"I am her lawyer, madam." He nodded with a smile that reached his coppery eyes. "Be sure to have your affairs in order, young lady. Your flight leaves at eight o'clock in the morning on Saturday, November ninth. Your detailed itinerary is inside the envelope. Someone will meet you at the airport in Victoria."

"Victoria, British Columbia?" Loribeth leaned closer.

"Have my affairs in order? That sounds ominous."

"I'll say. What's going on?" Loribeth asked. "You never said you had a lawyer, or that you were going anywhere."

I gazed from Foster to the yellow envelope then finally at Loribeth's ruddy cheeks before I drew in a deep breath. "I'm flying to Victoria."

"I never authorized any time off," she said.

"You don't need to authorize anything. I'm flying to Victoria, then going to Cedar Grove for a month to be a Writer-in-Residence." I hesitated as my words sank in. "By the way, Loribeth, I quit."

"I shall see you again soon Miss Cadell." Foster tipped his fedora.

My former boss's voice rose an octave. "You can't do that. I need you here. It's going to get even busier with the holidays coming. I need help to look after the shop."

I handed her my cotton-candy pink apron. "I'd stick around, Loribeth, but you heard the man. I need to get my affairs in order. See ya."

As I left the shop, second thoughts rolled in like a violent summer storm. I questioned my sanity over the entire twelve blocks home. I had some money set aside but would have to find another job when I returned. That or move in with my mother. On the upside, I'd have an entire month to panic.

I sent Emily a text to tell her I'd quit, then called my sister.

"Someone is paying you to go to Vancouver Island?"

I read the paperwork once more. "Yeah. That's exactly what they're doing."

"You do realize this guy could be some whacko who wants to lock you in his basement for twenty years, right?"

"At least I'd have time to write." I snorted. "I can also look for our dad."

"What do you mean?" my sister asked.

I hesitated. "Cedar Grove was Perry's last known address. It could be a coincidence, but..."

"Why didn't you say so? If this is what you really want to do, Ali, then go. I'll help you convince mom. I'll even help you pack. Heck, you can borrow some of my clothes. I'm sure the B.C. coast will be colder than here."

Considering my clothes came from clearance racks, it was more likely she didn't want me to embarrass her. I was glad for her help. Convincing Mom wouldn't be easy. Even though I'd asked for more information about our father since she dropped her bombshell, she hadn't budged. When it came to Perry Beyer, her lips were sealed—except for sips of martini.

***

On Saturday, November ninth, I clutched my stone in my pocket, worried I might wear off the etched pineapple. I was thankful for Emily already checking me in, so I had one less thing to worry about. My mom and her driver took me to the airport at eight-thirty for my eleven o'clock flight. Mom shed far more tears on the drive than she did in the terminal. I hadn't seen her so upset since I'd pestered her about the bumps and scars on my head and body.

"I can't believe Roxie convinced you to find that deadbeat," she said, adjusting the collar on my coat. "Why she's so determined to have him at her wedding is beyond me. He's never done anything for either of you since we..."

I waited, but she didn't finish her sentence. "This trip has nothing to do with him. It's a chance for me to focus on writing for a month. Becoming a Writer-in-Residence doesn't happen to every author. Besides, I don't even remember my father."

Mom sighed. Reaching into her purse, she took out a bright green envelope, her fingers white as she hesitated. "I don't understand why you have to do this, but I know you inherited his stubborn streak. Maybe this will help."

"You're handing me money? Usually, you just transfer it into my bank account."

"It's not what you think. Oh," she said, "I got you an extra bottle of your pills. Just in case. I know how you get when you run out. The last thing I want is for you to end up in the hospital out there."

With a quick glance at my watch, I stuck the envelope and the orange bottle in my purse to open on the plane. "Thanks. This trip is a great opportunity for me to write and build my career. I'm excited for the change of scenery."

"Then forget about Vancouver Island," my mother said. "If that's all you want, move back to your old room and listen to music like you did when you were a teenager."

As tempting as that sounded, I had no desire to move back to the three-bedroom downtown condo she shared with my stepfather, four dogs, two cats, and a budgie named Tweety.

"We've tried that. There's no such thing as quiet at your house."

"Then what about Cody?" she asked. "I'm sure he'd be happy to support you while you go through this little phase."

Little phase? I bit back my frustration as I corrected her. "Cory and I broke up months ago."

"Again? You two always make things work."

"If we made things work, we wouldn't keep breaking up."

"Gerald and I fight too, you know, but when we make up…" My mom fanned her face.

I'd witnessed far more making up than I'd cared to. "Oh, I know. But Gerald respects who you are. When I got my first book published, Cory gave me a card that said he couldn't wait to see what I tried next."

"That sounds supportive," Mom said.

I snorted. "Inside was a note to say he'd pre-arranged an interview at the candy store to be the assistant manager."

"Oh." Her fake elation faded. "How do you know this is for real? What if Roxie's right and someone plans to kidnap you? I might never see you again."

"Maybe. You're right. This might possibly be the worst idea ever, but an offer like this doesn't come along every day and I won't know until I get there." I tried to ease my white-knuckled grip on my purse as I inched toward security. "Relax, Mom, no one would create such an elaborate plan to kidnap a nobody like me. I'll call you when I land in Victoria. Love you."

She never said another word as I walked away and stood in the line to get through security. When I looked back, she and her driver were gone.

Mom and Roxie were right about one thing: I had no idea what I was getting into. As I boarded the plane, my anxiety peaked like white-crested waves in my chest. I focused on taking one calming breath after another until I could take my seat and pop an anxiety pill.

"Are you okay?" a flight attendant asked.

I cringed as I nodded. "This is my first flight."

"Oh, how exciting. Are you going to the Island on vacation?"

"I'm going to find my father." What on earth possessed me to say that?

"Good luck. I hope you find what you're looking for."

Once I found my seat, I buckled in and glanced out the window at the tarmac. I should've specified not to have a window seat. I'd probably spend the entire flight with my eyes closed clutching my rock. Twenty-five years old and I carried a rock with a crudely etched pineapple that I was slowly eroding with each rub of my thumb to keep me from panicking. I took one of my pills and swallowed it with the bottle of water I'd brought along.

To distract myself during takeoff, I dug out the envelope my mom gave me. The address in the corner was still legible. Definitely not Cedar Grove.

"Colvilletown. Where is that?" I muttered before I slid my finger beneath the flap and willed my heart to stop racing.

I slipped the card out of the green envelope. A photo of a googly-eyed skydiver was on the front along with a speech bubble that said, *'Thought I'd drop in and say hi.'* Now I knew where I got my sense of humor. It certainly wasn't from my mom.

As I opened the card, a folded piece of paper fell out and landed on my lap.

'Dear A.J.' My heart fluttered. *'I'm sure you've heard a lot of bad things about me, so I'm not surprised you never wrote back. Some people don't understand why I jump out of planes to fight fires. It's tough, dirty work, but I've loved every second of it even though it took me away from my family. Or should I say I drove you away from me? Sorry for not being there when you need me. Your mom needed to move on. To build a new life. Don't blame her for my arrogance.'*

No mention of an accident, which was odd.

I wiped away a tear. Why was I crying over a man who'd abandoned his family? Perry Beyer cut himself out of our lives and left my mom alone to carry on with two kids. Of course, it sounded like he'd written to me—to us—several times. I refolded the letter, unable to focus on anything else as I dug into my bag for my stone to ground me.

As I slid the card back into the envelope, I caught a glimpse of the date stamped on the corner. Either the card got lost in the mail or my mom had kept it hidden for the past ten years. The latter was most likely. I stuck it in my purse and sat back for takeoff.

How many other letters did he send that I never received?

Chapter Three

Mercifully, my flight across the country was far less dramatic than my departure. I savored my quiet time by ignoring the chatty man next to me and writing the outline for my next novel. The one I'd plotted while hustling candy and waiting on people either in an agitated hurry to get in and out of the shop or counting out one dime after another to pay for their purchases. People were odd that way.

As I disembarked around one-thirty Pacific time that afternoon in the midst of a herd of middle-aged businessmen, mothers with unruly kids, and shuffling seniors, I scrubbed my face with one hand. Three hours ahead on Ontario time, my stomach growled. I was grateful for the bag of chocolate covered peanuts I found in my bag.

I focused on the landing at Victoria International Airport, recalling every detail to write about later. The Canadian landscape was blanketed with patches of gold, white, and dark blues of vast lakes. To calm my nerves, I pictured the incredible views of the forests and fields below dotted with cities, towns, and lakes that stretched as far as I could see.

Once I figured out how to balance the purple suitcases, on loan from Roxie, I followed yet another herd toward freedom and the unknown. Excitement and terror made for a heady combination. I walked with confidence, yet my heart raced as my palms sweated. I still had no idea who had invited me or what I was really doing here, but hoped it was to be a legitimate Writer-in-Residence.

When Foster mentioned someone would pick me up, the writer in me pictured a tall, dark-haired, handsome man with chiseled features holding a large sign with my name in glittering script. No, scratch that. I'd prefer a man wearing a plaid flannel jacket and snug blue jeans with a couple days' worth of stubble on his sculpted jaw. His hair curled up at the nape of his neck and...

Heat rose from my belly. I needed to save that image for later. Focusing on my novel had sparked my imagination into high gear. The thought of my notebook filled with fresh characters, a storyline, and an almost ending spurred me toward the door. I was already on a roll, which made me giddy.

When I spied my name in block letters written in black marker on a sheet of plain paper, my heart sank. There was no stud with rugged features. Just Foster.

"Mr. Foster." I waved at the familiar face in the sea of strangers.

He lowered the sign. "Miss Cadell."

No one around us seemed to recognize me or my name. Not a surprise. I was still a fledgling author in the grand scheme of things.

"This way."

Before I could hand him my suitcases, my laptop bag, or my purse, he walked away. I blew out a sharp breath then slumped my shoulders in disappointment. The strap of my laptop bag slid down my arm. Being a writer-in-residence didn't come with as many perks as I hoped. Definitely not valet service.

As I carried my bags into the November air, a shiver wrapped me in a hug. As luck had it, he'd parked in the farthest possible row he could have found. I was starting to really dislike him now.

Foster didn't say much on the drive down Highway 17 toward Victoria. He asked a couple of polite questions about my flight, then made sure I was warm enough before he nudged up the heat. When I grew drowsy and yawned, he lapsed into silence. A catnap would refresh me what with the time difference and all the mental work I'd done on the plane.

Chilled from the weather and a lack of restful sleep, I gazed at the drizzle that gathered on the rolling landscape and clung to the trees. The next time I opened my eyes, it was dark. A huge, spot lit rock on the front lawn bore the words "Thistlewood Manor" framed by two beautifully carved thistles. Beyond that stood a majestic log building that resembled a ski chalet for the rich and famous. Tons of glass and stones were set into logs bigger around than car tires.

Something stirred inside of me as Foster parked. An odd feeling deep in my gut that I'd seen this place before. My stomach rolled and my palms sweated. I chalked it up to being tired from the flight and having to get up so early.

"This, Miss Cadell, is Thistlewood Manor," Foster said. "Welcome home."

"Are you serious?" I turned to stare, but he'd left the car and was heading toward the trunk. The man had a bad habit of disappearing abruptly.

I released my seatbelt and opened the door to a rush of cold, damp air. Sucking in a sharp breath, I reached into the backseat for my purse and laptop and climbed out of the car. As I wandered toward the large rock, I paused. "How many rooms are in this place?"

"Several." Foster set the larger of my two suitcases at my feet. "Good evening, Anna."

A mannish, middle-aged woman framed by the open doorway wiped her hands on a cloth. "Is this Miss Cadell?"

The wide front doors were dwarfed by massive log pillars that supported the porch roof. Many trees and years of labour went into building the place. An odd sensation of déjà vu swept over me as I glanced at a dimly lit window on the second floor. I pictured a cozy nook with throw pillows and a cup of coffee awaiting inside. The curtain in the window fluttered closed as if someone had peered out, then hid from sight.

Foster grunted, setting my second suitcase near the first. "Enjoy your stay."

"Uh-huh. Thanks." I gazed around me at the dark trees and bright lights. This place would make a great setting for a romance novel. My creative juices started to flow as Foster drove off into the fog that rolled in.

"Let's take your things to your room then get you a cup of tea to shake off the chill, shall we?" The woman in the doorway beckoned me inside. She curled a strand of her shoulder-length hair around her right ear but didn't venture into the light rain.

When no valet appeared, I picked up my bags and made my way up the flagstone walkway. "As Cedar Grove's Writer-in-Residence, you have a lovely room in the north wing that overlooks the Strait."

"The Strait?" I asked.

"The Strait of Georgia."

Rustic and warm were the first words that came to mind as I stepped inside the manor. A waist-height cedar counter stood to my left. It was adorned with a large bouquet of fresh flowers and a registration book. In front of me, a russet carpet runner led from the double doors to a pair of sofas with a live-edge coffee table in between. Beyond them was an open chef's kitchen with what promised to be a breathtaking view of the bay in daylight. To my left, a set of French doors opened wide to a large room with a stone fireplace at the far end. To the right of the sofas, a staircase rose into the ceiling and beyond.

"I'm Anna Larkin, I'm the manager." She motioned toward the stairs. "Let's take your bags to your room, then I'll show you around. You'll have time to freshen up while I fix you some dinner."

"I'll help." A tall, thin man around my age ran over like an enthusiastic four-year-old. He had thick brown hair, round glasses, and a shy smile. He was halfway up the stairs with both suitcases before I could thank him.

"I didn't think you offered valet service."

Anna tensed. "Owen loves to roll out the red carpet when we have guests, especially writers. Your room is at the top of the stairs."

"Why especially writers?"

"He has a soft spot for books and dabbles in writing his own stories. He has a vivid imagination," she said as we emerged into a large foyer between two corridors.

Part of the foyer was open to the front entrance below, which made me queasy. I didn't dare peer over the side.

Anna directed me toward the hallway to the left. "Your room has a lovely area to write and an amazing view."

My suitcases awaited in front of the door. The man who carried them up was nowhere in sight.

Anna opened the door then took a half-step back for me to get past. My eyes widened and a shiver swept through me. It was exactly as I'd pictured while standing outside. Without an awaiting cup of coffee. The décor needed an update to take it out of the eighties pastels and florals, but the room was simple and cozy. A queen-sized bed took up the far corner with a flowered, wing-backed reading chair nearby. An ornate white desk in the windowed alcove held a glass vase filled with pink carnations and a notebook with seashells on the cover. I peeked beneath the desk, relieved to find a close outlet.

I only wished I could see the Strait of Georgia, but that could wait. My stomach rumbled. Despite seeing the images online, I couldn't believe this place was real. "This is beautiful, thank you."

"I'm glad you like it." Anna handed me a key on a gold ring with a white tag embedded with an elegant gold thistle. "It's yours for as long as you plan to stay."

"According to the paperwork, I'll be here for a month." I set my laptop bag on the desk.

"That's great. I'll make sure Owen leaves you in peace."

In the north wing, near my room, was a bathroom and two other bedrooms. Across the hall from my room, someone played a scratchy record behind the closed door. It was an old song I recognized but couldn't recall the name of. Something about a dream.

"Is that a vinyl record?" I asked.

"It is." Anna waved a hand and rolled her eyes. "Bebe plays that song at all hours of the day and night. If the music's a problem, I can move you to another room."

"I'm sure it'll be fine. I've heard vinyl is making a big comeback. What's in the room at the end of the hall? Is that a honeymoon suite?"

"We don't use that room," she said. "It belongs to the owners."

"Oh." I was intrigued. "Do they come often? It would be great to meet them."

"No. I keep it ready. Just in case," she said. "Come. I'll show you around the rest of the manor."

The writer in me sensed a story. "Could I take a peek? It's not like I'd be disturbing anyone, right?"

She glanced down the hall. "I suppose a peek won't hurt. As long as you don't touch anything."

"I'll behave."

Anna led me down the hall, then pulled a gold key from her pocket. Her hand shook as she stuck it in the lock. It was all I could do to keep breathing when she turned the knob. The door opened with a creak.

"Need to oil the hinges," she muttered.

My pulse quickened as she stepped aside. Everything was draped in a thin layer of dust or a sheet. I crept across the hardwood floor to the stone fireplace that took up half the far wall. A large painting covered with a flowered sheet hung over the mantle. Possibly a portrait of the original owners. I itched to take a look but couldn't reach. The windows faced in three directions that I guessed gave a fabulous view of the Strait, the forest, and the front yard.

I gazed in awe at the king-sized canopy bed draped with gauzy white curtains. On each night table, stood a crystal vase of dried roses. This was a room for lovers. In the corner near the bed, an antique full-length mirror reflected the room. Next to it a small round table held a copper statue of a horse and rider that seemed so familiar. Had I seen it in my stepfather's man cave?

Taking pictures with my phone as discreetly as I could, an uneasy feeling swept over me. I was positive I'd been in this room and seen these things before. Was that even possible when I'd never been to Vancouver Island before?

"You have a chill," Anna said. "Come. I'll start a fire while you get settled."

She locked the door behind us.

"Actually, I'd rather see the rest of the manor," I told her. "That room and the view are stunning. You could make a lot of money if you added a hot tub and rented it out as a honeymoon suite."

Anna waved toward the south wing of the manor which had another bathroom, two bedrooms, a great room, and an office. Rather than show me any of them, she led me back to the main stairs.

I gasped at a gigantic chandelier made up of brass rings that held white ceramic candles. Beyond the lights was an insert in the wall with a wooden railing that hinted at a third level to the manor. Normally, looking up didn't bother me as much as looking down but nausea swept over me accompanied by a sensation of falling. I grasped the rail in front of me.

"What's up there?" I asked.

Anna froze mid-step. "An attic. The owners had plans to renovate the upper floor to expand, but the manor wasn't busy enough to bother."

When I took a picture of the chandelier and the railing, I realized there was an identical railing on the opposite side. "Could I take a look?"

"Another day," Anna said, her voice raised as her fingers turned white on the banister. Was it my imagination she seemed nervous? "You must be starving."

My stomach agreed. "Maybe some herbal tea if you have any."

Anna led me back down the stairs. "Ten different flavors, I believe. Through that door to your right is a utility room and the garage."

We strolled through the foyer into a room with an even larger fireplace. "Wow! This place was made for parties."

"Yes. The owners loved to dance."

"Loved?" I raised my eyebrows noting the past tense.

Anna either didn't hear me or pretended not to as she pointed out the fully stocked wet bar stood to the left facing the gigantic windows that overlooked the Strait of Georgia.

The wall next to the bar was dotted with holes surrounding a dart-board. Two large leather sofas sprawled in front of a stone fireplace that rose straight through to the next level of the manor. To one side of the fireplace, along the floor to ceiling windows, sat two highbacked leather armchairs with a round table in between. A hand-carved marble chess board sat in mid-game.

"This place is amazing." I turned slowly to drink it all in. "Do the owners live in Cedar Grove or are they based in Victoria?"

"We can talk more later," Anna said, as she added some wood and a couple balls of crumpled newspaper and started a fire in the hearth. "Tomorrow you can check out the property. There's a trail along the shore that will take you into Cedar Grove. Dinner is at six o'clock each evening and the house is usually quiet by nine."

"Works for me. I have a lot of writing and prep work to do for the library," I admitted. "I see a lot of cozy spots where I could work."

"Take your pick," Anna said. "Bebe and Owen keep to themselves, so I doubt they'll bother you much."

The moment she left the room, I pulled out my phone to snap more pictures. Emily would love this place. Plus, it was just the setting I needed for the novel I was working on. Since I was the Writer-in-Residence at the local library, I doubted the owners would mind if I took photos for my research. Maybe I'd even get to meet them. Of course, from the dust in the master suite, I doubted they were here often. They probably travelled the world when they didn't spend summers on the Island.

Wandering back to my room, I took dozens of pictures to send to Emily and file for my new book. I'd barely reached my room when the door across the hall opened. I took a reflexive step back as an elderly woman with thick, white hair falling to her elbows stepped into the hall.

The mysterious Bebe's gaze met mine. Her eyes appeared glassy, and I had the impression she didn't actually see me. Something about the way she waltzed across the hall in a pale blue chiffon dress that swirled around her calves both concerned and amused me. Her presence was oddly comforting.

Like I already knew her.

"Why good evening, Countess." Bebe paused to curtsy. "I do hope you're enjoying the party. If you will pardon me, I have to skip to the loo, my darling."

"I'm not a Countess," I told her.

She waltzed away from me then twirled again in front of the bathroom door while she hummed. Her skirt flared out like the Morning Glory blossoms that climbed the side of my mom's house each summer.

"What an odd woman." I chuckled as I unlocked my door.

Even though the vague familiarity of Thistlewood Manor made me uneasy, I studied the window nook. I reached for my laptop bag to grab my notebook to make a few notes while I waited for the bathroom door to open. The call of nature spoke louder than my desire to transcribe thoughts to paper. Or even text Emily who would be long asleep.

"Ah. There's my lovely, Countess." Bebe danced toward me. She pulled me into her arms and spun me around while she sang the song from her record. The sweet scent of flowery perfume twirled between us.

"You dance divinely, my darling," she drawled as she swung me speechless then burst into laughter. Her breath carried the acrid scent of alcohol.

"Have we met before?" I asked. "You seem so..."

"Why of course we have, Countess." When she smiled her blue eyes sparkled. "I know you like chocolate-covered strawberries. They're my favorite, too. Only I'm old enough to enjoy them with a glass of sparkling champagne rather than milk. It's so deliciously decadent. You should drop by one evening. We'll dine on strawberries accompanied by my special tea."

My face warmed. "That sounds wonderful. Why do you keep calling me Countess?"

"Then we shall conspire to find you a handsome young man. Maybe a hot firefighter or a wealthy lawyer." She winked. "Chocolate-covered strawberries should always be shared with someone you love."

I laughed. "I take it you've shared them with someone you love."

"Every chance I get, Countess," Bebe sang. "A wonderful man who held me in his arms and made me feel like the only woman in the world."

"Has he passed on?" I asked.

"True love never dies." As she held my face in her hands, I felt like I could dive deep into her watery, blue eyes. "Promise me you'll find a love like that, my darling. A love that not only sweeps your breath away but leaves you sleepless and giddy every single night."

I couldn't help admiring the woman. "I'll try."

"Trying is for sissies." Bebe tapped my cheeks. "Just do it, darling. Fall in love and fall hard. That's the only way to find your happily ever after."

I'd lamented to that reporter about being unable to find my own happily ever after, which was why I wrote romance novels. Had Bebe read that article? Probably not. I doubt any newspaper in Cedar Grove carried his column or that Bebe spent much time online. Did anyone west of the Rockies even get the Toronto Star?

Bebe kissed my cheek then twirled away and sashayed back to her room. Seconds later, the record player began to play as the scent of her perfume lingered like a wispy ghost.

I stood alone near the railing avoiding looking down at the entrance below. I itched to get back to my novel to capture that odd moment with the delusional woman who'd left a warm spot in my heart.

Right after I used the washroom. I hustled down the hall texting Emily and Roxie to let them know I'd arrived. I promised to send pictures later.

"Dinner," a man's voice seeped through the bathroom door.

"I'll be right down."

Owen and Anna joined me at the long, wood table with bark one each side. Live edge wood, which was popular in Ontario. While I ate reheated pasta with meat sauce, they enjoyed blueberry pie and tea.

"Isn't Bebe joining us?" I asked.

Anna shook her head. "She's already eaten. Besides, she took her dessert with a glass of brandy in her room."

That explained the alcohol on her breath. I guessed she'd had a glass before I arrived. I had so many questions, but wanted to respect the rules of the house, especially when Owen yawned so wide that I saw his tonsils.

By then, it was about ten o'clock Toronto time, seven on the Island. I excused myself, taking my pie and tea up to my room to do a little writing. despite the struggle to keep my eyes open.

I'd barely filled two pages with hastily scribbled bullet notes before I heard a knock. Curious, I peered into the hallway and saw Anna in front of Bebe's bedroom door with a silver tray that held a low-ball glass half filled with dark amber liquid. Beside the glass was a bowl of strawberries dipped in chocolate.

"Bebe, I have your nightcap," Anna knocked again while she called over the music.

More brandy. Did the elderly woman have a problem with alcohol?

"Sorry for disturbing you, Miss Cadell," Anna said, noticing me. "She must've fallen asleep."

"No problem. I'll get used to the routine in a day or two."

Anna took a keyring from her pocket to let herself inside.

I hesitated, oddly fascinated, until Anna re-emerged into the corridor with her hands empty. "Can I get you anything before I retire for the night?"

"No, thanks. I'm good." I nodded toward Bebe's room. "Do you bring her that every evening?"

"Her one request. You should join her one day. I'm sure she'd love the company."

"Perhaps I will." I hesitated. "What does she drink?"

"Tea," she said. "Bebe hates those fussy little teacups that barely hold a thimbleful, so I serve it to look like a cocktail. We all have our quirks. Good night, Miss Cadell."

"Good night." I closed my door and locked it. Bebe's drink hadn't looked like tea to me, although it was possible.

The lack of sleep all week finally got the best of me. I took my nightly medication and, pineapple stone in hand, crawled into the soft bed. I still had no idea who had invited me.

Would I be able to find the library on Monday and how would I get there?

I fell asleep before I could reach for my phone to find out.

Chapter Four

*B*ebe *swayed to the music while she giggled like a teenager in love. She held her hands in mid-air as though they rested on a man's shoulders. "Oh, Jack, you move like Fred Astaire. You're so light on your feet, my love."*

I wanted to speak up, but she seemed lost in her own little world.

She twirled with her invisible partner, chattering about the champagne going to her head and the divine strawberries robed in chocolate. How she'd never had such a delectable treat before she met him. Every so often, she reached down as if adjusting long skirts of a phantom gown.

"Bebe?" I spoke softly, careful not to startle her.

"Yes, Countess?" She gazed over her shoulder. "Oh, I am so sorry. Forgive my rudeness. Jack, darling, this is my dear friend, Anna. We're more like sisters really. She takes such good care of me."

I corrected her, "My name is Alison. I'm a romance writer from Toronto."

Bebe giggled as she glanced away once more. "Yes, that's right. Did I mention she's going to live with us for a while, darling? Just until she gets her feet on the ground. Her husband's a terrible man. Thankfully, he's gone now, so she can breathe easy."

"I've never been married. You have me confused with someone else. Should I come back later?"

"Don't go." Bebe grasped my wrist faster than I expected. "Don't leave me alone with them."

"With Jack?" I asked.

"Of course not." Bebe's face went blank before the rosiness of love bloomed once more. "Jack. Have I told you how much I love that man, Anna? We'll be together forever. We'll have half a dozen children and even more grandchildren. We'll fill this house with more love than anyone ever thought possible. And you, my dear, will be by my side for as long as you like."

"I will?"

Bebe took my hands then kissed my cheek before turning suddenly as if someone tapped her shoulder. Laughing, she danced away into swirling smoke flickering with orange flames.

I sat up gasping as though escaping from real fire. Less than a day in Cedar Grove and I was having strange dreams again. Who was Jack, Bebe's romantic partner or the one who got away? I rubbed my face and blew out a long breath. Why would I dream about them?

As I set Mabel on the desk, I shoved my curiosity aside and settled in to capture my thoughts while the house was quiet. The three-hour time difference between Toronto and Cedar Grove could work well for me until I adjusted. All I needed was a strong cup of coffee, but I didn't want to disturb anyone.

An hour later, at six o'clock local time, I tackled Mom's and Emily's long strings of texts. Each contained questions about Cedar Grove. Luckily, it was nine Toronto time. They were both at work. After that, I fielded Roxie's half dozen calls, texts, and emails. Each message she sent offered a new way to find our father.

One email. That was all she'd get.

Yawning, I became absorbed in my latest work in progress. I only half noticed when daylight broke, and the sky went from purple velvet to pinkish then blue.

My stomach grumbled, but I powered on. I didn't pay much attention to the hum of voices beyond the walls of my room. I brushed them off as being leftovers from my overactive imagination. As a writer, I'd become accustomed to hearing voices before putting their words onto paper.

It slowly dawned on me these voices were real and were seeping beneath my door into my room. I caught words like "money" and "heirs", but I didn't think much of it. I focused on making notes and creating another outline.

A woman's voice warbled along with the recording of that singer I couldn't place. Something about dreaming a little dream. Bebe loved that song so much I'd heard it in my dreams, too.

"Could be worse," I said aloud, delving back into typing. Just as my hero cradled the heroine's face in his hands and was about to plant a passionate kiss on his lady love, the lamp near my elbow flickered then died. Ten seconds later, Mabel's screen went black.

After three years and two books, I'd finally killed her.

"Oh, come on, Mabel. Wake up, baby." I fanned my face with my half-filled notebook. "We can't leave them like that. They were *this* close to sealing the deal."

No response.

I shut my laptop then ducked beneath the desk. Mabel was unplugged. I'd either kicked the cord or I hadn't plugged her in properly when I got here. No wonder she'd shut down. Good thing I'd learned early on to save my work every few lines. No more lost manuscripts like with my first book.

Just as I pushed the plug into the outlet, the lights went out.

"That's just great." I crawled out from beneath the desk as my stomach grumbled again. I'd missed both coffee and breakfast, but I'd written over a fifteen hundred words and done an outline of the next two novels in my new series. Shivering, I dressed in a thick sweater, blue jeans, and warm socks.

With the power out and Mabel's battery out of juice, I resorted to pen and paper. Outside, the abrupt change from bright sun to dismal gray made me cringe. The sky was gray. The beach was gray. Even the patches of snow seemed dismal and moody. Not that much different from Toronto really, but here I didn't have Emily to brighten my mood with stories of life at the newspaper office. Nor did I have my job at the candy shop for a distraction.

On the upside, Bebe couldn't play Ella Fitzgerald—that was the singer's name—with the power out. I stood to stretch a kink out of my shoulders then realized the lack of electricity wasn't about to stop her. She was singing like a drunken canary without her record for accompaniment.

I had two options. To tolerate her serenade while I wrote by hand, or to head out to see the little town I was going to spend the next month in. I draped my scarf around the back of my neck and pulled on earmuffs, more against Bebe's singing than any anticipation of cold. Toronto was quite a bit warmer than Cedar Grove today. I'd checked the weather app on my phone. Four times.

I tucked my phone and my pineapple stone into my pocket before stepping into the hallway. Locking the door to my room, I stuck the key next to my rock, and marvelled at the craftsmanship on my way down the stairs. The entire manor was a work of art and worthy of being a setting in one of my romance novels.

After a long morning of writing, it seemed I was a bit full of myself.

"You missed breakfast, Miss Cadell," Anna said. before I'd even reached the door. "Can I get you anything?"

"Alison, please." I slid off my earmuffs. "Good afternoon, Mrs. Larkin."

"Call me Anna. We missed you at breakfast. And lunch."

I flashed a sheepish grin. "I was inspired and got a lot of writing done before the power went out. Does that happen often?"

She nodded. "Usually only when there's a storm. I haven't heard what happened to knock it out this time. Next time, I'll bring breakfast up to you."

"That sounds lovely. Thank you. I tend to get distracted sometimes and lose track of time."

Anna lit a couple of candles. She was either going for ambience or preparing for a long, gloomy day. Either way, she appeared youthful in the flickering light. "I hope you have pens and paper."

"I do, but I might need to pick up more. Do you think it'll be off for longer than an hour or so?"

"Hard to say." A blonde woman wearing a dark blue uniform entered from the utility room. "Sounds like it was caused by a downed powerline. I heard it's out all over Cedar Grove."

Anna chuckled. "Alison, this is Sheila, our housekeeper. She keeps this place tidy and the laundry fresh."

"Pleased to meet you."

Sheila flashed a warm smile. "Speaking of, I'm off to change Bebe's sheets. Wear some gloves out there, Miss Cadell, it's chilly today."

"I will, thanks."

"Dinner is at six," Anna told me. "I'll barbecue if I have to."

"That sounds delicious. It's been a long time since I've had barbecue." I headed out into the midday gloom and pulled the door closed behind me. I checked the time on my phone then put on my gloves against the damp cold.

Ash gray skies and small, delicate snowflakes greeted me as I walked down the circular cobblestone drive toward the street. Cedar Grove wasn't exactly a cheery place when the lights were out all over town. No colorful traffic or Christmas lights. Even the few flakes that drifted from the sky seemed lackluster. Blah, for want of a better word.

Sheila called me Miss Cadell, yet Anna had only called me Alison when she introduced us. They must have talked about me earlier.

I crammed my hands into my pockets as I wandered toward the center of town with my mind on that abruptly interrupted literary kiss. Only one place in town had lights glowing and voices ringing out. The oddly named Burlap Diner. The coffee smelled good even wafting from a distance.

"Why not?" I could use a cup of coffee and maybe even lunch. Whether or not the electricity came back on, I could get coffee to go. That would give me enough power to write for the rest of the afternoon with pen and paper by candlelight.

The diner was packed. Presumably because every store around it had temporarily closed while waiting for the electricity to return.

I strolled past occupied tables toward the counter and chose an empty stool near the far end.

"What can I get you, honey?" the middle-aged woman behind the counter asked.

"I'd love a vanilla bean latte with soy, please."

She raised her eyebrows. "Excuse me?"

I glanced around the diner then recanted. "Coffee. With cream, please. Oh, and could I get a burger and fries with a side of gravy?"

"You bet, hon." The waitress pulled out a clean white mug. She poured my steaming coffee while she glanced at a man near the wall wearing a gray toque speckled with glittering water droplets. "How's your grandma doing, Mac? I don't see her out and about much lately."

Mac hunched over his coffee and a barely touched crossword puzzle. "She's good, Violet, better than that friend of hers who swears someone's out to get her."

I added cream to my coffee.

"Dementia will do that. She's had good reason to be suspicious." Violet wiped coffee splatters off the counter. "Did you get your ticket for the McKittrick Christmas party yet?"

"Why?" he asked. "So I can mingle with a bunch of nosy neighbors and pose under the mistletoe with girls my mom sets me up with that I don't like? No thanks. I'm working that night."

"It's over a month away," she said.

"I'll volunteer. Besides, I don't need anyone to remind me I'm single."

I cast a quick glance in his direction while I added a spoonful of sugar to my mug. Unshaven, he wore his wool hat pulled low, leaving a short fringe of dark hair sticking out. He wore a red and black checked, lined lumberjack jacket. My heart skipped a beat. He was the type of man I'd envisioned meeting at the airport. The same kind of guy I avoided while walking down the streets of Toronto. Here in Cedar Grove, he fit in with every other unshaven male.

Violet chuckled as she placed a plate with my burger and fries in front of me then said, "And a Merry Bah Humbug to you to, Ebenezer."

Mac flashed a brief grin as he pointed to his cup for a refill. "I don't hate Christmas. I'm the guy who strings up half the twinkly lights around town before the bloody parade in two weeks."

"My hero. One day you'll win some pretty girl's heart with talk like that." Violet fanned her face with one hand as she winked at me.

I raised an eyebrow, surprised he'd be stable on a ladder. While he looked like a tough customer, he didn't smell like anything unsavory, just faintly of citrus soap and sweat. I wasn't about to get closer for a better sniff.

His phone vibrated on the counter. "Back to work. Power should be back on soon. Can I get that coffee to go, Vi?"

"For you, darlin'? Of course." She poured his coffee in a paper cup. "Be careful out there, Mac. You boys could be in for a busy day."

Mac's gaze met mine as he laughed. His dark green eyes reminded me of a stormy ocean. "You seem to forget who you're dealing with."

Violet handed him his coffee. "So do you. I changed your diapers, remember?"

"You keep reminding me." His face reddened beneath the scruff. He tossed a five-dollar bill on the counter and left the diner.

"Can I get you anything else, hon?" Violet asked, as she wiped the counter.

"This is good." I gazed around the room. "The restaurant's busy."

"The owner installed a generator years ago. On stormy days, we're the only place on the block with electricity."

I raised my eyebrows. "It's gray out, but not stormy."

"One of the guys backed a truck into a power pole while they were stringing Christmas lights." Violet chuckled. "Coffee and Irish Cream will get them every time. That's why they get the boys from the firehall to lend a hand."

"That guy you were talking to is a firefighter?" I glanced toward the door.

"One of Cedar Grove's most eligible bachelors. A lot of women would love to get their hands on him."

"Count me out." I didn't need complications. I dipped a fry in the gravy. "Why is the diner the only place with a generator? That seems short-sighted."

Violet wiped a coffee spill off the counter. "Every place has one. It's just become habit for everyone to meet here for coffee until the power comes back on."

I stirred more cream into my mug. "They turn blackouts into social events?"

"You bet. We're a resilient lot. Are you new here, or just visiting?"

"I'm staying at Thistlewood Manor."

Violet seemed to stiffen. "Oh. Fancy. I hear there's a famous author staying there. Have you met him yet?"

"Anna never said anything. Who is it?"

"A.J. Cadell," Violet said. "I've never heard of him, but mostly because I'm more into movies than books."

Since I probably glowed like a shiny Christmas bulb, I bowed my head before asking, "What have you heard about the guy?"

Violet scanned the room to check on her customers. "Just that he's some uppity writer from Toronto who's here to work on his next book and do some stuff at the library. I'll have to ask around. See if anyone's met him yet. Excuse me. Back in a jiff."

A.J. Cadell seemed to be a bit of an enigma to the locals. Well, to Violet anyway. Considering she waited on and talked to nearly everyone in town, especially during a blackout, she would have the low down on local gossip.

Why would someone bring me to Cedar Grove if no one ever heard of me? As if that mattered, I wasn't well known in Toronto either. Aside from the woman I'd signed a book for in the candy shop and the weird reporter who'd done the impressive newspaper interview thanks to Emily. I was still able to travel across the country in complete anonymity, which wouldn't change anytime soon.

"Not with that attitude anyway." I chided my own negativity, then eavesdropped on the conversations around me.

Violet took orders and rushed past as I sipped my coffee and nibbled my fries. I made notes on napkin after napkin to finish that steamy kiss scene I'd started writing earlier. I stuffed my notes in my pocket and gulped the last of my extra-strength coffee. Paying my bill, I pulled on my hat and gloves.

I barely made it to the end of the block before electricity jolted the air. The hair on the back of my neck stood on end as the gray vanished in a snap. A burst of colors in a myriad of brilliant rainbow hues, as well as Christmas lights, blinked to life and a cacophony of sound assaulted my senses. The strains of *Santa Claus is Coming to Town* serenaded the entire street. Main Street, silent only a dozen rapid heartbeats ago, suddenly bustled with people as it shone with twinkling lights, glowing candy canes, and snowmen.

With still a month and a half to go before Christmas, my bravery to explore suddenly ebbed. I held my hand over my pocket to touch my stone. It was like some weird Christmas horror movie.

Thankfully, my phone rang, saving me from the overwhelming abundance of good cheer. I speed-walked toward Thistlewood to calm my nerves and get away from the swell of commercialism and noise. "Hey, Em."

"Hey, how's the new Writer-in-Residence in Cedar Grove?" my roommate asked.

"A total enigma." I groaned.

Emily chuckled. "Yup, that sounds like you. I meant the writing though."

I glanced over my shoulder to make sure no delinquent ghosts of Christmas cheer were following me like static-charged tinsel. "It was going great until the power went out and Mabel died."

"Mabel died? I hope you mean your laptop, not our old teacher."

"Yes, my laptop."

"Is there a party going on?" Emily asked. "It sounds like fun."

"I'm sure it is. If you're in the mood for loud music and bright lights." I dodged a couple of pedestrians who jostled past me with over-stuffed bags. It wasn't even mid-November, yet the Christmas season seemed in full swing in Cedar Grove. "The electricity just came back on. Now it looks like elves threw up all over town."

"That's not like you. Why are you out and why is Christmas so early? It's only a three-hour time difference, not two months."

"Aren't they already decorating in the Distillery District and putting wreaths on the light posts in Toronto before the Santa Parade?" I asked.

"Good point."

Why was I out here? I could have stayed at the manor near the fireplace with a glass of wine and a late lunch while I wrote by hand. Maybe not the wine. "The power went out, my laptop died, and I had nothing better to do. I did find a great coffee shop though. The Burlap Café. It's kind of retro. You'd love it."

"Ah, there's the Alison I know and love," Emily said. "You enjoy social interactions and excitement on your terms. No idea how you'd have survived the candy store for another Christmas."

"Necessity and anxiety medication. Give me a good cup of coffee and a romance novel any day. It beats being someone's pet project."

Emily huffed so hard I pictured her rolling her black-lined eyes. "Forget Cory. Surely there's someone out there who'll drag you out of your room."

"Speaking of." I brightened. "Since the power's back on, I can get back to work. A good book doesn't write itself."

"That's what I hear," Emily said. "Miss you. I'll talk to you later."

"Miss you, too." I paused and tried to capture the wonder and so-called magic for my novel. After a few minutes, I gave up. The upcoming holiday was lost on me. Without someone to share it with, Christmas was just another day. I had half a mind to stay in Cedar Grove to avoid it altogether.

I took my time sauntering back to Thistlewood while I collected ideas to add to that steamy kiss I'd written. I dreamed of finding that kind of love one day. The sweep-a-woman-off-her-feet kind of love that I only read or wrote about. The kind Bebe mentioned last night while we danced. Now, she was a true romantic and would make an endearing character. I decided to interview her.

Quickening my pace, I jumped as the wail of sirens pierced the air. A police car raced past closely followed by two firetrucks. They headed away from the downtown core in the direction of Thistlewood. People emerged onto the streets, pausing. Some followed to see what was going on.

My heart hammered against my ribs as a shiver swept over me. I ran toward the flashing lights as the acrid scent of smoke met my nostrils. Firefighters swarmed the scene. While I couldn't see flames, the stench of smoke became overpowering the closer I got to the manor.

"Mabel!" My first thought was of my writing. I darted across the thinning patches of snow on the lawn toward the manor, dodging first responders. My life's work was on that laptop.

A strong arm clad in a heavy canvas coat caught me across the stomach with enough force to knock the wind out of me. "You can't go in there, Miss. You need to stay back."

"I need to get Mabel! She's inside!" I shouted, struggling against him.

He tried to get a grip on me, but I fought hard. "Are you sure your friend's inside? Take a good look around."

I pried his hand off my arm. "I have to get her out of there."

"It's not safe," he yelled, grabbing my shoulders and looking me in the eye, making sure he had my full attention. "I'll go get her. You wait here. Which room is she in?"

"I know where she is!" I yelled.

The firefighter waved to get his supervisor's attention. The instant his focus flickered away, I yanked out from beneath his hand and bolted for the front entrance. Smoke reached my nostrils as I stubbed my toe on the bottom stair. No time for pain or fear of heights. Mabel's life was in danger. The firefighter was behind me. I had to move fast. Hopefully, his heavy turnout gear would slow him down to give me time to rescue Mabel.

Not seeing any flames, I sprinted up the stairs holding a hand over my nose. I tried to breathe through my mouth, which was no better. The air was thick with smoke. My eyes burned and tears rolled down my cheeks. Several smoke detectors screamed at me to get out.

I heard the firefighter's boots clomping up the stairs behind me. His shouts reached my ears as I grabbed the door knob and struggled to shove my key into the lock.

Heart racing, I got the door open and gulped a greedy mouthful of fresh air before the smoke billowed in from the hallway.

"Where is she?" he asked, as he caught up to me. He was in way better shape than I gave him credit for. "We have to get out of here."

"Once I get Mabel, I'll get out. I promise."

"You don't have a choice. Where is she?" He yanked open my closet door while I grabbed my laptop and shoved it into the bag.

"There's no one in here." He pointed to my bag. "What's that?"

"My laptop. Mabel."

Growling, the firefighter lunged across the room and grabbed the back of my coat as other firefighters hustled past my door. "That's what you came up here for? I ought to throw you out the window. We need to get out. Now!"

"I'm going." I coughed, then tried to dodge past him, but those heavy gloves had latched onto my coat like lobster claws. There was no escape.

Before he could throw me out the window or down the stairs, I pointed to the door across the hall. Bebe's music was still playing.

"Someone's in there," I shouted.

"Yeah? What's that laptop's name?" he asked.

I coughed. "It's Bebe."

Shouting to another firefighter, he shoved me toward the stairwell. "Get this girl outside."

He placed a hand on the closed door before reaching for the knob. When he noticed me frozen in place, he yelled, "I told you to get out!"

As he pushed open Bebe's door, smoke billowed out. I could barely breathe. This was something right out of my horrific, haunting dreams.

I had to escape. Dazed, I kept one hand on the wall and felt my way onto the landing. The banister guided me toward the bottom of the stairs, but my feet were heavy and my head started spinning. Afraid I was going to fall, I froze. I clung to the banister as I clutched Mabel to my chest.

Suddenly, I was flying.

My feet skimmed each step as a strong hand gripped my coat. The firefighter propelled me down the stairs and through the open door to the outside.

I gagged as I gulped the crisp afternoon air. My nose stung. My eyes watered profusely. Tears chilled my cheeks. I doubled over with my lungs in spasm. I retched, my dignity long gone.

I squeezed Mabel to my chest as I sat on the icy ground waiting for a lecture about risking both our lives for a replaceable computer.

No lecture came.

My firefighter stooped to lay a woman with long white hair on the asphalt. He checked her pulse.

"Is she okay?" I croaked, then coughed so hard I nearly threw up.

"Stay back, Miss." He pulled off his helmet to perform CPR.

I wanted to creep closer, but a paramedic was shining a light in my eyes. I watched the firefighter's steady rhythm of breaths and chest compressions until one of his colleagues took over.

My firefighter backed away and shone his flashlight on Bebe, illuminating the ashy blue of her skin. She was so pale and still, it made my heart ache. Dark marks dotted her neck, as if someone had grabbed and choked her, leaving the outlines of fingers on her flesh.

Those marks weren't there yesterday.

A tear cut through the soot on my firefighter's cheek. He obviously knew Bebe. He cared about her. He helped the paramedics bundle her onto a gurney to whisk her to the nearest ambulance.

The strains of Bebe's favorite song echoed through my mind as someone steered me toward a second ambulance. I remembered that scratchy record and watching Bebe dance. I'd probably hum that song in my sleep for weeks.

Tears streamed down my cheeks. I didn't even know the woman.

One of the paramedics was asking me questions as Bebe's ambulance departed with lights flashing and sirens wailing. I barely heard his questions. Someone else fastened an oxygen mask to my face. I didn't resist. My mind was a million kilometers away.

I looked around for my brave firefighter, but I couldn't see him. How did he know Bebe?

Stupid thought. Cedar Grove wasn't Toronto. Everyone had to have known her.

Some probably even loved her. Except whoever tried to strangle her.

While there was a lot of smoke inside the manor, there were no flames flickering against the gray sky. And no sweltering heat radiating out from the inside.

"Are you okay, honey?" Anna appeared out of nowhere and pulled me into a hug, oxygen mask and all, as a wave of nausea gripped me. "I heard you helped find Bebe. I'm so grateful. I hope she's okay."

My face warmed as I nodded.

She wagged her finger. "What possessed you to run into the fire?"

I clutched my laptop bag to my chest as fresh tears swarmed my eyes.

"Your computer." Anna's expression softened.

I tugged the oxygen mask to one side. "Stupid, right?"

"Yes, but you might've saved Bebe's life."

My breath stuck in my throat. Why hadn't Anna noticed Bebe was missing before I showed up?

"They would have searched the building," I told her, my voice raspy from the smoke.

When I coughed, a paramedic replaced the mask. I sighed as I gazed past Anna to search for the firefighter who'd pulled us from the building. From where I sat, they all looked alike. Heroes wearing dirty turncoats and helmets.

"I need to speak to someone about alternate accommodations," Anna said. "Stay right here so I can find you. Promise?"

I nodded.

A few flickers of flame lapped the insides of the windows at the far end of Thistlewood Manor. The room at the end of the hall near mine and Bebe's. The former love nest for the owners of the manor. All of those portraits, the four-poster bed, the romantic, gauzy white curtains would be gone. I closed my eyes and prayed the firefighters could stop the flames before they reached our rooms.

I tried to imagine how the owners would feel if they knew what was happening to their dream home.

Anna returned a few minutes later. "How are you doing, Alison?"

Still masked, I gave her a thumbs up.

"Ken Archer owns a bed and breakfast down the road. He's offered you and Owen rooms for as long as needed."

The paramedic checked my vitals one more time before he removed my mask.

"What about you?" I asked. "You won't be allowed inside for days. Not until they make sure there's no structural damage. Where will you stay?"

Anna chuckled. "Are you sure you write romances and not mystery novels?"

"I've been told my father was a firefighter."

"Was?"

"According to my mom, he was a smokejumper. One of those crazy people who jump from planes into remote forest fires. She thought he was a bad boy and fell hard." I rubbed my hands as I babbled, not even sure I made sense. Shock had set in. I was cold and shaking. "It didn't take her long to realize he was an adrenalin junkie and not ready for a wife or kids."

"Is he still a firefighter?" Anna asked, glancing around.

I shrugged, searching my pockets for my phone. "Up until a few weeks ago, I thought he was dead. Now my sister wants me to find him in time for her wedding. Cedar Grove is where my search ended. I told my sister she was delusional, but then Robert Foster brought me that offer."

When a passenger van pulled up nearby, driven by a woman, Anna seemed relieved. "There's your ride. Ken and his staff will take care of you. With luck, Thistlewood should reopen tomorrow."

"I'll keep my fingers crossed." I said, filled with doubt as I gazed toward the manor. "At least everyone got out in time. Who called the fire department?"

"No idea. Considering where the fire started, I wouldn't have even noticed until half the building was gone."

I raised my eyebrows. "Where were you?"

"In the kitchen making dinner," she said.

"Who was home besides you and Bebe?"

"What are you, the FBI?" Anna asked. "Owen was here, and Sal was in the garage taking care of the shuttle van. We've been having issues with it lately."

"The garage is right below the—"

Anna smiled as she touched my cheek. "You're jetlagged and in shock, honey. Why don't you go get some rest?"

As she herded Owen, who was carrying a small cage, and me into the passenger van, something else bothered me. I hugged Mabel and kept my mouth shut. Why didn't anyone realize Bebe was missing and tell the firefighters, especially since she wasn't cognizant enough to leave on her own? Something about the whole fire stunk, besides the smoke.

Ken Archer's bed and breakfast sprawled along the cove on the other side of Cedar Grove. The main house was a smaller version of Thistlewood and made of large cedar logs that glowed golden in the lamp light. Five smaller cottages clustered around the backyard closer to the shore. Every structure was built from cedar logs.

There was even a large rock at the end of the driveway engraved to announce, "Georgia Shores Cottages." What kind of machine did they use to carve such large boulders? Possibly the same ones they used to create tombstones. I shuddered. Not a cheery thought.

"Welcome to Georgia Shores," the driver announced. It was then I recognized her. Sheila, the housekeeper at Thistlewood.

Too tired to make sense of things, I closed my eyes as she parked the van near the front door of the main house, then hopped out to open the passenger door. She led me inside.

A glittering chandelier lit the main lobby of the two-story main house. The aroma of a hot dinner welcomed us.

Owen and I were joined at the table by a young woman who introduced herself as Teena Archer. Dinner was spaghetti with a hearty meat sauce and warm, homemade garlic bread. I wanted to ask Teena how she was related to Ken but there was little conversation. Everyone seemed stunned into silence.

Ken still hadn't appeared by the time we'd finished eating. Getting approval from Sheila, Teena showed me up the blue-carpeted stairs to my room.

Lean with long legs, she seemed as eager to look after me as Owen was when he'd first brought my luggage to my room at Thistlewood. She unlocked the door and handed me the key. "I've left you some pajamas, a pair of yoga pants, and a sweater. There's a toothbrush and toothpaste in your bathroom, too."

"That was really thoughtful, thank you."

Teena tossed her long curls back as she flashed a sheepish smile. "Actually, I have an ulterior motive for being extra nice."

"You do?" I asked, meeting her gaze.

Her cheeks grew rosy. She fluttered her long eyelashes as she handed me the room key. "Bebe told me all about you and I've read both of your books. Is it true you're here to work on your next one?"

As I debated whether to tell Teena the whole story, another yawn sidetracked me. The time difference plus the fire had finally defeated me. I struggled to keep my eyes open. "Yes."

Teena bit her lower lip. "I'm sorry, Miss Cadell, you've had a long day. I'd love to hear all about Toronto sometime. I've never been there. Actually, I've never been anywhere, except to our cottage and into Victoria."

I set my laptop bag on the bed and peered into the small bathroom. Just as she said, there were daffodil yellow towels along with a bar of green soap, a blend of lime and lemongrass, by the sink. On a shelf sat a small pile of clothing that was topped off by a pink toothbrush, a travel-size tube of toothpaste, and a comb.

"As much as I'd love to take a shower, I'm wiped. Maybe you can tell me about Victoria tomorrow and I'll you whatever you want to know about Toronto."

"That sounds awesome," Teena said. "Towels are in the bathroom with a bar of this amazing soap my mom and I make. I sell it at the local farmer's markets. You'll love the scent. Have a good night."

"You, too. Thanks for the clothes, the soap, everything."

The room wasn't as big as my room at Thistlewood. But the décor was more up to date and every bit as cozy. I changed into the silky blue pajama pants and t-shirt, took my anxiety medication, then plucked my stone from the pocket of my jeans. Clutching it in one hand, I collapsed onto the bed, my fall cushioned by a thick feather duvet. Releasing a long sigh, I melted into the softness.

When I closed my eyes, all I could picture was Bebe lying on the ground with the firefighter struggling to save her life. The marks on her neck seemed to glow like embers in my dream. Did she clutch her throat when smoke filled her room, or had someone strangled her?

Chilled, I crawled beneath the covers with one last thought fluttering through my mind. Where was Bebe's family? Would they take care of her while she recovered?

If she recovered.

My sleepy thoughts jumbled into a series of nightmares about fire. Family. My father. My mother. Bebe. A faceless boy. As usual, none of it made any sense.

During one of the many times I awoke in the night, something Teena said came to mind. I stared at the stippled ceiling with my eyes half open as the thought took form. How did Bebe know about me before I arrived?

Chapter Five

The next morning, I gazed around the room, struggling to remember where I was. The smell of smoke brought it all back. The fire. The firefighter. Bebe.

I pulled the duvet around me as sadness washed over me. While my fictional characters never seemed to mind bad smells of any kind, I was sure Ken and his staff wouldn't appreciate the stink of smoke in my hair and on my skin.

As I rolled out of bed, my foot hit my laptop bag. I stuck my pineapple stone in one of the side pockets, then tucked the bag beneath the covers.

I wandered into the bathroom. Turning on the shower, I stepped into the claw-foot tub and released a sigh when the rush of water carried away the smell of smoke. Scrubbed and refreshed, I dressed in the yoga pants and shirt, glad to find Teena had thought to provide me fresh underwear as well.

I wandered into the hallway, lured to the stairs by the scents of coffee and freshly baked bread. All along the hall hung photos of Cedar Grove from various time periods. I took pictures of the ones that caught my eye. The aerial views were breathtaking.

I went downstairs hoping there would be good news about both Bebe and Thistlewood.

"Good morning, Miss Cadell," a tall, gangly man with bright blue eyes and hair the color of cold ashes turned to face me with the coffee pot in one hand. Dark circles shadowed his eyes, but his infectious smile set me at ease. "Cream or sugar for your coffee?"

"Both, please. You must be Mr. Archer." I glanced around the kitchen at the tidy, granite-topped counters. The delicious scent of fresh baking that had wafted through the entire house emanated from cooling racks covered with loaves of bread and muffins. "Looks like you've been busy."

"Call me, Ken. Please," he said. "I've had help today. Teena gives me a hand, then takes off for a run before she delivers our complimentary breakfast baskets to the cottages."

Sheila, the housekeeper from Thistlewood, sat at the kitchen table sipping from a handcrafted mug. Across the table, Owen bowed over a notepad writing furiously. His hair stuck up in all directions.

"Can I get you some breakfast?" Ken asked.

I was tempted by the muffins. "No, thank you. Coffee is fine. I was thinking of heading to the diner, so I'm not underfoot. To get some work done."

Ken raised his index finger. "Ah, Sheila said there was a writer staying at Thistlewood. Is that you? And you're not underfoot. You're a guest."

"A.J. Cadell. You can call me Alison." My face grew warm.

"Isn't that counterintuitive, going to a busy diner to write?"

I shook my head. "Not really. The hustle and bustle and variety of people can be inspiring. Have you heard from Anna?"

"Not yet. I'm not sure where she ended up. I doubt the fire marshal let her stay at Thistlewood with all that smoke." When the phone rang, he checked the number before his smile faded. "Sorry, I need to take this."

"Make yourself at home," Sheila said, as Ken left the room. "There are some great places here for you to work. There's a beautiful stone fireplace in the front room already lit. It's a nice place to relax with a cup of coffee and a warm muffin."

"Thanks. Do you work here as well as at Thistlewood?" I asked, eyeing the muffins.

Owen snorted. "She lives here, silly."

"Be nice." Sheila shot him a scowl. "Alison's our guest."

Our guest? I raised an eyebrow as I gazed out the patio doors at the Strait. Another gray day. "This place reminds me of Thistlewood. Were they designed by the same architect?"

"Same builder, too," Owen spoke around a mouthful of muffin. Melted chocolate clung to his lip.

"What are you working on today?" I sat next to him.

When his gaze met mine, I nearly laughed out loud. He reminded me of an image of Mozart I'd once seen with that untamed hair and those wild eyes. Something in that gaze made my stomach lurch even though he didn't utter a word.

Ken broke the spell when he returned to the room. "I was going to make pancakes. Are you sure you don't want to join us for breakfast?"

I swallowed hard. "No, thank you. I'm going to take a walk and get some fresh air. I'm still a bit agitated."

"I can toss your clothes in the laundry while you're out if you'd like. Just leave them in the bathroom with the towels." Sheila got up to refill her cup. "Hopefully, we'll hear from Anna soon and get you moved back into Thistlewood in a few days. It doesn't sound like there was much damage outside of—"

"Sheila," Ken warned.

She shrugged. "I'm sure Alison would feel better once she's settled in her own room."

The look he shot her made me cringe. I shrugged and told them, "Considering it was only my room for a day, I'm not that attached. I'll leave my clothes upstairs."

Although I did miss the view at Thistlewood. I gave in and took a muffin before I savored my coffee. The scent of chocolate chips and walnuts made me swoon. Emily would be in muffin heaven.

"I should've brought Jelly downstairs. I hope he's okay," Owen said, his voice muffled as he continued to write.

Sheila frowned. "I'm sure he'll be happy in the little cage for a few days."

"Who's Jelly?" I asked.

"My hamster." Owen beamed. "Bebe gave him to me for my birthday."

I turned to Ken. "Speaking of Bebe, have you heard any news yet?"

Sheila said nothing. Ken cleared his throat and looked at his phone again. Tension seemed to fill the room.

Deep in the pit of my stomach, I knew whatever news there was had to be bad. Was it possible Ken tried to get rid of the competition? Not likely since Sheila and Owen were here. I didn't hear any arguments last night, although I'd been focused on Bebe and the firefighter.

Setting my empty cup in the sink, I excused myself and left the kitchen. The atmosphere inside the house was so stifling I itched to rush out into the crisp air. The moment I reached the stairs, the whispering began. I couldn't make out anything more than Ken asking, "Doesn't she know?"

I made sure Mabel was safely tucked in my laptop bag and set my smoky clothing on the edge of the bathtub before I pulled the strap over my shoulder. The Burlap Diner was sounding better by the second. If I wasn't careful, it could become my happy place while I was in Cedar Grove. I even thought about immortalizing it in one of my books.

As I walked to the end of the driveway, I paused beside the etched rock. Georgia Shores Cottages stood on the edge of Cedar Grove, about a half kilometer from Thistlewood. A smaller version of Thistlewood Manor, it was comprised of five small cottages, which appeared filled to capacity. The entire place was cozy and homey, especially with the smell of fresh baking to greet guests.

By the time I arrived, the Burlap Diner was quiet. I contemplated taking over a booth near the window, but I chose a stool at the counter instead. After all that happened the night before, I was positive I'd hear several theories. All I had to do was stay within earshot of Violet.

I'd barely settled onto a stool before she was pouring coffee into a white mug in front of me. "I hear you helped find Bebe last night. When Mac came in, I got an earful about the crazy lady who nearly got him killed."

"Mac?" I groaned as I pictured those dark green eyes, then deflated at how she assumed it was me. "He was the firefighter who dragged us out?"

Violet's eyes lit up. "Ha! I knew it was you."

"And I'm sure he'll be happy to never run into me again."

"Is it true you ran inside for your laptop and he had to haul you out?" she asked.

"Yes." I pretended to focus on adding cream and sugar to my coffee. "In my defense, my entire life is on that laptop. If anything happened to it, I'd be ruined."

"Yeah, well, he's pretty steamed about it." She slid a piece of lemon meringue pie onto a plate. "Breakfast is on me. It seems like your first couple of days in Cedar Grove haven't exactly been a joy ride."

I stirred my coffee and thought about the scary look Owen gave me earlier. It seemed my arrival had stirred up some bad things. "I have a feeling things won't get easier any time soon."

Violet patted my hand on her way to grab the pot of coffee. "Just stay away from Mac until he cools down and you'll be fine."

"I'll try." I blinked away tears. The guy must hate me by now. "Have you heard anything about Bebe?"

Before she could answer, a tall, thin man slid onto the stool next to me. He ordered a cup of coffee and scowled in my direction. "Hey. You're one of them Thistlewood people, ain't cha?"

"I'm staying there, yes." I stuck a forkful of pie in my mouth and wished he would go away before I was tempted to correct his grammar.

The thin man did move away, but only a fraction of an inch. "Did you hear the old gal was murdered?"

"Sal, what are you talking about?" Violet asked, sliding a cup in front of him.

"Bebe. Someone killed her."

My throat tightened. I needed a swig of coffee to wash the pie down. "Murdered? Is that what the police said?"

"Maybe," he said. "You gonna eat that pie?"

I pulled my plate away from him. "Yes. Where did you hear she was murdered?"

"Rumor has it someone killed her before they set the fire."

"A rumor. Of course." Violet threw up her hands before she took the coffee pot and walked away.

"You're that writer from Toronto," he said.

"I am."

Sal frowned. "Were you there last night?"

"I was there when someone rescued Bebe." I left out the part about being the crazy lady.

"And now she's dead. Is that a coincidence?" Sal leaned closer and whispered. "Did you kill her?"

"I didn't touch her. Were you there last night?" I clenched my jaw. From the marks I saw on Bebe's neck, murder was possible.

"No."

His answer surprised her since Anna had told her he was in the garage at the time. "Then who told you someone killed Bebe?"

He glanced around us then leaned close. "Chloe at the hair salon told Maisie from the gas station, who told Roger at the Stop'n'Shop who told me."

"Is that it?" I stared.

"What more do you want? It's only nine o'clock. Nothing's open yet."

"I thought you'd be hard at work cleaning up after the fire." Violet said when she returned.

Sal held up a hand. "Just got back to town. We were at the cottage last night."

I narrowed my eyes. "You weren't working in the garage?"

"Nope. I was up near Buttle Lake. Anna asked me to come back early this morning and meet her at the police station. I'm off to see how much damage there is. I'll be by for lunch later, Vi. Be a doll and save me a piece of that blueberry pie."

"Of course." As soon as Sal left the cafe, Violet leaned cross the counter. "Doesn't that make your mystery writer senses tingle? Anna told me after the fire last night that you're A.J. Cadell. I can't believe you didn't tell me. Here I was under the impression you were a guy."

I banged my cup on the counter. "I'm a romance novelist."

"Romance. Mystery." Violet shrugged. "If you ask me, there's not a lot of difference between the two. Not in my experience, anyway."

"Mine, too." I thought for a long moment. "I did think it was strange Bebe had finger marks on her neck."

"I didn't hear that part," she said.

"It's probably one of those details the police won't make public."

Violet swiped a finger across her lips. "Then I'll keep that nugget to myself."

For the sake of a police investigation, I hoped she would. "How well did you know Bebe?"

"I knew of her mostly." She wiped the counter with a blue cloth. "Bebe was a recluse for the past ten years, which is why Anna ran Thistlewood. The rare times Bebe came into town was for doctor appointments and the annual McKittrick Family Christmas Party."

"The way you talk, it sounds as though Bebe owned Thistlewood."

Violet paused to greet an elderly man who entered then continued as if I hadn't spoken, "That Christmas Party is a big deal around here. It's always fun to see what new things the McKittrick family comes up with every year."

A steaming coffee waterfall streamed from the carafe as she filled my cup again. "Speaking of family," I said, "did Bebe have family in town? There must be someone taking care of her arrangements."

Violet seemed to hesitate then shrugged. "I'm sure Anna and Foster have contact information. Anna's lived with Bebe for years and Foster's been her lawyer since the Stone Age."

"Oh really?" I took one last sip of my coffee and wondered if Bebe could've been my mysterious benefactor. "I'll talk to Anna. Bebe couldn't be alone in the world."

Violet winked. "Now you're thinking like a mystery writer."

"Which I'd be happy about if I was a mystery writer," I told her, then asked, "Is Sal a firefighter?"

"Just the caretaker at Thistlewood."

Which was why Anna thought he was in the garage. Didn't she know he was going to his cottage? He had an alibi and, possibly, a witness. Odd.

I thought about why I'd accepted Foster's offer then asked, "Have you lived here long?"

"My whole life. Why?"

I glanced around. "Writing a book wasn't the only reason I came here. I'm looking for someone."

"Ooh, the plot thickens. Is it an old boyfriend? I know a few single guys, but most of them are single for good reasons. Mostly Mommy issues."

"Too much information." I covered my eyes with one hand.

Violet laughed. "Why else are you here?"

"My sister is getting married in May. We both thought our dad was dead, but Mom insists he's still alive. I've tracked him down to this part of the country but other than that he's as elusive as Bigfoot."

Violet leaned on the counter. "Maybe I know him. What's his name?"

"Perry Beyer."

Her eyes grew wide. She let out a breath and turned away, avoiding my gaze while she busied herself wiping the counter. "Yup, that one's right up there with Bigfoot alright."

My breath seemed stuck in my chest. "You know him?"

"I did. Years ago," she said. "Back when we were kids. I had a huge crush on him for years. I wish I could help."

I sighed. "Me, too. It would be great to get my family off my back."

"You might talk to Sergeant Sharpe. He knows everyone around here." Violet pointed toward a six-foot-something man in a Royal Canadian Mounted Police uniform who entered the diner and took off his hat. "Since you were with Mac when he found Bebe, you should have a word with him before he hunts you down to ask what you know about the fire."

"That's a good idea." With my thoughts on Bebe, I grabbed my belongings before approaching the RCMP officer, who took a seat near the window. "Excuse me. Sergeant Sharpe?"

The middle-aged man with a thick moustache and a thicker middle glanced up. "How can I help you, Miss?"

"I'm A.J. Cadell, the Writer-in-Residence staying at Thistlewood." I held out my hand as I took a shaky breath. "I wondered if you had any update about Bebe's murder."

He raised one eyebrow. "Now what makes you think Bebe was murdered? You a mystery writer like that Murder She Wrote woman on television?"

"Romance writer." I glanced around the diner, wary of Mac showing up to tear a strip off me. "I was there when that firefighter pulled her out. There were bruises on her neck."

The Sergeant narrowed his eyes to study me for a long minute. "Have a seat."

I slid onto the chair across from him, clutching my bag against my stomach. My heart raced as I stumbled over my words. "I only saw Bebe once since I arrived even though she lived across the hall. I want to extend my condolences to her family. Do you know where I can find them?"

"A.J. is it?" he asked.

"Short for Alison Jane." I wiped my hand on my pant leg.

He waved his coffee cup to Violet. "How exactly did you come to be Writer-in-Residence here in Cedar Grove, Alison Jane Cadell, when you live in Toronto?"

"Robert Foster gave me an offer to come to Cedar Grove to teach workshops at the library and stay in Thistlewood for a month. It seemed odd, but…" I flashed a worried smile, pausing when Violet poured me another cup of coffee. "I was barely here a whole day before the fire. Now Bebe's dead."

"And you're worried I'll think you killed her." Sharpe dumped two creamers into his cup before Violet poured his coffee.

"Why would I be worried?" I asked. "I didn't even know her. Well, aside from dancing in the hallway with her."

His eyes grew wide. "You're sure you didn't know her before then?"

"Why are you doubting me?"

Sharpe held up a finger. "I believe you, Miss Cadell. You and I'll talk more after you meet with Foster."

"He's going to send me home, isn't he?" I studied him for a reaction, but he had a great poker face.

"You want anything else today, Frank?" Violet asked. "Fries and gravy? I've got a slice of deep-dish apple pie with your name on it."

"No, thanks, Vi," he said, patting his stomach. "If I keep packing on weight, my wife will start sending me celery for lunch."

"All the more reason to drop by." She winked as she walked away.

The Sergeant turned his attention back to me. "Do you go by Alison or A.J.?"

"Alison." I added one cream and emptied a sugar packet into my coffee. "Did you know Bebe?"

He stirred his drink. "Young lady, everyone around here knew Bebe. She was a local treasure. We'll likely have to hold her funeral in the arena. She and her husband finished building Thistlewood about twenty-five years ago and threw a big party that July."

Around the time I was born. "What happened to him?"

The Sergeant tapped his spoon on the rim of his cup. "Jack was a volunteer firefighter. He was killed in a fire."

Vague information but enough to make me gasp. "I didn't know that."

"Why would you?"

"I've been doing research on Cedar Grove. I think my father might live around here." I paused. "He's part of the reason I came to town."

The Sergeant tilted his head. "Who is he? Maybe I know him."

"Perry Beyer."

"I see." His face went blank. "Are you pulling my leg, girl?"

"No, sir."

"And you seriously have no idea who Bebe is?"

My mouth had gone so dry I needed a sip of coffee but was afraid I'd choke. "Until a couple weeks ago, I had no idea my father was even alive, let alone what his name was."

Sergeant Sharpe leaned his elbows on the table, then rested his chin on his folded hands. "It seems an awful coincidence you appear in town right before Bebe died. Especially with that kind of money on the line."

"Money?" I frowned with no idea how the two were related. Why did I feel like I'd dropped into the Twilight Zone? "Am I a suspect in the murder of a woman I met one time?"

"Should I think otherwise?"

I avoided touching my coffee cup even though it was already covered in my fingerprints. My hands shook so badly, I'd spill half of it anyway.

"For the record, Foster came to me, so you can strike me off your most wanted list." I jumped up to leave in a huff, colliding with a tall man whose coffee dumped between us.

"Sweetheart, you and I have to stop running into each other," Mac said.

The sergeant chuckled. "Ah, Mr. McKittrick. Always a hit with the ladies. I take it you two have met."

McKittrick? Mac must be one of the branches of the local tree.

He reached for a handful of napkins. "Alison was at Thistlewood last night."

"That's what I heard."

"Did she also mention that I found Bebe because she ran back inside to get Mabel?" Mac waved to Violet who brought over the coffee pot and a fresh cup.

"Mabel?" Sharpe asked.

"My laptop." My face burned.

The sergeant broke into a grin. "Did Mac lecture you?"

I cast a sheepish glance at my abandoned cup. "He was busy with Bebe."

"Good enough for me. Thanks for the chat, Alison. We'll talk soon." He waved toward the chair I'd vacated. "Mac, have a seat. We need to get to the bottom of a few things."

My turn to stare. "Wait. What?"

Mac placed a hand on my shoulder, then sat close to the wall. "Suits me. I need to let my pants dry before I go out in public."

I slung the strap of my laptop bag over my shoulder. "I need to go anyway. I have a lot to do."

"Writing or packing?" Mac asked as Violet placed his new cup on the table.

"Writing." I grimaced. "I'm working on a new book, which is why I came to Cedar Grove in the first place."

"Do you write mysteries?" the sergeant asked.

When Mac chuckled, I started to wonder what was wrong with him.

"She writes romance novels," Violet gushed.

Sharpe pulled out a notebook. "Huh. Alison Cadell, right? I'll have to tell my wife to check out your books. As long as they're not those steamy ones. I don't think she likes those, or if she does, she keeps them hidden from me."

"A.J.," I told him. "My penname is A.J. Cadell."

"Oh really? Interesting."

Why was he so interested in my name and the timing of my arrival in Cedar Grove? I edged toward the door wanting nothing more than to bolt from the diner.

Sharpe wrote more beneath my name in his little book. "Violet mentioned your luck in finding a benefactor. I'd like to hear more about that arrangement. Like exactly who your benefactor is."

Since he didn't seem to be done with me after all, I sat across from him once more. "You and me both. I'm the Writer-in-Residence at the Cedar Grove Library. They gave me a room at Thistlewood Manor during my stay."

"You have no idea?" Mac asked.

Sharpe made another note and muttered, "Interesting."

I was starting to dislike that word. "I have the papers Foster gave me, but it doesn't say much aside from my itinerary."

"Did Foster mention how this benefactor found you?" Sharpe asked.

"There were no other names on the paperwork." I reached for my cup and took another gulp. Forget fingerprints. I hadn't done anything wrong. "I can call Foster and ask. You might need a warrant though."

Mac tilted his head. "Are you okay?"

"Yes. I don't know." I left the diner in such a frantic rush that I was halfway back to Georgia Shores before I realized I hadn't paid for my coffee or my lunch. With any luck, Violet would cover for me until tomorrow. My thoughts were one big jumble.

Footsteps pounded the pavement behind me until Mac caught up. "Warn me the next time you're at the diner, will you?"

"I'll ask Violet to post a warning on the door," I told him. "I thought you wanted to talk to Sergeant Sharpe?"

He pointed over his shoulder with his thumb. "He had to leave."

"Is that why you're hounding me instead?"

"I have an ulterior motive," Mac said, reaching into his pocket. "I found this at Thistlewood last night and thought you might've lost it."

The napkins I'd written on in the coffee shop. "Did you read it?"

He grinned. "You really are a romance writer."

My internal temperature rose like a freshly struck match. "You can throw them away. I rewrote that."

He shoved the napkins into his pocket. "I'm sure the new version's better."

I unzipped my coat a couple inches before asking, "Didn't you like what I wrote?"

"I did. In fact, I bought one of your books for my mom."

"Sure, you did." I laughed. "I can't believe I didn't bring any copies with me. I was trying to pack light."

"Were those napkins for the book you're working on?"

"Yeah. I started working on it on the plane." Why did talking to him about my writing make me so uncomfortable?

Mac took my discomfort to a whole new level when he asked, "Do you have a boyfriend?"

"Nope, no boyfriend."

"That's a shame, especially if you kiss as good as you write." He winked, then veered off to walk toward the rocky shore.

Taking a deep breath, I fanned my face. That darn firefighter was as good at starting fires as he was at putting them out. If Mac wasn't careful, he'd inspire the hero of my novel.

As much as I wanted to track down Anna and find out more about the fire, I needed to be alone with my thoughts. It was as good a time as any to check out the local library.

When An RCMP car drove past, Sergeant Sharpe waved on his way out of town. I slowed my pace. Why would he want me to talk to Foster before we spoke again?

Chapter Six

O n my way to the library, I tried to call Emily. Her phone went straight to voicemail. I sighed as I checked the time. Two o'clock in Ontario. She was either in a meeting or on a deadline.

The Cedar Grove library was a block west from the diner. I let myself inside the brick building and wandered the stacks. It had been months since I'd wandered a library. The quiet and calm soothed me. I browsed through the mystery section, then headed toward a comfy chair in one corner.

I should've brought copies of my books for when I did my reading and book signing. When I spoke to Emily later, I'd have to ask her to mail some from the stash in my bedroom closet. I could also donate a copy of each book to Thistlewood Manor, although I hadn't seen a library there yet.

"Hey, A.J." Teena, wearing fashionably ripped jeans and a short, pink sweater, walked toward me followed by another girl about the same age who wore similar ripped jeans and a matching red sweater.

"Hey, what are you doing here?" I asked, pulling out a new notebook.

She held up a physics textbook. "Our afternoon class was cancelled, so we came here to study. Are you working on your next book? Jewels, Alison's the author of those books we read."

Jewels shrieked, making patrons around us raise fingers to their lips and shush her. She leaned closer and whispered, "They were so good. I can't wait to read the new one."

"Thanks. I'm surprised you've both read them." I dug out a pen.

"We read them at the same time," Teena said. "The library has a few copies."

"That's amazing."

Jewels checked her phone when it vibrated in her pocket. "Oh, brother. My dad saw us come in. I need to meet him outside. It was nice to meet you, Alison."

"I'll come with you," Teena said. "See you later, Alison."

Stunned, I sat back. I couldn't convince our local library to carry my books, so why would the Cedar Grove library have more than one copy? Especially since no one else I spoke to had heard of me.

Motivated by the girls, I wrote several pages by hand before my mind wandered to my conversation with Sharpe. More specifically to his and Violet's odd reactions when I mentioned my father.

Was my father a notorious criminal? Cedar Grove was where his trail had ended. He had to know Bebe, or at least know of her.

Rolling my head, I stretched my neck. My entire body was stiff, and I needed to move. Payback from trying to outrun a firefighter. As I loosened the kink in my neck, I caught sight of the clock. Barely one. I wanted to write a few more pages today, then, hopefully, get a good night's sleep. My stomach growled so loudly I thought everyone heard. Time for something to eat.

On my way out, I stopped at the front desk. A middle-aged man peered over his narrow, wire-framed glasses at the computer.

I waited for him to finish, but he didn't seem to notice. "Excuse me."

His gaze darted in my direction, but he didn't stop typing. "Yes?"

"I wanted to thank you for carrying my books in your library. Hopefully, people are enjoying them." I flashed a smile hoping I wasn't being creepy.

"Okay."

That was it? Not eager to be brushed off, I continued, "I'm A.J. Cadell. If you'd like me to sign them, I'd be happy to."

"Someone borrowed them."

"Oh. I could come back later in the week. I'm staying at—"

He looked down his nose at me. "Thistlewood Manor."

"Did someone donate them?" I tried again, feeling like a diva.

His entire body tensed like he wasn't used to talking to people. "Yes."

Disappointed by his lack of information, I turned to leave. "Thanks."

"They're a gift from the owner of Thistlewood Manor," he said. "I thought you knew that."

When the phone rang, he pounced on it like a fox on a rabbit. I didn't feel like sticking around to talk to him about my workshop schedule.

Tucking aside my barrage of questions, I pushed open the front door and stepped outside. Did the owner donate my books to get the locals interested in my arrival? It hadn't worked. Aside from Teena, Jewels, and the mysterious owner of Thistlewood, no one knew who I was.

I started to head back to Georgia Shores Cottages when I spotted Jewels arguing with a lanky man in a baseball cap. Sal. Teena stood a few feet away checking her phone and looking like she'd rather be anywhere else.

My stomach growled again. That was when I noticed a deli across the street. I grabbed a sandwich and soda. Sitting on the beach would've been a peaceful spot to think. Too bad my benefactor didn't invite me here in the summer.

Munching on my ham and Swiss as I walked, I thought about the next chapter in my novel and only snapped out of my dream-like state when I stopped in front of Thistlewood Manor. I'd passed Georgia Shores half a sandwich ago. Lights blazed inside and a familiar black car sat out front.

Foster.

Not seeing any fire or smoke damage on the exterior of the building, I strolled past his car toward the front door. Talking to Foster seemed like a good idea. I had questions I hoped he'd be willing to answer.

The front door was unlocked. I pushed it open and stepped into the foyer. It smelled like floral air freshener with smoky undertones. From upstairs came the hum of fans.

Anna stood ten feet away with a phone in one hand and a relieved smile. "Welcome back. How are you after all the commotion?"

"I'm fine. How about you?"

"Shaken. I can't believe Bebe's gone. It's awful."

The damp, cool air sent a shiver through me.

"That wind cuts right through you today," Anna said, then hesitated. "I've been trying to track you down. The fire marshal cleared us to return to Thistlewood."

"Already? That seems fast."

"I guess it wasn't as bad as it looked. You look chilled to the bone. Why don't you go sit in front of the fire? I'll bring you a cup of tea."

"That sounds great. First, I'm going to change into warmer clothes," I said, glad my sister had thought to outfit me with some of her winter wardrobe, although it probably all smelled like smoke right now.

She hesitated. "Actually, you have a visitor who's already made himself at home."

"Foster? I wonder what he wants."

"Guess you'd better go find out."

Intrigued, I wandered toward the fire blazing in the hearth of the sitting room. Images rocketed through my head too fast to make sense of. Another shudder swept over me as my chill settled in deeper. I reached into my bag for my anxiety medication.

Robert Foster sat in one of the wing-backed chairs someone had moved closer to the fireplace. A thick manila envelope lay on the empty chessboard. He set his glass on the table, then stood when I entered the room.

"Good afternoon, Miss Cadell. I trust your accommodations last night were acceptable. Hopefully, you were able to work on your novel despite the minor inconvenience."

Minor inconvenience. Did he mean the fire or Bebe's death?

"Georgia Shores is great. I'm glad Thistlewood wasn't badly damaged, although I am surprised." I continued toward the second chair, aching for the warmth of the fireplace. "The news about Bebe was unnerving."

"Yes. My condolences." He took a sip of amber liquid from the cut-crystal glass. "This will be a difficult time for everyone."

Not sure what he was talking about, I took a wild guess. "I think I know why you're here to see me. Bebe owned Thistlewood, didn't she? I'll pack my things and book a flight back to Toronto as soon as I can."

"Is that necessary?" Foster asked.

"Now that she's gone, I assume the executor of her estate wouldn't approve of me freeloading." I pulled a dill pickle spear from my lunch bag.

He handed me the inch-thick envelope. "Before you make any plans, you should read this."

I finished the pickle then wiped my fingers on a thin paper napkin. "What is it?"

"Bebe's last will and testament." Foster passed me two gold keys. "These are the keys to her rooms."

My stomach lurched as I took them. "Her rooms? I don't understand. I didn't even know the woman aside from listening to her play the same record over and over again."

"Do you know a man named Perry Beyer?"

For someone I didn't know and couldn't find, he was quickly becoming a bigger part of my visit. "I understand he's my father."

"Yet you've never met him?"

"If I did, I don't remember him."

"Nor do you remember Bettina Beyer. His mother."

"Bettina Beyer?" I frowned, puzzled until I read her name in print on the envelope. "Bebe."

Foster nodded as he raised his drink. "Bebe."

I sat back in the chair and stared into the crackling fire. The keys dug into my palm as I gathered my wits.

Foster strolled to the bar. He returned a minute later with a second glass containing amber liquid. No ice.

"The mystery benefactor who brought me here was my grandmother," I whispered.

"Now you've caught on," he said.

"Why would she want to pay my expenses so I could come here to write?"

Foster tented his fingers. "I'd tell you to ask her, but..."

But she was dead.

I took a gulp from the glass. Straight whiskey. My mouth and throat burned as I asked, "Why didn't she tell me who she was?"

"I do not have that answer, Miss Cadell," he said. "Bebe gave me the contents of that envelope to hold onto, then swore me to secrecy."

"Doesn't attorney-client privilege end when the client dies?" I stared at the manila envelope while my mind whirled.

"I promised her I would look out for you. Technically, you have become my client by default. My promise to her, however, did not allow me the privilege of knowing what she was up to or why."

The reverse side was plain except for a seal made from dark red wax. Blood red with a pineapple design like on my rock. Or was it a thistle? Tiny fireworks seemed to go off before my eyes.

"Have you read what's in here?" I asked.

"Bebe closed it before she arrived at my office. She pressed the wax seal in my presence, then tucked it into my safe until your return to Toronto." He hesitated. "Or upon her death, which she also specified."

"Did she have a premonition someone might kill her?"

His cheek flinched. "Bebe was old, Miss Cadell, she predicted death around every corner."

That didn't sound like the woman I'd danced with in the hallway. "The seal is kind of old school, isn't it?"

"Bebe was kind of old school," Foster said.

"How did she know about me?" I asked. "Where I was and that I'm a writer."

"She loved to read and enjoyed a good mystery. All I know is that she dragged me halfway across the country to find you."

"Bebe was in Toronto?"

"Indeed, she was," he said.

"But I never saw her, just you." I thought back to the woman who asked me to sign a copy of my book. My mouth fell open. She'd been far more lucid than the Bebe I'd met in Thistlewood.

"Is there something I can help with?" Foster asked.

"Bebe asked for my autograph in the candy store."

He nodded. "Indeed, she did."

"Why didn't she tell me who she was? Why the secrecy?"

"Would you have believed her?"

Considering I thought she could be a stalker, I might not have. "I was looking for Perry by then. If she would've told me, I..."

Foster was right. I would've thought she was crazy.

"Perhaps she was afraid you would call the police." As Foster stood, his face softened as he voiced my thoughts. "You have a great deal of reading to do, Miss Cadell. You have my number if you have questions."

Too numb to think, I gulped the rest of the whiskey, causing more little fireworks to pop before my eyes. I tucked the envelope beneath my arm and clutched the keys in one hand. I needed privacy. Whatever Bebe placed inside that envelope was nothing I wanted to share with anyone else. Not yet.

The door at the end of the hall was strung with yellow caution tape. A stark reminder of the heavy smoke only a night earlier. Hands shaking, I paused in front of my door and fingered the keys. If Perry was still alive, I needed to become acquainted with my past. For all our sakes.

My room smelled of smoke, yet someone had opened my windows. I stuck the envelope in my laptop bag, setting it on my desk before I walked across the hall. One of the gold keys opened Bebe's door.

The stifling scent of smoke greeted me. Once my nose adjusted, I detected something else. The faint scent of Bebe's flowery perfume.

It clung to the floral comforter, the zigzag patterned wingback chair, and the blue velvet curtains. As outdated as the décor was, I hugged my stomach and gazed around the room of the woman who'd waltzed me down the hallway.

My grandmother.

Tears welled in my eyes as I turned to leave. Then stopped.

The wall was filled with images of the past. A quote framed by dark wood made me sigh. *What happens at Grandma's house, stays at Grandma's house.*

What had happened at Grandma's house that she'd wound up dead?

Thistlewood Manor—my family home—held a lot of secrets. Were those secrets why my father's trail ended here? I peered into the hallway. Seeing no one, I took dozens of pictures of the room, the photos on the walls, and her possessions.

I wasn't sure how much time I had before Anna wanted the room emptied for paying guests., but it wouldn't be long enough to solve Bebe's murder and figure out what had happened to my family.

I caught my breath. Since I was Bebe's next of kin, did Anna even have a say in what would happen?

I'd have to break the news my sister. Maybe to my father. How could I tell him that his mother was dead when I didn't even know him or where he was?

If someone killed Bebe, something in her room might hold a clue. A journal, some paperwork, a photo. I needed to call my sister and talk to my mom. She must've known Bebe, or at least knew of her.

What happened in Thistlewood that she never told us about Bebe or Perry?

A copy of my book *Moment of Weakness*. I wandered over for a closer look, knowing I'd find my name scrawled inside. What I wasn't prepared for was the pink sticky note beside my signature. *"Perry, you should be proud of your little girl. She turned out great despite everything."*

My breath stuck behind a lump in my throat. Bebe intended to give the book I'd autographed to my father. I took a picture of the book both open and closed, then shut my eyes to gather my courage.

When I opened my eyes once more, my gaze fell to the charred metal garbage basket near Bebe's armchair. Everything inside was reduced to ashes. The side of the chair was slightly scorched. Something shiny caught the light as I walked by. Glass?

I took a tissue from the nearby box, then paused to take a couple pictures first. If the police and fire marshal had checked the place out, why hadn't anyone taken the basket? I needed to do like I'd seen on television. If a character in my next book was a cop, I'd have to do some research.

Using the tissue, I sifted through the ashes and pulled out a few shards of soot-covered crystal. Thick, heavy glass like an old ashtray or serving bowl. Similar to the glass Anna had brought to Bebe's room the night before the fire, and the ones that Foster and I used earlier. Had someone snuck in to remove the basket while the fire marshal was here, then replaced it later? Why?

I was becoming paranoid.

One by one, I set each shard on a clean tissue. Bundling them together, I'd figure out where they came from later. For now, I needed some fresh air and to wash my hands.

On my way to the door, my gaze fell on that framed quote. *What happens at Grandma's house, stays at Grandma's house.* If only I'd known Bebe was my grandma before she died. I would've loved to learn more about her firsthand. Instead, I had to rely on the memories in her room. The urge to track down the father I hadn't seen since I was little surged as tears trickled down my cheeks.

Why didn't I remember Perry or Bebe let alone recall Thistlewood?

Going next door to the bathroom, I splashed cold water on my blotchy face while sobbing. Once I'd caught my breath, I returned to Bebe's room. A lone figure stood inside running his hands through his thick, dark hair.

"What are you doing here?" I asked.

Mac's face was gaunt and drawn. He wore a handknit blue sweater that hugged his muscular body. "Anna asked me to take care of Bebe's things once the fire marshal was done."

"Why did she ask you? How did you know Bebe?"

"She was my grandma's best friend. At least she meant more to me than some computer," he said.

"That's not fair."

"I could still have you arrested, you know," Mac told me. "You risked both of our lives to get a laptop from a burning building, then dumped hot coffee all over me in the diner. The way I see it, you owe me."

I placed my hands on my hips. "Well, if it wasn't for me, you wouldn't have found Bebe until—"

I stopped and closed my watery eyes. It was already too late when we found her. Going to my room, the urge to break the wax seal on the envelope overwhelmed me. I wished I'd put Mac in his place as eloquently as one of my heroines rather than having a meltdown. I sat on the bed and hugged the envelope.

"Are you okay?" Mac asked.

My heart ached to hear Bebe's song one more time. I averted my gaze as I fought an onslaught of tears. "Go away."

"I'm sorry. I forget people need compassion after things like this. Even after they do stupid things." Rather than leave, he sat next to me on the bed. "Why do you have an envelope with Bebe's name on it?"

"Foster gave it to me."

"To you? Why?" he asked, narrowing his eyes.

I met his gaze to tell him to get out. Just my luck, his eyes were that mesmerizing green people like me write about in romance novels. It took a full minute for me to say, "Because Bebe was my grandma."

"I thought you didn't know her."

The sudden silence stifled me. I clutched the envelope to my chest. "I don't remember. You need to leave. I need to sort this all out."

"Sounds like you've had one surprise after another lately." Mac said, he put his arm around me and gave me a quick hug.

I wiped a stubborn tear off my cheek as I inched away. As much as I was comforted by his warmth, I didn't even know the guy. "You could say that."

"Why don't we both get out of here for a while?"

"Why should I go anywhere with you?" I asked. "I don't even know you."

"Because I saved your miserable life from a fire." After a long minute, he held out a hand. Unmanicured, but clean with a couple scrapes and a cut. The hand of someone who worked hard. "I guess we haven't formally met, have we? I'm Mac McKittrick."

"I know that."

His hand didn't waver. "Humor me."

"Alison Cadell." I didn't take his hand but did meet his gaze again. Big mistake.

That green that I'd described so many times in my novels and short stories reminded me of the apple gumballs kids bought at the candy shop. So much for romantic. I was comparing the color of a man's eyes to gumballs while holding the last will and testament of the grand-mother I'd never met.

What was wrong with me?

"How did you find Bebe when you went into her room?"

"It wasn't hard," Mac said. "She was in her favorite chair."

"Her room was full of smoke, right?"

His cheek flinched. "Yes."

"Then why was she just sitting there?" I asked. "If my room filled with smoke and I was able-bodied, there's no way I'd sit there and wait for some Prince Charming. I'd run screaming and clear the building as I went."

"With Mabel in one hand, I'm sure." Mac smirked. He jumped up, then peered out the door. When he turned back to me, his expression was somber. "You also would've grabbed the extinguisher near the stairs and yelled for help."

"Exactly."

He held up a finger. "Wait. Did you just call me Prince Charming?"

Did I? My cheek burned as I tucked the envelope into my laptop bag. "Can you focus? This is a serious conversation."

"You're right. This is no time for comic relief or flirting."

"If that was flirting, it's no wonder you're single."

"So are you."

"By choice," I said, grabbing his arm and pulling him across the hall.

"Same here."

My thoughts came at such a frantic pace that I almost sat in the chair she died in. "Are you sure she was alive when you carried her out?"

"We thought the building was on fire. I didn't stop to check her vital signs. I grabbed her and hauled you both outside."

"I know, and I'm grateful you did," I told him.

"You have a funny way of showing it. Just saying."

"Wait a sec. What do you mean you thought the building was on fire?"

"Lots of smoke. Few flames," he said.

"Does that happen often?"

He shook his head. "It's not common, but it happens."

I hesitated. "There were marks on her neck when you shone your flashlight on her. Could those have happened when you lifted her over your shoulder?"

"I saw them when I checked for a pulse," Mac said, running a hand through his short, dark hair. "Are you a cop or something?"

"Actually, I'm a romance novelist, remember?"

He grinned. "Oh, I remember. Did you ever think you might be working in the wrong genre?"

"No." I turned to leave then spied that sign again. *What happens at Grandma's house...* I needed to take it down before it gave me nightmares.

Mac pointed to the photos. "Do you know these people?"

I tapped the glass of one photo. "That's my father."

"Whoa." He flinched. "You're Perry Beyer's daughter?"

"I didn't even know I had a father. That he was still alive, I mean. I recognize him because of pictures I saw online," I said, then asked, "Did you know him?"

Mac raised his eyebrows. "Perry's the reason I'm a firefighter. I grew up listening to him tell stories. My favorite ones were when he talked about suiting up with a hundred pounds of gear to jump into fire zones. He made the job sound scary and glamorous all at once."

Before he retired, he was one of the best smokejumpers in Canada."

I moved to another photo as a lump grew in my throat. "He seems like the hero type all right."

"He's a good storyteller. Once he starts talking, you don't want him to stop."

"I wouldn't know."

"Are you sure you didn't know him?" Mac asked.

"I really don't remember," I told him, then asked, "Why did Bebe live here?"

He frowned. "Didn't Foster tell you?"

I placed my hands on my hips. "Can you just tell me what I'm missing and stop being so dramatic?"

Mac's gaze met mine as he said. "Bebe owned Thistlewood Manor. Now that she's gone, you and Perry will inherit the place."

"Wouldn't Thistlewood go to Perry? He is her son."

"It would if he wanted the place," he said. "Not many people know where to find him."

"Do you?" I asked.

He glanced back at the photographs then cleared his throat.

"The letter." I practically shoved him out of the way in my rush to get out of Bebe's room.

"What letter?" Mac followed me across the hall.

I reached for my purse then took out the green envelope. "My mom gave it to me at the airport. I got so busy working on my novel, then the fire, and..."

"What does it say?" he asked.

Holding it out to him, I indicated the address in the top corner. "Where is that?"

"Colvilletown. Weird. I can't see him ever living that close to Nanaimo," Mac said, peering over my shoulder. Not a stretch since he was easily six inches taller than me and smelled like Teena's lemongrass soap. "The smaller islands in the Strait of Georgia are more his style. He must have used someone else's address."

I wasn't ready to share what was inside. Sure, Mac had saved my life, but I didn't know him well enough to soak his shirt with tears. "Did Perry visit Bebe?"

Mac took a step back as if he sensed my hesitation. "Depends on where he was or if he was working. Why don't I ask Anna if she has some boxes, so we can sort through Bebe's things?"

We. "I don't feel up to sorting anything. I need to read the papers from Foster and then call my sister. She might want to see things for herself. At the very least, she'll have a chat with Mom."

"No rush," Mac said, then paused near the door. "Is your sister more like Perry than you are?"

"What do you mean?"

He chuckled. "You're a writer. Seems to me that's the farthest thing from a daredevil there is."

"Oh yeah?" I folded my arms across my chest. "Have you ever had to face an editor? That's as close to jumping out of an airplane as I'll ever get."

Mac ran a hand through his hair. "For me, it was dealing with my high school English teacher. I don't like to read or do book reports."

"Is that why you fight fires for a living? Because it's safer?" I asked, tapping the envelope against my leg. "Math and science were my downfall."

"Why don't we go grab a coffee?" he suggested. "You owe me one. Actually, you owe me two."

I allowed a small smile. "Only if you tell me more about Bebe and Perry."

"You got it. Right after you tell me what's on that laptop worth risking lives for. It better be military secrets or the formula for making gold."

My book. I fingered the envelope. "Then I'll pass. I have things to do."

"Are you clinically insane or just incredibly annoying?" he asked.

"According to my mother, a bit of both."

Anna chirped from the doorway, "Oh, good. You two have met. Isn't it exciting, Mac? Thistlewood has a best-selling Writer-in-Residence."

Best-selling? I wished. All this author wanted was to be left alone to let recent events sink in.

Mac folded his muscular arms across his chest. "It's your book, isn't it? You named your laptop Mabel and risked both our lives to save it because of the book you're writing. Have you been locked up in your room since you arrived?"

"You know I haven't," I snorted.

Anna chuckled. "She had to leave when the power went out."

I shot her a scowl. "You're not helping."

"I wasn't trying to."

Mac shook his head. "All the more reason why I should drag you out for a cup of coffee. Isn't it the life blood of writers?"

What I wanted to do was read the documents that Foster left, and to figure out how to tell Roxie and our mom what was going on.

"Are you even listening?" he asked.

"Sort of."

He burst into laughter. "Well, if you change your mind, I'll be at the diner having coffee and blueberry pie."

"Go get some fresh air, Alison, "Anna said. "I'll lock Bebe's door and look for some boxes. You can tackle those later."

"I already had pie."

Mac's expression softened. "I offered to help when she's ready."

Anna flinched as she turned away. "Bebe would be honored. She always thought highly of you."

I put both envelopes in my laptop bag before I joined them in the hallway. Mac and Anna headed down the stairs while I locked my door. I itched for another peek inside the room at the end of the hall. Was that what the second gold key was for?

"Alison, can you give me a hand?" Anna called up the stairs.

I caught a whiff of roast chicken, vegetables, and apple pie. It was all worthy of an appreciative sigh. "I'll be right there."

"Mmm, it smells good in here," Mac said. "Masks the smell of smoke. You should open more windows upstairs to air the place out."

"We will," Anna assured him. "Why don't you stay for dinner?"

Mac met my gaze. I got the impression there was something else he wanted to say, but not with Anna nearby. He nodded toward the door.

"Thanks, but I should go. Maybe another night."

"I'll hold you to that." She wagged a finger.

"Walk me out?" Mac asked as he nudged my arm.

I frowned as my phone rang. Emily. Of all the bad timing. "The door's right there. See you later."

Anna motioned for me to go. "When you get back, you can set the table. Owen usually does it, but he's probably still at Ken's."

"Guilt trip," Mac murmured.

"No problem. I'll be right back." I grabbed my boots and coat before Mac and I stepped onto the porch. Despite the chill, I closed the door behind us, and whispered, "Have you seen where the fire was?"

We both flinched as a window opened several feet away.

He shook his head. "No. Have you?"

"Not yet," I whispered. "Doesn't it seem odd that more of the building didn't burn since it's all cedar?"

Mac hooked his arm around mine and led me to the end of the sidewalk. "I thought that, too. Someone must've called it in before setting the fire. Can you get a key for that room at the end of the hall?"

A breeze had sprung up since I'd left the diner earlier and I shivered. "I think I already have one. Foster gave me two keys. One is for Bebe's room, but I haven't tried the other yet." I hesitated. "Is it possible whoever set the fire called 9-1-1?"

"I'd say so, but why?"

My writer brain whirled with possibilities. "Maybe they only wanted to scare Bebe, not kill her.

"Most arsonists set fires to cover up their crimes," Mac said. "I'm surprised you didn't know that."

"As a romance writer?"

"Right. The napkins." Mac winked, then placed his hands on my shoulders. He leaned over to kiss my forehead as though he'd known me forever. For all I remembered, he might've. "You'd better get back inside. You have a table to set and a book to write."

"Yes, I do." Since my entire body tingled, I knew I wasn't dreaming.

"I'm looking forward to reading more napkins," he said.

"You are?" Staring into those green eyes again, I was suddenly breathless and weak in the knees. Dumb move. "I guess I'll have to write on some more then."

Mac's grin made my pulse quicken and my cheeks warm. "You and I need to have a long talk one of these days."

"About what?"

"Things," he said.

"You know where to find me." I blew out a breath, grateful to have time to figure out what was going on. Not only with Bebe, but with Mac.

My entire body had a strong reaction to him that I'd never felt before. Warm cheeks. Weak body. Out of breath.

As I returned to the house, I realized maybe I was getting sick. It could be my symptoms had nothing to do with Mac but with the stress I'd been under. Had I missed a dose of my medication due to jetlag?

"You must be cold. Your cheeks are red," Anna said. "Set the table for three. Owen's on his way back and Sal's preparing the property for winter."

I raised my eyebrows. "He still has to eat."

"I'll save him a plate to grab when he's ready." She reached into the cupboard and removed a plastic plate with a cover. "Dinner will be ready in fifteen minutes. You have time to wash up."

I set the table then made my way upstairs, pausing to glance at Bebe's door before I entered my room.

My plan for the evening was simple. Read the paperwork from Foster, then call my sister. I removed the card with the photo of a skydiver on the front from its envelope.

The letter inside landed on my foot. Seeing the writing—my dad's writing—rattled me now that I knew more. I refolded it, then pulled out my pineapple stone to ground me.

Shaken, I traced the rough pineapple pattern on my rock with my thumb.

Being back in Thistlewood wasn't as easy as I thought. Reading Bebe's paperwork wouldn't make things any easier. I wandered down to the kitchen to make a cup of herbal tea before dinner. Owen sat at one end of the table writing in a little red notebook. I walked past him in a daze, aware he looked up.

"Are you okay?" Anna asked, stirring the mashed potatoes.

I reached for a package of peppermint tea. Comfort in a cup. "So much has happened. I guess it's all hitting me at once."

"Help me get dinner on the table before Owen eats the napkins, will you?" She patted my arm. "I'll save you an extra piece of pie for later."

"That'll help keep me going while I work on my book."

With my mind still laser-focused on the fire, Perry, and Bebe, I ate in silence while Anna made several attempts at conversation. Owen and I spoke little except to ask for the chicken, gravy, or mashed potatoes.

Until the lights flickered.

My entire body tensed. Across the table, Owen's gaze met mine. The last power outage hadn't ended well.

Anna jumped up to light several candles. When she returned to the head of the table, she took a gulp of wine.

"Are you okay?" I met her gaze.

"This might be bad timing," she said, "but there's no rush for you to leave Thistlewood. You can stay as long as you like."

Why would she think I planned to leave right away? I was one of Bebe's main heirs and had several reasons to stay. I couldn't make any decisions until I'd read the paperwork. "Thanks."

I had just piled my utensils on my plate when Owen gazed at the ceiling and said, "I flew in a plane once when I was a kid."

Surprised, I remained seated. It was the first time he'd really spoken. His descriptions of the clear sky, clouds, and white-capped waves kept me entranced until he finished.

"You're a really descriptive storyteller," I told him.

He scurried into the kitchen before I could add that he inspired me. Writing for a few minutes would clear my head before I tackled the legalese.

I put my dishes in the sink, made a cup of tea, then took a handmade red mug and a large slice of apple pie upstairs. Sitting at the desk, I pulled up my work in progress. Owen was onto something. After the events of the week, I needed a distraction. Delving into my fictional romance for half an hour before pulling out Bebe's envelope would help to calm me.

The lights flickered again when I was deep into chapter four.

I saved my work. "Oh, come on. Three times in one night isn't funny."

Then the power went out.

For a fleeting moment, I heard a few quick strains of music from Bebe's room. That was impossible. She wasn't there. I hadn't seen her record player earlier either.

My hands shook as I unplugged Mabel, then reached for my cell-phone to use as a flashlight. I needed to see if I was hearing things.

The hallway was empty. Not only was the house semi-dark and quiet, but the door to Bebe's room was locked. I was hearing things.

Scrubbing my face with both hands, I realized jetlag had caught up to me. There was no way I could sleep until I read what was in that envelope. I returned to my room, then changed into my fleecy pajama pants and a thick sweater. The chill that had set in earlier had yet to subside. I needed more tea. Tugging on woolly socks, I clutched the envelope to my chest and crept downstairs trying not to disturb anyone. I was so on edge that if anyone spoke, I would've leaped to the chandelier.

The open concept staircase and foyer made me cringe more than normal. I kept my focus ahead of me and froze when I heard creaks. What was I so afraid of?

I was surprised to see a low fire crackling in the hearth with no one to tend it. Perhaps Anna had stepped away for a moment. After the recent ordeal, to not keep an eye on the flames seemed like a bad idea.

Setting my phone and the envelope on the chair closest to the fire, I added a small log to the embers. I grabbed my phone and used it to light my way as I crossed the room and poured a small glass of wine before curling up in the chair.

I took a couple sips of pinot grigio to calm my nerves, then popped the seal and eased open the flap. A handful of pictures slid out first. Some were copies of the ones in Bebe's room. Photos of me and Roxie with Mom and Perry and people I guessed were grandparents and other family. Not one triggered a memory, although some seemed vaguely familiar. One little boy had the same grin as Owen. Another resembled a much younger version of Mac. Was that possible?

A series of photos showed Thistlewood Manor in various stages of construction. Part of me knew these people were family although I had no idea who they were aside from my mom and sister.

I set them on the chess board, then closed my eyes and wiped my clammy hands on the legs of my pajama bottoms. I swore I heard a woman whisper, *"What happens at Grandma's house, stays at Grandma's house."*

Sitting upright, I waved my flashlight around the lounge. There was no one else in the room besides me. Once I settled back into the chair, I pulled out Bettina Beyer's last will and testament.

I took another gulp of wine before digging in.

Among the legalese, I learned Perry was to receive half of Thistlewood along with a substantial amount of money and holdings valued in enough zeros to stagger me. The other half of her possessions were to go to me and Roxie.

The shock that took my breath away was quickly followed by a wave of nausea. As I finished the last mouthful of wine, I nearly gagged when the acidity hit the back of my throat. I'd just gone from struggling to pay my rent, to owning a quarter of Thistlewood Manor. Plus inheriting a great deal of money. I had to be dreaming.

According to the documents, Bebe bequeathed fifty thousand dollars to Foster, who'd likely been paid handsomely over the years. Anna and Sal would each get twenty-five thousand dollars. Owen, Teena, Jewels, and Mac were to receive ten thousand each for their unwavering support and assistance. Lastly, a charity called Sunrise Shelter would get half a million dollars.

My glass was empty.

Were any of those amounts enough for anyone to want to kill Bebe?

According to the breakdown, me and my sister were suddenly wealthy women. Roxie could start her photography studio, pay for her wedding, plus have a fabulous honeymoon. I would never have to work another dead-end job, especially if we sold Thistlewood.

To do that, however, I needed to talk to Roxie, and find our father.

Mac knew Perry. Maybe I should've asked for his phone number. I covered my mouth to stifle my laugh. That would've seemed desperate. Which I suddenly was.

Something creaked somewhere in the manor. I listened for voices or footsteps. Anything. All I heard was the wind outside.

Then I reached for my phone.

Rattled by everything I'd read, I wanted to refill my glass. Instead, I sent a text to my sister. *We need to talk.*

She called immediately, even though it was nearly midnight in Toronto. "Did you find Dad?"

"Not yet." I kept my voice low and hoped sound didn't carry far in spite of the polished wood floors and cedar walls. "I have other news."

"I'd prefer to hear that you found Dad."

"Do you remember a woman named Bettina Beyer?" I asked. There was a long silence as I rifled through the photos. Had she hung up on me or did I lose the signal in the wind? "Roxie?"

"Bebe," she whispered. "Did you meet her?"

Why did everyone know who these people were but me?

"Briefly. She was my mysterious benefactor. She died yesterday and I have her will in my hands. I keep wondering why no one mentioned our grandmother lived here after I told you and mom I was coming here."

"Why do you have Bebe's will?" she asked.

I hesitated. "You, me, and Perry are her main beneficiaries. You and I each inherit a quarter of Thistlewood Manor plus some money."

"Are you serious?" Roxie's voice dropped to a whisper. I guessed her fiancé was nearby. "How much are we talking about? Enough for my wedding?"

"Enough for your wedding, a six-month European honeymoon, a brand-new car, and whatever else you'd like."

She gave a stifled squeal. "Ali, that's amazing."

"Roxie, our grandmother died. Have a little compassion."

"What compassion? The woman didn't bother to keep in touch after..."

When she didn't continue, I asked, "After what?"

"Send me the info. We'll talk later." With that, she disconnected.

I gazed into the hearth where the fire burned down to glowing embers. The eerie glow triggered the ball of nerves inside my stomach, and I wanted to be ill. Why were there so many skeletons tucked into our family closet, and why was I the only person unaware of them?

As I finished reading Bebe's will, I decided finding Perry was now at the top of my to-do list. Hopefully, he could explain what was going on. It made no sense why Bebe didn't tell me who she was. And why I had no memories of Thistlewood.

I hugged the will to my chest with a deep sigh. What had happened that I couldn't remember my own father?

Chapter Seven

"So, how's the new romance going?" Emily asked over Skype the next morning after showing me her Mediterranean omelet.

"The what?" I asked, then yawned.

Not only hadn't I adapted to the time difference, but I didn't get much sleep after all the surprises yesterday.

"Your novel," she said. "What did you think I meant?"

"Nothing. I'm tired."

Emily gasped. "You met someone. Is he cute?"

"It's the three-hour time difference." I ran my fingers through my sleep-knotted hair. "That and I've been trying to figure out what happened to Bebe."

She narrowed her eyes. "You mean the woman who died in the fire? Why are you so caught up in what happened to her?"

"It turns out Bettina Beyer, aka Bebe, was Perry's mother." Talking to Emily suddenly made things real. I fought to keep my tears at bay.

"Does Roxie know?" she asked.

"I talked to her last night," I told her, then paused. "I think someone killed Bebe and other people have said the same. I want to help figure out who it was."

"You write romance novels, Ali," she said. "What do you know about solving a mystery?"

I tossed my pen on the desk. "Absolutely nothing. She was family, Em. I guess I'll just have to do what the police do."

"What's that?"

I gazed out the window. I needed to go for a walk later to burn off some nervous energy. "Ask a lot of questions."

"I guess that's a start. In the meantime, I can do some digging online when I get to work. Who knows, I might get a great story from this. And a raise. I'll let you know what you find. Did you meet any good-looking guys yet?"

"Just the firefighter who rescued me," I admitted. "He's cute in that tough, rugged sort of way, but a bit on the grumpy side."

"You like him," she said, sounding amused.

"And I need his help. Mac's lived here his whole life and knows Perry. He was also close to Bebe."

"A rugged guy named Mac, huh? What a surprise," Emily said. "Please tell me the guys out there don't preen like the ones in Toronto."

I laughed. "You mean like my ex? Not that I've seen."

"A firefighter, huh?" Emily asked. "Does he have a page in a local calendar. I'd like a copy for Christmas."

"He doesn't seem the type. He is tall, dark, and handsome, but humble. And, before you ask, there's nothing going on between us. Aside from me spilling coffee on him a couple times."

"That's one way to get his attention. Not only will he smell good, but he'll look at me twice when I come to visit you." She winked, getting up with her mug.

I sighed. "Unless he's in jail by then."

"What?" Emily sat back down. "I was going to suggest you solve the murder together. Suddenly the hot firefighter's a suspect? Life's not fair."

"I don't know if the police suspect him, but I do. He found Bebe then gave her mouth to mouth."

"How dare a firefighter rescue her then try to save her. Why does that make him a suspect?" she asked. "He might not have found her if it wasn't for you."

Deflated, I tucked my chin to my chest. "True. But she still died."

"I love you, Ali, but stick to writing romance novels. Leave the detective work to the police. You're a better writer than a cop. But your firefighter friend probably knows your suspects."

"And Perry. I just have to convince Mac to help me find him." I caught a glimpse of a man jogging along the shoreline wearing a bright orange jacket and blue shorts. "Speaking of, I think that's him running on the beach."

"Your dad?" Emily's voice rose an octave.

"Mac. The firefighter."

"What's Mac short for?" she asked.

"I have no idea. We're barely on a first name basis."

Emily wiggled like she was trying to see past me, which was pointless. Mabel's screen faced away from the window. "Can you still see him?"

"Yes."

"Then either turn the camera around or send pictures," she demanded. "What's he wearing? Let me guess, jogging pants."

"Shorts." I grinned.

Emily fanned her face. "Does he have nice legs? Never mind. He's a runner."

"It's hard to tell from here, but I'd say yes."

She whooped. "Go get him, Tiger, and send pictures."

"Bye, Em. Love you."

The last complication I needed was a man. I was on a roll with my writing career and my book sales were climbing—well, inching like a wounded turtle—up the best-seller lists. Plus, I needed to sort out my newfound family and figure out what happened to Bebe. Still, Mac did have great legs, even if he was cranky and arrogant. Maybe I could repay him with those two cups of coffee while I asked a few questions.

Like how to find my father.

"Go get him, Tiger. Yeah, right," I muttered, checking my emails.

The local library suggested pushing back my duties as Writer-in-Residence by a week due to Bebe's sudden death. Hopefully, that wouldn't affect my departure date at the end of November. It would give me more time to write and prepare for my workshops.

I closed my laptop then tucked Mabel and the paperwork in my laptop bag, so no one found either by "accident." Shrugging on my coat, I pulled the strap of my bag over my shoulder, then locked my door. I was startled to see a figure in the upper foyer.

Owen's hair stuck straight up and his tongue peeked out one corner of his mouth as he concentrated. "Good morning, Owen."

"Oh. Hello." He glanced up from where he sat cross-legged on the floor. "Anna told me you're a writer. Is that true?"

I approached slowly as though he were a squirrel that might bolt when I got too close. "Yes."

He grimaced. "Do you write smut?"

"No, I write romance novels."

"Same difference." He narrowed his magnified eyes and asked, "Were you the crazy lady who ran into the fire and found Bebe?"

Fidgeting with the zipper on my coat, I told him, "Sort of."

"Someone told me you knocked out a firefighter before you rescued her single-handedly."

I shook my head. "That's not how it happened."

"Because if you did, that makes you a hero."

"Whoa, I'm no hero. The firefighter who got us out is the hero, not me."

He jabbed his pen against his notebook. "That's too bad. I don't like Mac."

"Why not?" I joined him on the floor away from the railing. I'd always had a fear of heights. I was certain if the wood broke, I'd fall to my death near the door below.

"When he came to visit Bebe, he'd never let me hang around," Owen said. "He said they had business to discuss."

"Business? Interesting."

I was starting to sound like Sergeant Sharpe. Did Mac have another reason for helping me besides being a nice guy? Maybe I'd learn more as I dug through Bebe's belongings. "How well did you know Bebe?"

Owen squeezed his eyes shut and tapped his foot against the hard-wood. "That's a dumb question."

"Why's that?"

"I know how she took her tea. Black with two sugars and a squeeze of lemon. And that she had two sons and grandkids. And loved straw-berries in chocolate."

Two sons? I frowned. Aside from me and Roxie, Perry was the only other family member named in Bebe's will. "What else can you tell me?"

His mouth twitched. "I know she and Foster were boyfriend and girlfriend. He visited her all the time. Even more than Mac and Jewels did."

"Are you sure that wasn't because he was her lawyer?" I asked.

"Foster's a lawyer?"

"He invited me to come here." I paused. "It's weird that Bebe came to see me."

His gaze darted past me down the hallway as though he'd heard something. "Why's that weird?"

"I didn't know her."

He looked like he wanted to say something then wrote a couple short sentences before glancing up again. "You're from Toronto, right?"

"I am. Where are you from?"

"Pincher Creek, Alberta, ma'am," he said. "I was a cowboy until I fell off a horse and got kicked in the head. Some days my brain doesn't work the way it should. It's like a TV channel being off the air. Noisy and full of static."

"Mine feels that way sometimes. I take medication to help. Was your brain full of static the night we had the fire?"

"Which time?"

A hollow sensation settled in my stomach. "What do you mean which time?"

Owen shrugged. "We had two fires. The one where Bebe died and the one where they took the stairs away."

My back stiffened. "Why did they take the stairs away?"

"Dunno."

While I wanted to push for more information, I didn't want to scare him off. "The fire two nights ago?"

Owen hummed, then said, "I was writing. I smelled smoke, then I told Jelly we had to go outside. I took his little cage but stuck him in my pocket to stay warm. Anna doesn't like him, because the last time he escaped, we found him in a bowl of raspberries she'd washed to make jam."

"Is that why you call him Jelly?" I asked, aware of Anna peeking through the railing on the staircase.

Owen pushed his glasses up the bridge of his nose. "Nope. Because I like peanut butter and jelly. I had a hamster named Peanut Butter, but he died."

"Jelly still isn't welcome in the kitchen," Anna said.

Owen bowed his head as color bloomed in his face. "Sorry, Anna."

"But I'll give you some sunflower seeds for him," she told him. "Maybe even a piece of cookie if you think he'd like one."

His face lit up. "We love your shortbread cookies best, especially the ones with bits of caramel."

"Those do sound good," I agreed.

Anna smiled. "Shortbread it is. You and I need to let Miss Cadell get back to work on her book. Did you know she's an author?"

He stared at me. "You are?"

My mouth opened in surprise. I guessed his television, as he called it, had gone off the air. "Yes, I am. I write romance novels."

Anna had probably overheard our entire conversation. "Owen, would you like to come down to the kitchen to get some cookies?"

"Jelly and I love cookies, especially shortbread ones." He clambered to his feet, then followed Anna down the stairs to the kitchen.

I sat for a moment with my eyes closed, not daring to look down into the kitchen. Could Owen have set the fire and not remembered? Before I could get to my feet, he raced back up to his room at the end of the hall to my left.

"Alison?" Anna called up the stairs.

As I made my way down, she set a mug on the table, then waved a hand like she'd done a magic trick. Aside from making Owen disappear. "I thought you might like some tea and cookies. Shortbread with caramel. They're Jelly's favorite."

I set my laptop bag onto a chair beside me. "That's wonderful. Thank you."

"I'm sorry if Owen bothers you. He wasn't the same after his accident."

"He told me he was a cowboy in Alberta. Pincher Creek, right?"

Her face paled. "Is that what he said?"

"That's not what happened, is it?"

"Owen suffered a traumatic brain injury from a fall." She broke a cookie in half. "On the upside, he's become an amazing storyteller."

"What happened to him?" I asked.

"He doesn't like talking about it."

I bit into one of the cookies. Jelly had good taste. Anna's shortbread was delicious. I'd have to get the recipe for Emily. "Has he lived here long?"

She sipped her tea. "His whole life. His perception of reality is...well...skewed. He's not always able to separate reality from his stories."

"That's so sad." My heart sank.

"It is what it is," she said. "Be his friend. Just don't take everything he says at face value."

"That explains why he thought Foster was Bebe's boyfriend." I sipped my tea, which tasted odd. She must've added sugar. I tried hard not to make a face.

Anna nodded. "That's one example."

"How long has Sal worked here?" I changed the topic before she could grow more uncomfortable.

Her gaze wandered toward the front entrance. "Sal knew Bebe's husband for years before he came to Cedar Grove. He's done maintenance and the landscaping ever since."

"Really? Where did he live before?" I asked.

"The Mainland, I think. He doesn't talk about his past much. One of those strong, silent types. Like Mac."

I finished one cookie, then wrapped the other in a napkin. "I won't keep you. I'm sure you have work to do. I'll take a cookie for the road."

She peered into my cup. "You didn't drink your tea."

"It's too sweet for me." I reached for my bag. "I take sugar in my coffee, but not in my tea. How weird is that?"

Anna forced a smile. "I should've asked. I'll keep that in mind."

My phone pinged in my pocket. Roxie had to wait. "I'm going to try writing in the diner today and see if anything inspires me. I've been a little distracted."

"That's understandable." She remained seated as I left.

The morning air was damp. I pulled on my gloves before strolling down the road. My link to Cedar Grove was stronger than I'd imagined. What else would I discover?

It was about a kilometer from Thistlewood to the diner. Enough time for me to mull things over, yet not go too deep down the rabbit hole. If I wanted to find my father and figure out what was going on at Thistlewood, I had to start by asking some serious questions.

Chapter Eight

The Burlap Diner was busy by the time I stumbled in. I should've felt refreshed and energized by the walk, but I needed a strong cup of coffee instead. All the tables were taken, but one seat remained open at the counter. While I preferred to work at a table, the stool was where Mac sat the first time I saw him. Maybe I'd be inspired.

I slid onto the stool, took out my notebook, and set my bag on the floor beside my feet before taking a moment to collect my thoughts. Why couldn't I shake off the cobwebs in my head. Must be jetlag.

"Mornin', hon." Violet slid a steaming cup of coffee in front of me. "How's your day going?"

"Good." I yawned as I added cream and sugar to my cup. While she made her rounds, I wrote a list of all the people in Bebe's will. Anna. Sal. Owen. Foster. Mac. Sunrise Shelter.

"What are you working on today?" Violet set the coffee pot on the burner.

I circled Sunrise Shelter. "Just thinking about Bebe."

Violet stopped in front of me. "Me, too. Why would anyone kill such a sweet old lady? And to strangle her? It's horrible."

"It was personal. Television detectives would say it was personal." I closed my notebook, tempted to stick a straw in the coffee pot. I toyed with a thimble-sized creamer container. "I never thought her playing that song repeatedly was enough to kill for."

"What song?" Violet asked.

"One Ella Fitzgerald used to sing."

She blew out a heavy breath. "Owen said she played that record a lot. I'm sure it got annoying."

The guy beside me grunted as he slid off his stool.

"It still plays on continuous loop in my head."

"That could be enough to make anyone cranky." Violet turned to the shiny metal shelves that separated the dining area from the kitchen. She grabbed a plate of fries and a cup of gravy before setting them in front of me.

"I didn't order these."

"The fries are on me," she said. "You need comfort food."

I smiled. "You're the best. Thanks."

"Least I can do. You've been through a lot lately."

Rubbing the back of my stiff neck, I reached for a French fry. "Do you think I killed her?"

Violet shook her head. "You didn't even know her. Careful, love, those things are hot."

"Thanks, but I've had fries before." I dunked it in gravy, then stuck it in my mouth. While I fanned my mouth, someone slid onto the stool to my left. "Ah! Hot!"

"Yes, I am." Mac chuckled.

"Don't tease the poor girl, her face is melting," Violet told him, then asked, "What can I get you, hon?"

He didn't bother to cover his yawn. "Chocolate milkshake and large fries. It was a long night."

My tongue hurt, but I dug in for more. I was as hungry as I was tired.

He stole a fry off my plate. "Hot fries?"

"Yup." I gulped half a glass of water while slapping his hand.

"You're not very good at making friends, are you?"

"Oh, and you are?" I nudged his persistent hand away as he made another attempt. This time he managed to snatch one fry. "Could you please sit elsewhere? I'd like to enjoy my lunch without fighting you off."

Mac chuckled, then asked, "Would you really like me to leave?"

"Yes, I would." I met his gaze. When would I learn not to do that?

He leaned so close his breath warmed my face. He smelled of stale coffee. "Then no."

I huffed but didn't move. "You're a jerk."

"You used to—"

"Yes, he can be," Violet interrupted as she set a large silver cup and a long straw in front of Mac. "When he's not putting out fires or chasing crazy women into burning buildings. Keep it down, kids, you're scaring customers."

I wanted to look away, but Mac hadn't averted his stare. Our simple eye-gazing had become a competition. My stomach lurched. What did this guy want from me?

"She means you," Mac said.

Violet huffed. "I mean both of you."

"So there."

He winked. "My but that's a lovely shade of red you're wearing."

"Did you honestly just use the word lovely?" I asked.

"Imagine that and I'm not even a writer." Small lines radiated from the corners of his eyes. "I do have the ability to read, you know. I pick up new vocabulary now and then."

"From safety manuals or food labels?"

Violet guffawed as she walked away.

"Sometimes lost napkins." Mac stole another fry without breaking eye contact.

I tensed my jaw. "Not funny."

He dipped the purloined fry into his milkshake and ate it. Just like that, the spell was broken.

My gaze darted to his milkshake. "Did you seriously just do that?"

"What?" Mac dunked another fry.

"That's disgusting."

"Have you ever tried it?" he asked, offering me the fry as drops of chocolate rolled down to his fingers.

I shook my head. "Not a chance."

Mac popped it into his mouth. "That's funny. I mistook you to be more adventurous."

"Why's that?" I took a fry off my plate before he took any more.

"Because you travelled across the country on a whim to a place you've never been, then ran into a burning building without batting an eye to rescue a laptop."

Violet set the coffee carafe on the burner as she barked a laugh. "Forget adventurous, girl. You're just crazy."

"Gee, thanks." I let my shoulders droop.

"Besides that, if you're Perry's kid, it's in your genes," he said.

"Will you stop that?" I groaned as he dipped another French fry. "I'm losing my appetite."

After he stuck it in his milkshake, he shoved the fry into my mouth.

I sucked in a surprised breath and wanted to spit it out. Then the ice cream bathed my tongue. The combination of sweet and salty made me sigh. "Mmmm."

"Still think it's disgusting?" he asked.

"It's okay." I glanced at my fries, then at the silver milkshake cup glistening with sweat.

"Wanna share?" He grinned.

I hesitated. "Tempting."

When Violet placed a steaming plate of fries in front of him, he announced, "Too late. You have to get your own milkshake. I don't recommend dipping them in coffee. It doesn't work well."

"You've tried?"

He shrugged. "I'm an adventurous guy."

"You're crazy," I told him. "With several good reasons why you're single."

"Ouch." Violet chuckled.

Mac took my left hand in his. "No ring on your finger either."

I snatched my hand away to eat in silence then realized my list of suspects was in plain sight. I closed the notebook.

He leaned his elbows on the counter. "Wanna talk about it?"

"About what?"

"Whatever you're hiding."

"Nope."

After several more fries, he said, "Everyone I know adored Bebe. Who would get mad enough to strangle her?"

I blew out my breath. "I've never been that mad at anyone. Mad enough to think about it but not mad enough to do anything."

"Not even me?" He nudged my elbow.

I studied his profile while he sipped the rest of his shake. "Amazingly enough, not even you."

"So far." Mac grinned. "That's a good surprise."

"What's so good about it?" I asked.

He leaned a couple inches closer. "Violet said I should talk to you about the fire. She thinks I might stop being mad if I understood your motives. Her words."

I stared at my nearly empty plate. "I guessed they were too big to be yours."

Mac pushed his empty dish away and lowered his voice. "When I saw you in Bebe's room, I realized how upset you were even though you barely knew her. So, I decided to give you a chance."

"You decided to give me a chance?" I gawked. "Are you for real?"

He leaned away. "Is that a bad thing?"

"You're..."

Violet leaned over his shoulder. "Mac, you need to work on your people skills. Particularly, your female people skills."

"You..." I slapped some money onto the counter then grabbed my laptop bag.

"At least you write better than you talk," he told me.

I jumped off my stool. "You're an awful person, Mac McKittrick."

Before I'd gone three steps toward the door, Sal stepped in front of me. His gray eyes grew wide beneath his Toronto Blue Jays baseball cap as he gave a nod. "Alison."

I took a reflexive step back and bumped into someone.

"Hey, Sal," Mac said, placing a hand on my shoulder. Comfort or possession, I wasn't sure.

"I talked to Sharpe this morning." Sal didn't meet my gaze so much as bore holes through me with his glare. "He thinks I might have something to do with Bebe's death." He narrowed his eyes. "Where would he get that idea?"

"Me?" I asked. "Why would I say something like that?"

"No, she doesn't know," Mac interrupted as he tightened his grip. "She's been busy writing and hasn't seen him since the other day."

Sal's hard gaze never left mine. "Is that true?"

"Yes." My heart banged against my ribs from the pressure of Mac's hand as he gave my shoulder another squeeze.

Mac could've left me to flounder, yet he hovered. The fact he hung around protectively alarmed me. What did he know that I didn't?

"I hear you're the one who inherits the whole shebang Bebe left behind," Sal said. "My money's on you, lady. I'll bet you killed her."

I snorted. "Yeah, your money and half the town's. Except I was nowhere near Thistlewood when the fire started. I was here. Violet and Mac can vouch for me."

"When it was discovered, you mean," Sal said. "It might have smoldered for a while. Anna said you left the manor when the electricity went out."

That thought hadn't occurred to me. Was it possible someone killed Bebe, then set the fire long before anyone noticed? There was smoke, but few flames. If someone had started a small fire in the room down the hall..."

Sal placed his fists on his hips. "Don't look at me that way."

"I wasn't looking at you in any way," I told him. "I was thinking."

"I had that day off. I sure as sugar didn't drive all the way back to Thistlewood to burn the place down. What would I have to gain by that?"

"I never thought you did."

"You didn't?"

Not since I first spoke to Sergeant Sharpe anyway.

"Can I get you some coffee, Sal?" Violet called out. "I've got a slice of cherry pie with your name on it."

He pushed back his cap. "I'll take both please, Vi."

"Great. Have a seat and let the young ones go about their business."

"Yes, ma'am." Sal gave a nod before he glared at me and Mac.

"Thanks. I'll talk to you later, Vi." Mac tossed money on the counter keeping a grip on my shoulder. He steered me around the busy tables and out the door.

While I tried to wait patiently for an explanation, my curiosity won out. "What was that was all about? A little male posturing, perhaps?"

"You said he made you nervous." He crammed his hands in his coat pockets. "I got you out of there as fast I could without getting us both in more trouble."

"I did say that."

He walked alongside me in silence for half a block. "I suppose you're going back to Thistlewood to work on your book."

"That's the plan." As well as taking pictures of Bebe's paperwork to send to my sister who'd texted me three times since I left Thistlewood. It was also a good time to follow up on some leads I'd come across to find Perry, since we seemed to be in the same part of the country.

"I have a big favor to ask," I said, turning to face him. "Two, actually."

"Just because I saved your life, doesn't mean I owe you." He smirked.

"Fine. I'll find it myself." I turned to walk away.

Mac followed like a hound dog. "What are you looking for?"

"It's okay. I'll ask Violet."

"Alison..."

Reluctantly, I stopped and asked, "Where is Sunrise Shelter?"

"Why are you looking for the homeless shelter?"

"It was mentioned in Bebe's will. I thought I'd see why."

He nodded up the street then stuck his hands in his coat pockets as he walked beside me. "Bebe and Ken donated a lot of money to make sure the place was not only up to code, but accessible and comfortable. Bebe helped arrange for grants up until she couldn't get out anymore."

That didn't sound like the woman I'd met in Thistlewood. She seemed as sharp as a rusty razor. "I thought she had dementia or something."

"I don't know about dementia, but I know she wasn't her normal self."

"What do you mean?" I sniffed the air as we passed a bakery. Tempted to do a U-turn and dig into a pastry or two, I kept my gaze on the street ahead.

Mac took so long to answer that I glanced over to make sure he hadn't disappeared into the bakery. "She seemed out of it sometimes. Like she'd taken sleeping pills in the middle of the day. Other times, she was in her own little world and talked about dancing with her husband or seeing him in her room."

"That's creepy."

"I didn't think much of it at first," he said. "We all have off days. Lately though, she seemed dazed a lot. At a loss for words."

"Drugged, maybe?" I asked, thinking about her nightly snack.

He shrugged. "Maybe. Just don't go accusing Anna of poisoning the food or there'll never be another guest there again."

I caught a glimpse of Sunrise Shelter across the street from the hospital. "Pretty nice for a homeless shelter. How did Bebe come into so much money?"

He shrugged. "That you'll have to ask Foster or Perry. All I know is that her family had made some good investments. Did you want to go inside?"

"Not right now. I need to do a little research first." Where did the money come from? Why a homeless shelter? That sort of thing.

In the meantime, I needed to figure out how to ask for a second favor.

"I was going to ask if you wanted to go for a hike," he said. "I need to burn off some of those fries we inhaled."

My opportunity. "A hike? Isn't that for people who want to be healthy?"

"Like firefighters?" He laughed. "Yes."

"I'm a city girl, remember? I'm not much of a hiker. I get winded climbing stairs."

"Yeah, I saw how fast you moved up those stairs the other night. I don't believe you." He gave me such a nudge that I lost my balance and staggered. "Whoa. You okay?"

Shaking off the brain fog, I nodded. "Yeah. Fine."

"Come on. A little fresh air's good for you. It'll get those creative juices flowing. Besides, there's a great trail along the shore that ends up near Thistlewood."

"Which means you'd be walking me home." I tried to hide my smile.

Mac seemed amused by the idea. "Essentially."

Tough choice. Option A, I take the shortcut back to hole up in my stuffy room to write. Option B was a hike with a firefighter cute enough to pose for a calendar. Mr. December, perhaps.

No brainer. I turned away. "See you later."

He burst into laughter and grabbed my arm. "No way, Sweets. You owe me."

"What do I owe you for?" Emily would never forgive me if I didn't go with him.

"For risking my life."

I rolled my eyes. "Oh, please. You were never in any danger."

A grin tugged at the corner of his mouth. "More than you know."

"What's that supposed to mean?" I stopped.

Mac kept walking.

Seriously? I huffed. What kind of danger did he think...?

"Oh." My temperature shot sky high. The guy was trouble.

By then he was several feet ahead of me. He glanced back and chuckled, probably at my new shade of strawberry red. "You spend way too much time in your room. It's time we got you into the real world."

"Why is that?" I trudged along the path behind him.

"Research." He winked.

Southern Ontario summers were nothing compared to the heat that radiated off me. I probably melted any patches of snow within a ten-foot radius.

We walked for what seemed like an entire kilometer before he faced me. "What was the other favor you wanted to ask?"

"Huh?" I'd already forgotten.

"Let me guess. You want me to pose for your book cover." He grinned, flexing his arms.

Boy, did I ever. "That's up to my publisher."

"Tell you what," he said. "Let's hike to the top of the bluff, then have a seat. After you catch your breath, you can fill me in on what's going on."

"You already know." I paused a couple feet in front of him in the middle of the trail. "Bebe died. I'm her granddaughter. I have to find Perry to tell him what's going on. Since you know him, I hoped you'd help me find him."

"Are you sure you want to open that can of worms, Sweets?" he asked.

"It's been opened wide without my help. I don't have a choice but to dive in. If I don't get my sister some answers—"

"Wait, are you doing this for her or for you?"

I wiped a bead of sweat off my face. "Roxie asked me to find Perry to invite him to her wedding. After I read Bebe's will last night, I realized Perry's the only one who can fill in a lot of the blanks."

Mac's eyes widened. "Is that what was in the envelope you had?"

"Yes. She left you some money." Tears filled my eyes.

"I told her to give it to charity, but..." He paused. "Does that make me a suspect?"

"Of course not. You tried to save her life. Do you think I killed her?"

"If you had killed her, you would've taken your laptop bag when you left," he said. "You wouldn't have dragged me inside."

"Drag you? You chased me." A weight seemed to lift off my shoulders. "I hope the police think the way you do."

Mac chuckled. "Come on. We're almost to the top. I'm sure Sharpe will be eager to talk to you now that you've read the will."

We walked in silence until we emerged from the woods and stood on a bluff that overlooked a quiet part of the Strait of Georgia.

"This is incredible," I gushed as I took several pictures of the blue-gray water and wispy clouds. I also snuck a couple snapshots of Mac for Emily. "Thanks for bringing me here."

"What did you mean Perry's the only one who can fill in some blanks?" He stuck his hands into his pockets while he took in the view.

I debated how much to tell him then went all in. "I thought I was born and raised in Toronto. My mom said our dad died when he and I were in a bad car accident, which was supposed to keep us from asking questions."

He raised his eyebrows and tugged the zipper of his coat up against the wind. "What kind of questions?"

"Who he was. Why he wasn't with us. About a month ago, she announced that Perry was alive. When I searched for him online, I found dozens of images. My search ended here."

Mac's right eye twitched. "Which is why you came to Thistle-wood."

"Someone offered me a spot as Writer-in-Residence, which I start next week. Turns out Bebe was my benefactor."

"And since I know him, you think I'll help you meet him."

"I'm hoping," I whispered. "You know my dad and I can't even remember him."

While I snapped a few more pictures and tried to collect my emotions, Mac suddenly said, "Yes."

"What?"

"I'll help you find Perry," he said. "It might take a day or two to get in touch with him, but all you want is answers, right? He can't say no to that."

"That's great, thank you." I threw my arms around his neck before I realized what I was doing. As my feet slipped on some loose stones, I fell against him.

He caught me in a hug, moving us away from the ledge. "I appreciate the enthusiasm, but could you try not to kill us again so soon?"

"Deal. Sorry." I backed away from the heat of his strong body.

As I readjusted my laptop bag, I remembered that Owen said he didn't trust Mac, yet Mac had saved my life twice now. Both times because of my own stupidity. My vision blurred for a split second. Had I remembered to take my medication?

"Are you afraid I'll push you over?" he asked.

"Owen told me you visited Bebe to discuss business. What sort of business did you have with her?"

Mac recoiled like I'd slapped him. "Owen said what? Alison, Bebe was my friend. I did errands for her on my days off. Like picking up things from the pharmacy and mailing packages for her."

"Aren't those things Anna did?" I asked.

"Most of the time," he said. "Sometimes Bebe would ask me. Since she and my grandma were good friends, I did what she asked. One time she got me to pick up fries and a strawberry milkshake from the diner. With her dementia, sometimes she got suspicious that someone was poisoning her."

My thoughts went back to the glass shards in Bebe's trash can. I'd forgotten all about them. "Do you think someone could've poisoned her?"

"She had good moments and bad. Didn't you say she danced with imaginary men?"

"I only saw her twice. When she came to Toronto, she was lucid and sharp."

Mac frowned as he met my gaze. "When was Bebe in Toronto?"

"A couple of weeks ago." I put my phone in my pocket. "She came into the candy store the same day Foster gave me the offer."

"No wonder Anna said Bebe wasn't seeing visitors. I thought she was ill."

I folded my arms across my stomach. "She didn't tell you? That's weird. And why would Foster take Bebe across the country if she was in a bad state?"

"But you said she seemed lucid."

"She was lucid and knew all about me and my sister, which was creepy at the time. She certainly wasn't off in her own little world." Yet she didn't recognize me in Thistlewood and called me Countess. "Was she on any medications for dementia?"

He shook his head. "All I ever picked up for her were vitamins."

"If she had dementia, would she think someone poisoned her food?"

"Possibly. Most days she had a long list of chores for me. Little things like getting chocolate-covered strawberries or a bouquet of flowers, just because she wanted a man to give her some like Jack used to."

The image of yellow daisies flashed through my mind.

"She gushed about chocolate-covered strawberries when we danced. They were her favorite. Did you ever see her when she couldn't think straight."

"You mean like Owen gets sometimes?" he asked. "Maybe once or twice. Anna and Owen loved Bebe. That's why they looked after her. There's no way either of them would've hurt her."

"Thanks. I was starting to have my doubts." I avoided glancing over the bluff before I followed Mac past a small cedar cottage nestled in the woods as we headed toward Thistlewood.

Chapter Nine

I picked at my lasagna, unable to eat much after my chat with Mac. My phone buzzed in my pocket as I was about to excuse myself from the table. Roxie. I groaned. The will and Bebe's paperwork. I'd already forgotten. Where was my head today?

"Thank you for dinner, Anna. I need to call my sister before she thinks I'm avoiding her."

"Okay. I get your pie then," Owen said.

Anna shot him a scowl. "Be nice. I'll bring you tea and a piece of pie later."

"You don't have to do that. I'll need a break in a couple hours anyway." I set my plate in the sink before I ran upstairs.

Fishing the yellow envelope out of Mabel's bag, I placed each sheet on the desk one by one to take photos of them. Once I'd texted them all to Roxie, I swiped to the next picture.

Mac stood on the bluff with the trees and the strait in the background.

My next text was to Emily. The photo of Mac. Considering she was currently at work and had a date later, I wouldn't hear from her until morning. Hopefully, Roxie was busy as well. I studied Mr. December for another minute before plugging in my phone next to the bed and muting the volume.

I'd barely started to work when someone knocked at my door.

Anna stood in the hallway with a mug of tea and a little plate with a thick slice of blueberry pie. "You didn't come back for dessert. How's the book going?"

"Okay. I have a major scene to write and just have to dig into it. The tea will help. Thanks."

"Did you talk to your sister?" she asked.

"I sent her the information she needed. She'll call later."

Anna nodded. "I'm going to watch a movie. Enjoy your evening."

"You, too." I watched her walk across the foyer.

Back at my desk, I threw myself into my novel while nibbling at the pie. It was a few minutes after eleven before I took a break. The house was quiet. Somehow, I'd managed to block all thoughts of Mac, Bebe, and Perry out of my head. My eyes burned from too much screen time, but I'd managed to add several pages.

With the writer in me sated for the moment, I stretched and tried to ease a couple of kinks out of the middle of my back.

I'd completely forgotten about the tea, more than likely from past experience. I sipped just enough to wet my mouth, then gagged. Anna seemed determined I had to drink my tea with sugar. I ate the rest of the pie before dumping the tea into the toilet. I could take the dishes down in the morning.

Since everyone else was settled for the night, I crawled beneath the covers and stared at the ceiling. My thoughts rambled until one dominated my ruminations. I needed to talk to Owen without Anna around. What did he know about Bebe?

As I started to doze off, I jolted awake. My heart raced. Bebe's favorite song played somewhere in the manor. Even after I covered my ears, the volume didn't change. The music was in my head. The song played just as loud and scratchy as it had the day I'd first arrived.

Unable to stand the deafening silence, I decided to go for a walk before anxiety set in any further.

I reached for my phone and turned on the flashlight. Not so much to see where I was going, but to blind anyone—or anything—that tried to attack me in the dark.

Grabbing my keys, I turned on the light before reaching for my coat and pulling it on over my flannel pajamas. It wasn't like I'd run into anyone at this time of night. I crept down the stairs and was careful to make sure the back door was unlocked as I left the house.

A cold wind blew off the Strait of Georgia and attacked my skin straight through my thin pajama pants. I zipped my jacket to the top as I passed Sal's cottage. I'd barely reached the rocky shore before I murmured, "Who'd want to kill a harmless hermit like Bebe?"

Her will had made me curious about a few things. Our family dynamic for one. Owen said Bebe had two sons yet only Perry was mentioned in the will. Had she cut off her other son, or had he died?

Maybe I was overthinking things. Perhaps someone in Thistlewood Manor wasn't a music fan, which was no reason for murder. Breaking her favorite records, perhaps, but not murder. I hummed as I walked, then paused when I realized it was Bebe's song.

Great. On top of everything else, I was losing my mind.

As the icy wind whipped small snowflakes at me, I stepped over pieces of driftwood that littered the beach. Some smooth and stripped of bark, others worn and weathered. Rocks of all sizes created a rugged shoreline. Everything from large boulders to pebbles and sand. Why couldn't I be Writer-in-Residence somewhere tropical instead of Vancouver Island in the winter?

Close to the water, a dark figure leaned over to pick something up. I slowed my pace, turned off the flashlight, and tried not to make noise. My efforts were wasted when I tripped over a rock and nearly fell.

The man turned and walked straight toward me. "Rough day, Miss Cadell?"

"Sergeant Sharpe." I laughed in relief. "Yes, and it's Alison, please."

He turned up his coat collar to protect his neck from the wind before he picked up a stone and tossed it in the water. "Feels like snow tonight."

I'd only been in Cedar Grove a few days and was already sick of the weather. Toronto was damp and gloomy, but the cold here seemed to seep into my bones and left an awful chill behind.

He chuckled. "Enjoy this while you can. We rarely get snow, just cold and damp. Did you get settled back into Thistlewood?"

"Aside from the smells of smoke and cleaner, you'd never know there was a fire." I stuffed my hands in my pockets.

"Odd, isn't it?" He picked up more stones.

"What is?"

"How there was so much smoke, but not much damage," he said. "Almost like someone wanted the building structurally intact for when they inherited it."

My mouth went dry and gritty as I picked up a rock. "Foster told you about Perry and the will."

"Yes, ma'am, he did." He handed me a rock to throw. "He showed me proof you're Bebe's granddaughter and a copy of the will. You, young lady, stand to inherit not only a great deal of money, but part of Thistlewood Manor."

Which not only left me as a suspect, but at the top of the list. I squeezed the stone in my hand. It was roughly the size of my pineapple stone I'd left on the nightstand.

"Unless we can find Perry," I said. "I asked Mac to help me track him down, but I hoped you might have some leads. Do you know much about my father?"

The Sergeant threw another rock. After a long couple minutes, he said, "I owe you an apology, Alison. I wasn't forthcoming when we spoke before. You're new in town and I'm looking for a killer."

"And I'm at the top of your list. That's understandable."

"Not at the top." He grinned.

"Funny."

Handing me another stone, he asked, "When's the last time you saw Perry Beyer?"

"Apparently, twenty years ago when my mother left him. She dragged me and my sister to Toronto. I would've been five," I told him. "Did you speak to my mother? I'll bet she's on your list."

He chuckled. "Yes, but Toronto's a long way to fly to strangle someone. If Perry was the victim, I'd look her up."

"Don't forget my sister." I rolled the rock in my hand.

"She's cleared," he assured me. "Anyone else I should consider?"

"Everyone else who lives at Thistlewood. Maybe even Sheila," I told him before I finally launched my rock over the crests. "I'll bet it was an inside job."

"I forgot you're a mystery writer."

"Correction. Romance novelist. I've never read a mystery in my life. I'd like to know who killed Bebe though." I stuck my cold hands into my pockets. "Are you only talking to me because I'm her granddaughter?"

When he scooped a whole handful of pebbles, I had a feeling our talk was about to take a turn. "Where did you learn about solving crimes?"

"The Internet. Television."

"Interesting." There it was. His favorite word.

"What's the other reason we're talking now?"

He threw three pebbles in a row before he said, "Alison, I've known Perry for a long time. We grew up together. He's low on my suspect list. As for Owen, he's like a kid brother. We have to protect him."

"Do you think Owen killed Bebe?" I asked.

Sharpe shook his head. "Honestly? No, but I do know he's prone to doing odd things. If he knows anything about her death, it won't be easy to pry it out of that bank vault he calls a brain."

"Especially with Anna around," I muttered, rubbing the rock in my pocket while I thought.

"Why do you say that?"

I exhaled out a cloud of steam like some kind of dragon. "Every time Owen and I talk, Anna appears. It's like she's keeping watch over him."

"She does live there."

"I know that, but..." I waved a hand. "You're right. She's probably just doing her due diligence."

"Do you know Owen writes?"

As a gust of wind pierced my pajama bottoms, I hunched my shoulders closer to my ears. "I've heard. Have you read any of his stories?"

He stepped in front of me as if to block the wind. "A couple years ago, he gave me a story about a man dying in a fire. I told him he had a lot of talent and should keep writing. Then I noticed similarities between his story and Jack's death."

I shivered. "Jack who?"

Sharpe met my gaze. "Jack Beyer. Your grandfather."

Jack. My grandfather, the love of Bebe's life, died mysteriously as well? I tried to shrug it off, but my thoughts kicked into high gear.

"And before you say anything, that doesn't mean Owen's a killer," he said. "Although he may know more than he realizes.

"Maybe he just has a vivid imagination."

"Maybe." He didn't sound convinced. "Did you know Mac wanted me to press charges against you after the fire?"

"He didn't say anything when we went for a hike earlier. Besides, we're both fine and he rescued Bebe."

"Yes, but you didn't know she was in there at the time, did you?" he asked. "You did endanger your life and his."

"He reminds me when I see him, which is why I don't think he'll press charges. It's become a running joke."

Sharpe chuckled. "I'm glad to know you've called a truce. Mac's a good man. I know the fire investigators and crime scene crew went through everything, but there are a couple things I'd like to check on."

I scooped up a small, flat rock and warmed it in my icy hand. "That won't be a problem. How well did you know Bebe?"

"As well as anyone else around here, I guess."

"Did she have any enemies?" I realized how odd my question sounded, but curiosity gnawed at me. "Maybe a disgruntled employee or a family member."

Sharpe ran a hand over his jaw. "Trying to solve her murder, are you? It's late. We're both tired. Stop trying to do my job."

"Someone strangled her," I reminded him. "Unless you have another explanation for the marks on her neck."

He folded his arms across his chest. "Who do you have in mind?"

"I don't trust Sal."

"That's exactly what he said about you."

"What did I ever do to him?" I asked.

"Aside from looking at him like he's a killer? Nothing, I'm sure. What did he ever do to you?"

The fact was, I'd barely spoken to or even seen Sal aside from at the diner. Technically, he hadn't done anything.

"Sal adored Bebe. He'd do anything for her and Thistlewood. No matter what."

"That sounds like everyone around here. It's hard to make a suspect list when everyone loved her."

Sharpe grimaced. "Tell me about it."

"Where was Sal the night of the fire? He said he had the day off."

"He was fishing with a couple buddies all day then spent the night at his cottage with his daughter before they drove back to Cedar Grove early the next day. He heard about the fire on the radio."

My eyes grew wide. "Sal has a daughter?"

"Yup." He threw another stone. "You might have met her. Jewels works at Georgia Shores part-time and studies medical books the rest of the time. She wants to be a nurse or a support worker after she graduates. She would help Bebe once a week to give Anna some free time."

Medical books. Jewels could have found out what medications Bebe was on and how they would interact. I cringed at my own wild imagination and brushed the thought off.

"I know what you're thinking," he said. "Jewels was with her dad at their cottage near Buttle Lake over two hours away. She has an alibi."

"Yeah. Sal. Except he was the one who told me Bebe was murdered."

He raised his dark eyebrows. "When?"

"The next morning. Maybe around nine. He heard it from Roger at Stop'n'Shop who heard it from Maisy at the gas station who talked to Chloe at the hair salon. At least, I think that's how the rumor chain went."

Sharpe rubbed his jaw. "You don't say."

"What if they worked together?" I asked. "Jewels drugged Bebe using medication and Sal strangled her. I'd look into their alibis if I were you."

He walked me back to the back entrance of Thistlewood Manor. "If I were you, Miss Cadell, I'd stick to writing romance novels and not worry about police business."

"That's pretty solid advice," I told him. "I might actually take it."

"I would appreciate that."

As we strolled toward Thistlewood, the two lights on either side of the door grew dim. I stopped. Not burned out. Simply dimmed. Before I took another step, they grew bright again.

"How odd."

"What is?" he asked.

I pointed to the entrance. "The lights. They almost went out, then brightened again."

As if on cue, the lights dimmed and brightened several more times like someone sending Morse code.

"Could it be an electrical short?" I asked.

"Maybe, but usually a short goes off and on faster. Like a flicker. It doesn't do that." He hesitated. "Maybe it's Bebe."

"A ghost? It can't be. I don't believe in them."

"You don't need to believe in things for them to be real," he said, making me nervous.

"I'll leave a note for Anna. Maybe she can call an electrician in the morning."

The lights dimmed once more. Just when I thought they'd finally gone out completely, they grew increasingly brighter until both light-bulbs exploded simultaneously.

Both Sharpe and I turned away to shield our faces.

"Still don't believe in ghosts?" he asked.

"It could be a power surge." My voice shook. "We'll get someone to check on it tomorrow."

"You do that," the sergeant said. "For now, watch your step."

Was that a threat? "What do you mean?"

"There's glass on the porch. I don't want you to get cut." He swept the shards to one side with his heavy soled boots.

"Right. Thanks." Stepping over the remnants of lightbulbs, I recalled the shards I'd found in the trash can.

Sharpe was already gone.

I locked the door behind me. I turned on the kitchen light, then rummaged for a piece of paper in a couple kitchen drawers. On the smaller table near the window sat boxes of glittering white envelopes like the one Foster gave me from Bebe. The invitations next to them were for the McKittrick Christmas Ball. Why would Anna have them in Thistlewood?

My stomach squirmed. She had to be helping out friends. It seemed to be something she often did. I pawed through a drawer and found a piece of scrap paper. I also came across a pill bottle with Bebe's name on it for something called flurazepam that was filled at a pharmacy in Toronto. I took a picture and closed the drawer leaving the pills where I found them.

Having left a note for Anna about the lights, I crept up the stairs in the dark with my mind whirling. Could Sharpe be right about Bebe causing the bulbs to blow up? Was it possible Sal and Jewels killed Bebe, started the smoldering fire, and still had time to flee to their cottage in Buttle Lake? I had to find out how far that was from Cedar Grove and...

Before I crawled into bed, I checked out the drug I'd found in the drawer. Flurazepam was a powerful sleeping pill that could become addictive and cause confusion and hallucinations in some people. Was that what Anna was giving Bebe with her nightcap?

How was I ever supposed to sleep while I became more suspicious of the people around me with every passing moment?

Chapter Ten

After my late-night stroll on the beach, I was too tired to focus. I stumbled downstairs for a cup of coffee before I even got near my laptop. At least I remembered to bring down the empty mug and plate. Maybe she had a thermos or a carafe I could borrow.

"Good morning." Anna handed me a clean mug before I could ask. "Did you sleep well? I hoped the herbal tea would help you sleep. I thought I heard you go out last night."

I poured some coffee then added cream and sugar. "I was trying to work through a scene and got so absorbed, I forgot it was there. Sometimes a walk helps me think. Next time I'll dress warmer. It was too cold out for pajamas last night."

"No doubt. I saw your note about the lights. I'll have Sal take a look." She opened the oven to check on a batch of muffins, then pointed to a bowl on the counter. "Could you give me a hand? Just give that pancake batter a stir while I put the bread in to bake."

"Sure." I set my cup aside to grab a large bowl with chicken designs on the sides. While I stirred the batter, Anna placed three loaves of bread dough in the oven, then flipped the muffins onto a cooling rack. "How long have you worked here? It's like you're one with the kitchen."

Anna refilled her cup then added two teaspoons of sugar. "I started working here a few months after it was built. Bebe had her hands full with reservations and staff. Then Jack died and I couldn't let the place fall apart, so I offered to run things while she grieved. Only she never came out of it. Jack was her whole world."

I scraped a layer of batter off the side of the bowl while she heated a family-sized griddle Emily would drool over. "It must be difficult for you to do everything on your own. Was Bebe able to help?"

"Sheila looks after the cleaning and laundry. I take care of everything else." Anna pulled a pint of blueberries and a strainer filled with strawberries from the fridge. "Some mornings Bebe would bake and entertain, then be half asleep by dinner. After I cleaned up, I could prep for the next day and watch a little television without worrying she'd leave on a burner or wander into the Strait."

I dropped a splatter of water on the griddle. It sizzled and danced across the hot surface. "This is a beautiful place to spend a vacation. I'll bet there's a lot to do in the summer."

"Kayaking. Hiking. Farmers' markets. This place and Bebe take..." Anna paused. "They took up a lot of my time. I miss the routine. I feel lost without her."

"I wish I'd known her." I poured puddles of batter onto the griddle, making six four-inch pancakes. "Is this good?"

"You're a natural," she said. "Do you cook at home?"

"My roommate's the chef. She'd love the chance to work in this kitchen. I just eat. When we were kids, my mom was always on a diet, so I never learned." I kept a close eye on the griddle as I asked, "What kind of routine did Bebe have?"

Anna raised her eyebrows. "No wonder you're a good writer. You're full of questions, aren't you? Some things..." Whatever she was going to say, she stopped herself.

As I flipped the pancakes, a flash of a memory raced through my mind. My dad.

Then it was gone.

"Bebe got up early and drank her tea while we made breakfast. Then she'd roam around talking to herself before going to her room to play her music and nap."

"Sounds good to me. I listen to music while I write."

Anna continued, "Every evening after dinner, I brought her a glass of brandy or champagne with some strawberries. She'd play that record until she fell asleep."

"So I heard." Hadn't she told me she brought Bebe tea every night?

"I guess you would've," she said. "Some nights I had to turn it off and tuck her into bed."

I lifted the golden pancakes off one by one and placed them on a nearby plate. "Did she have dementia? Is that why you had to tuck her into bed?"

"Some nights she'd fall asleep in her chair." Anna sliced strawberries into a separate bowl from the blueberries. "Others, she'd look at her pictures."

"Pictures of Jack?" I poured more batter onto the griddle.

Anna flinched then averted her gaze. "She lived in the past a lot. I took her to the doctor, but she was so stubborn and wouldn't admit she wasn't well."

"Did she take any medication?" I plucked a blueberry from the bowl.

There was an edge to her voice when she asked, "What's with the questions?"

I reached for my coffee, sure the answer would be obvious. "She was my grandmother, yet I never knew anything about her. You knew her best."

"I'm sorry," she said, patting my hand. "It's easy to forget that. You've been here such a short time."

Owen sauntered into the kitchen and reached for a coffee cup. "Bebe didn't need pills. She was as healthy as a goat. Loony as a ferret some days, but healthy."

I laughed. "Loony as a ferret?"

"Haven't you ever watched those things?" he asked. "They're nuts. I think Bebe was nuts because of her husband dying and all that other stuff. I think it made her sad that she lost her grandbabies."

Me and Roxie.

"Don't mix the berries together." Owen called over his shoulder as he poured a cup of coffee then left the kitchen.

Anna rolled her eyes. "Obsessive Compulsive."

"Loony as a ferret." I chuckled, making her laugh as I flipped the pancakes.

"Bebe always said you were just like Perry," she said. "She'd talk about how you'd come back to Thistlewood to help take care of things."

"And when I didn't, she came to find me." I blinked back tears. "When I was a kid, I wrote stories about a log house. I even had an imaginary big brother. My mom told me I was creative but had to get my homework done, so I could get a good job one day since writing isn't a real job."

Anna dropped a sliced strawberry onto the counter. It left a faint red stain on the wooden cutting board. "What about your dad?"

"I grew up thinking my dad had died, then my sister got engaged and wanted his medical information. Mom said Perry was alive but had no idea where he was."

"She must've had her reasons."

"I'm sure she did." I piled six more pancakes onto the serving platter, then scraped the last of the batter from the bowl. "Do you know my dad?"

She nodded. "I did. Once Jack died, the whole family fell apart. Perry and Bebe were never the same."

"What happened to Jack?" I asked, watching her for a reaction.

Anna turned away to bring the berries to the table. "I need to check on the laundry. Sheila's taking a couple days off, so I have to freshen up some rooms. Christmas will be busy. Lots of out-of-towners coming to the McKittrick ball."

Disappointed, I sipped my coffee. "Go ahead. I'll clean out Bebe's room today."

Anna hadn't returned by the time the pancakes were ready. I carried the platter to the table where Owen sat hunched over a notebook writing at a frantic pace. When his pen left indents in the paper with no more ink, he shook it.

I placed the tray on the wooden table, then returned with the coffee pot. "More coffee?"

Owen seemed startled to see me. He covered his paper with both hands.

"I didn't mean to interrupt. You looked busy."

"My pen died."

"There's another one at the end of the table. Would you like more coffee?"

"Yes, please," he said, then reached for the other pen.

I topped up both cups, then took a seat and shivered despite my thick sweater. "It's as cold and damp here as it is in Toronto."

A grin tugged at his mouth. "Yeah. Winter's nice though. At least it doesn't get so cold your nose freezes shut."

"That's true," I agreed. "What do you do to keep warm?"

"I drink hot chocolate in front of the fireplace during the winter. Do you like hot chocolate?"

"Oh, yeah, especially with lots of marshmallows or whipped cream."

Owen's face lit up. He relaxed enough to uncover his writing, which resembled some odd form of hieroglyphics. "Don't tell Anna, but I put both in mine. Where is Anna anyway?"

"Your secret's safe with me." My stomach growled. "Anna's doing laundry. How long have you lived at Thistlewood?"

"My whole life. I didn't move away like you did." He slurped his coffee, then bowed his head as he continued to write.

A heavy weight seemed to settle on my chest. "What do you mean like I did?"

He stared at his notebook for a long minute before he frowned and packed up his notebook. "You must have hit your head harder than I did."

"I didn't hit my head," I told him. "And I don't remember being here before."

As his gaze met mine, his eyes grew twice their normal size behind his thick glasses.

Anna cleared her throat behind me. "Owen, can you tell Sal breakfast is ready?"

"Yes, Anna." He frowned then shuffled to the back door.

"Everything looks great, Alison. I'll just grab one more setting for Sal."

"Yeah, sorry, I wasn't sure who'd be here this morning."

"Just the four of us for today. I'm sure Jewels is off to wherever." Anna returned with the extra plate and cutlery just as Owen returned with Sal.

"Is she still here?" Sal growled.

I focused on my breakfast, not wanting to stir up more trouble. The best way to stay out of everyone's way would be to clean Bebe's personal effects out of her room before guests arrived. The only sounds were the scrapes of cutlery on plates and Owen repeatedly clearing his throat. A nervous tic, I guessed.

Sal stood, ready to bolt from the table. "Thank you for breakfast, Anna."

"Are there any empty boxes I could use?" I asked. "This might be a good day to pack Bebe's personal things so someone can use her room."

"Don't touch her stuff," Owen snapped.

Sal placed a hand on Owen's shoulder. "Bebe's not here anymore, son. I'm sure the girl could use a hand if you're not busy."

"Don't worry, dear," Anna said. "We'll let you keep a treasure or two." She met my gaze. "Right?"

"We'll keep all the important stuff."

"It's all important," Owen said.

Knowing what he meant, I asked, "Why don't you come up and take what you'd like to remember her by?"

"There you go," Sal announced, as he headed out the French doors to the backyard. "Problem solved."

Owen tightened his lips and flared his nostrils. "I want everything. Leave her room alone."

"We can't do that, honey," Anna told him. "The Manor will get busier for Christmas. We need the room for guests."

Owen huffed. "We don't have guests. We have Alison."

She gave an exasperated sigh before turning to me. "Alison, Sal put some boxes in one of the cupboards in the garage. They're tied with twine, so you won't have a problem carrying them. There's tape in there, too."

"Thanks."

Anna wrung a cloth napkin in her hand. "Owen, why don't you help Alison carry the boxes to Bebe's room?"

With an angry furrow between his eyebrows, he led me to the garage and helped me find the boxes. "I don't like this. Bebe shouldn't be gone."

"I agree. I never even got to know her. Maybe you can tell me about her."

"I'm sad about that," he said.

What happens at Grandma's house, stays at Grandma's house was the first thing I took off the wall to place in a box. Maybe I'd give it to my mom when my sister had kids.

"I was supposed to call Sergeant Sharpe before we touched anything." I pulled out my phone.

Owen set the boxes in the center of the room. For a couple of seconds, he looked like he wanted to say something before he scrambled away at top speed.

"Hey," I called after him. "Aren't you going to help?"

He froze in the doorway with his eyes wide. "All I want is the picture of her and me that's in the little egg frame."

"Egg frame?" I scanned the wall then saw the photo of Bebe holding a boy. I took a picture of it before handing it to him. "Is that you? You were so cute."

"Yup. That was before…" He took a step back.

"Before what?" I tilted my head, but he darted down the hall.

Left alone, I turned a full circle. I had no idea where to begin, so took photos of the entire room before I called Sharpe. He told me to send him the photos before I touched anything.

The furniture and bedding I'd leave for Sheila or Anna to deal with. It would all have to be washed in order to rent the room. Finally, I ignored the photographs and personal mementoes to face the numerous books on the shelves. Romance and mystery novels mostly. Even a few I recognized.

"Writing books?" I sat on the floor and flipped through a couple that caught my interest as Sharpe gave me the go-ahead to pack things away.

Each was signed by the author. It seemed Bebe had met many great writers I admired. I put the books I wanted to keep into one box, then tossed the rest into a box for charity. Maybe the shelter. By lunch, I'd ended up with three boxes of stuff—mostly books—I wanted to keep and five bags filled with Bebe's clothing.

I slid the three boxes into my room, then took my favorite off the top. Stephen King's book *On Writing*. I had a copy in Toronto. Where my copy was riddled with notes, dogeared, and highlighted, this copy was brand new, and autographed. To Bebe.

Who was this woman?

After a hot shower, I pulled on my jacket and grabbed my laptop bag. The house was quiet. Anna was either in her room or had gone out for the afternoon. As I headed toward the front door, I caught a glimpse of Owen near the large fireplace at the far end of the manor. His pen scratched the paper in the silence.

I hoped he wouldn't run off before I could talk to him. "Hey, Owen. What are you working on?"

"I like that you're a romance writer," he said. "I decided to write a book, too."

"Oh yeah? What's it about?"

"I don't have much written," he said.

"That's okay. You can tell me later."

He gazed up, his eyes wide. "Would you help me write a book?"

"Sure. Why not?"

"But you don't even know me."

I sat next to him. "I don't have any friends here and you seem to know everyone in town. Maybe you could introduce me to people you know."

"I'm not sure about that," Owen said, his face growing red. "If we spend too much time together, people might think you're my girlfriend."

"Good point."

He slid his thick glasses up his nose before reaching for my hand. "I'm sorry, Alison. It's not that you're not pretty and I wouldn't like to learn about writing from you, it's just..." He glanced around us then whispered. "I already have a girlfriend."

"You do? What's her name?" I asked.

"Promise you won't tell?" The redness crept into his ears as he held out his little finger, which was nearly twice as thick as mine. "Pinky swear."

My breath stuck in my throat. His gesture triggered a familiar warmth even though I'd never done a pinky swear before. I took his finger with mine. "I swear I won't tell a soul."

Satisfied, he leaned in so close I smelled the stale coffee on his breath. "Violet."

My eyes grew wide before I whispered, "From the diner?"

"Yup." He flashed a lop-sided grin. "Girls my age look at me funny. She treats me nice."

I wanted to ask if she knew they were an item. "That's exciting. How long have you two been dating?"

"Since the day I saw her open the front door of the Burlap Diner twenty years ago. It was October tenth at six-oh-five in the morning. The last waitress quit, and it was Violet's first day." A dreamy expression settled over his face. "The same day your mom took you and your sister away in that big black car."

All the blood seemed to drain from my head, and I grew numb as I asked, "What are you talking about?"

"That's what I want to write about." He looked toward the foyer before he said, "The secrets."

"What secrets?" My heart raced. What if Owen was right?

He put his pen down and held the paper between both hands. "Here's what I have so far. 'They shared the last box of half-price chocolates from the corner store, then the girl tossed a pink teddy bear into the fire.' That's all I've got."

Something about his story tickled the depths of my mind. If it was a memory, it refused to let me coax it out of hiding. Was it the chocolates or the teddy bear that triggered my unease? "Why did the girl burn the teddy bear?"

Owen shrugged. "It was from someone she didn't like."

"Fair enough. I like the part about the half-price chocolates. Can I use that in one of my books?"

"That depends. Do I get royalties?"

"That's not quite how it works. I could give you an autographed copy when it comes out and a dedication."

"Hmm. Maybe," Owen said, tapping the paper against his mouth.

The other side was a letter. I tried to read it, but he tucked it in his notebook before I got a good look.

"I'll get back to you." He left the room with the paper in one hand.

Curiosity got the best of me. I couldn't let him get away, so I followed. "Could I read that for myself? Maybe we can add to it and turn it into a great book you can publish one day."

Owen hesitated and tapped his foot before he handed me the letter. Then he made me pinky swear again. "Make sure you give it back when you're done."

"Why did my mom take us away?" I asked. "Did something bad happen?"

He took a few steps back. "I can't tell you. Anna told me not to and made me pinky swear."

Two seconds later, I was alone with the fragment of Owen's story while he raced up the stairs. To get answers, I'd have to talk to Anna or Foster. I was sure one or both knew the truth. Rather than read Owen's scrawled printing, I flipped the page over.

"Dear, Mrs. Bettina Beyer." A letter from an insurance company regarding the damage from the fire. Damage I still hadn't seen. It was dated twenty years ago. Anna had probably taken care of Bebe's business correspondence for years. Why had she left it for anyone to see, or write on? I tucked the letter in my pocket, then picked up my laptop bag.

Numb, I wandered into town and found Foster's office. Hopefully, he could elaborate. His secretary, a middle-aged woman with short blonde hair and a bright blue dress that hugged her curves, insisted he was out for the rest of the day. Yet I heard the hum of his voice beyond the closed door behind her.

Writing my name and number on a notepad, I told her he could find me at the Burlap Diner.

She raised an unkempt eyebrow as I turned to leave.

I found a table near a window. Rather than open my laptop, I pulled out a notebook, nursed my coffee, and hoped something would inspire a scene in my novel. All I could think about was the odd family I was discovering. Why did my mother take us away from them?

Just as I pulled out my phone to try and ask her again, Foster sat across from me. "You look like you lost your best friend."

I immediately thought of Owen. "Possibly. I guess I'll never know."

"My secretary said you were looking for me. Is everything okay?" he asked.

Unsure how to answer, I doodled small spirals on my page. "I'm considering staying here to look after Thistlewood. I think that's what Bebe wanted."

His expression was unreadable as Violet poured him a cup of coffee. "Perhaps that was why she had me search for you. I should think you would appear happier about your decision."

"Yeah, well between my mom, Perry, and Anna, I'm starting to have second thoughts before I've finished having the first ones." I sat back to meet his gaze. "I need a few answers first."

The corner of Foster's mouth twitched beneath his moustache. "What sort of answers?"

"I'd like to see Thistlewood's financial records, for a start," I told him, hoping I sounded businesslike. "Plus, information about the people who live and work there."

"Is that all?" Foster fidgeted with a sugar packet.

"Employment records for Anna, Sal, and Sheila." I got the sense he was mentally building a stone wall in between us. "I don't think Anna wants me there."

"Why would you say that?" he asked.

"Every time I try to talk to Owen, she rushes him away from me. She also has a bad habit of sending us to our rooms. It's like living with my mother."

Foster gave a smirk. "Perhaps she hopes you will work on that book you came to write rather than worrying about things out of your control. Besides, I understood you had responsibilities as Writer-in-Residence."

"Next week. The head librarian thought that might be best under the circumstances. Are you sure Anna's not trying to get rid of me?"

"If she was trying to get rid of you, she would send you to the diner or the library to write," he said. "It sounds more that she doesn't want Owen to get in your way. Besides, there are a lot of great spots in Thistlewood to work, so you are not likely stuck in your room all the time."

I chuckled, sheepish at the thought I was overreacting. "You're probably right. I do have one more question."

"Fire away, Miss Cadell."

"Why did Bebe start to look for me after all these years?"

Foster raised his eyebrows. "She hoped you would return to Thistlewood on your own accord. When she discovered you were an author, she thought inviting you here as a Writer-in-Residence would be an offer you could not refuse."

"What made her think I wouldn't refuse?"

"What self-respecting writer would refuse the opportunity to travel across the country and escape the real world, all-expenses paid, to write?" he asked.

"Good point." I waved to Violet for more coffee and a glass of water. "How did she know where to find me?"

Foster's jaw tightened. "She hired a private detective. While she had an idea where your mother was, Ingrid refused to tell her where she was going."

That sounded familiar. "How did she find me then? The detective must've been good."

"Not really." He moved back as Violet topped up our coffees. "He saw you at your mother's house then followed you to the candy store. If Bebe was able to drive, she would have gone without me."

"Why didn't she tell me who she was?" I asked.

He took a small notebook and a slim silver pen from the inside pocket of his suit jacket. "Tell me honestly, Miss Cadell. Would you have believed her?"

"Probably not."

"Then there is your answer." He waved the pen like a magician doing sleight of hand. "Is there anything else I can help you with, young lady?"

I hesitated. "Owen said my mom took me away from Cedar Grove twenty years ago." I paused. "What happened?"

His eyes widened a fraction of an inch. "I have no more information than what Bebe imparted to me."

Earlier he said he'd known Bebe since before she and Jack built Thistlewood. Suddenly, he was playing dumb. "I hoped you could trigger a memory or two that might help me remember."

"You have no memories of Thistlewood at all?" he asked.

"None."

"Generally, when our brain locks memories away from us, Miss Cadell, it is to protect us from something. After Owen's accident, his memory was far from what it used to be. I'm sure he has met plenty of young ladies who vacationed at the Manor over the years. Maybe he mistook you for one of them."

"Except that I've never vacationed here before." I reminded him. "You and Bebe knew each other for a long time, didn't you?"

He made a note in his book. "Jack and I grew up down the street from each other. We played hockey on his family's pond."

"My grandpa played hockey?"

"So did your grandma," he said with a wink. "Bebe had an amazing slapshot. She was not one of those wives who had dinner on the table at six o'clock with all of Jack's clothing cleaned and pressed."

I smiled at the image. "That doesn't surprise me, but her running Thistlewood does. Is that why she hired Anna?"

"Indeed. As much of Bebe's sweat went into building Thistlewood as anyone else's. She loved those boys of hers and would do anything for them."

"Boys? She had more than one?" My breath stuck in my throat. "The book she asked me to sign in Toronto. It was for Perry."

"Yes, it was," he said. "Speaking of, how is your new book coming along? Has Cedar Grove inspired you?"

"I've been inspired by a few things." Odd how he'd side-stepped the topic of Perry Beyer and his mysterious brother.

"Bebe would have been happy to hear that," he said. "She was elated to learn you were a romance novelist."

Was it my imagination or had he emphasized the word "romance"? He probably spoke to Mac or Sergeant Sharpe and heard I was being nosy. Either that or I'd drunk way too much caffeine.

"Tell me about this inspiration. Is he anyone I know?" he asked.

My eyes grew wide. Forget deer in the headlights. I was a writer in the gaze of a lawyer, which was far more unpredictable. I thought back to the fire, then to my first night at Thistlewood. I could avoid topics, too.

"I danced with her you know," I told him.

"With Bebe? When?"

"The night I arrived," I told him. "We ran into each other in the hallway. She sang while we twirled around the foyer. It was like I'd known her forever. She called me Countess."

Foster nodded. "Ah. Bebe had developed dementia, which is why she could never go anywhere alone. Anna was worried she would leave the stove on, or a candle burning and burn the place down. She always needed supervision."

The back of my neck prickled. Was it possible Bebe had started the fire?

"That was why Anna moved into Thistlewood after Jack died. We were worried about her."

"How did my grandfather die?" I asked.

Foster paled, then shifted in his seat as he cleared his throat. "You shall have to speak with the sergeant about that."

What was wrong with people around here? How come no one would give me a straight answer? I fished for a clue about my father. "Where did Bebe's kids go after Jack died?"

Sergeant Sharpe appeared at the end of our table. "Mr. Foster. Miss Cadell."

"Sergeant." Foster suddenly relaxed, as though he'd been rescued from a lion's den. "What can I do for you, Sergeant?"

"I'd like a word with Miss Cadell, if you don't mind," he said, glancing in my direction.

Foster's smile stiffened. "If it regards Bebe's death, keep in mind I am Miss Cadell's lawyer. You can speak in front of me. I have been the family's lawyer for many years."

"I see." Sharpe raised his eyebrows.

"I'm sure it's nothing to worry about, Mr. Foster," I told him. "Sergeant Sharpe and I have had some great chats while I've been finding my way around."

Foster didn't seem convinced. "Only if you're sure, Alison."

Alison? What happened to Miss Cadell? I flashed a glance toward Sharpe, who gave a subtle shake of his head.

"I promise I won't lock up your client." He seemed amused. "If I do, you'll be the first to know."

"Gee, thanks," I muttered.

Foster huffed before he stood and straightened his suit. Placing a ten-dollar bill on the table, he excused himself then left the diner.

Rather than sit, Sharpe gazed around the diner like a king surveying his domain. He strolled toward the counter to chat with Violet while he placed his order. After a long moment, he returned with a cup of coffee and two slices of pie before he sat across from me.

"Is something wrong?" I asked.

"Tough day at the office. You?"

"Same. Thank you for this." I checked out the peach pie. "I wrote a scene for my book last night which made perfect sense until this morning. It's a disaster. I think I have writer's block, or at least, writer's distraction."

He frowned. "Sounds serious. Is there a cure?"

"Inspiration."

"I see. And what does it take to inspire a novelist?"

"Some days, anything. A photograph. The way the sun hits the water. The thought of my father jumping out of a plane into a fire. The taste of peach pie."

The sergeant raised his eyebrows. "I get why you have writer's block. There's a lot going on in that head of yours."

"What did you want to talk to me about?" I asked.

He sliced off a piece of pie with his fork. "You seemed uncomfortable when Foster was here. Was there a reason for that?"

"Same old story. I ask questions and people shut down. It's hard to get a straight answer out of anyone around here."

"Tell me about it," he said. "Part of it might be Perry. No one wants to get on his bad side. Not that he's a violent man or anything, but he likes his privacy."

As I gazed from him toward the chalkboard on the wall at the far end of the counter with the daily specials, a thought struck me. Did Owen mimic my dad and jump into a fire?

"I have to go..." I slapped some money on the table and grabbed my notebook. "You just inspired me."

He grabbed my hand. "Sit. Eat the pie."

"But I—"

Still holding my hand, he pointed to the pie.

The moment I finished eating, I darted out the front door. If my memories were bubbling up to the surface, I'd need Owen's help sorting them out. Even though he knew what happened, would he tell me if I was on the right track?

Less than a block from the diner, someone grabbed my arm. "Whoa there. You look like you're on a mission."

Startled by reality, I flinched. "Huh?"

Anna chuckled. "I was just on my way to do some shopping before you nearly ran me over. Would you mind giving me a hand? Since Thistlewood's rightfully yours, I thought you'd want a say in the menu."

"You're doing a great job. Why would I change anything? Besides, I need to get some writing done."

Anna turned away with a sigh.

What was I thinking? She'd been good to me since I'd arrived. I walked alongside her. "You're right. I should know what's going on. If I plan to take over."

Her step seemed to falter. "Take over?"

"I figured you could teach me everything you know. Just in case. Before I make any decisions, I need to talk to my father and my sister."

Anna paused in front of the grocery store. "Can you cook?"

Only if soggy noodles and charcoal chicken passed as cooking. "Like I said, my roommate does all the cooking. You'll have to check out her blog."

"You'll have to learn," she said. "As well as change all the bedding, do the laundry, and pay the bills."

"Just like at home."

She shook her head. "Only for twenty people, not one. Some weeks Thistlewood is completely full."

"I'll bet Bebe enjoyed that."

"She loved a good party."

Anna taught me about picking the best fruits and vegetables, the best cuts of meat, and all the necessary things to stock. A couple hundred dollars later, she drove me home. On the way, she pointed out all the local landmarks while we drove through Cedar Grove.

I helped her unpack the groceries, then wandered through the manor, seeing it with new eyes. This was no longer some place I was invited to. This was my place. My home. From what Owen told me, it had been since I was a baby.

When Anna went to her room, I poked around by the front desk near the door. The hotel register was tucked below the counter as though someone was trying to hide it. I flipped it open to the current week. Mine was the only name inside. The same for the next six weeks.

After all her talk about guests and renting rooms, it was a shock to see no bookings. What was going on?

When a door closed upstairs, I tucked the book back in place before making my way to my room. Why was part of me blocking memories of living here?

Was I in an accident that wiped them out?

I walked up to the second level as if lost in a dream, placing a hand on the railing that overlooked the open kitchen below.

My stomach lurched. I stepped back, afraid I'd fall.

The brass chandelier that hung from the ceiling caught my eye. It had almond-shaped bulbs, yet the main body was decorated with a floral print. It had to be Bebe's touch.

My gaze settled on the railing one level above. I'd been so fixated on Bebe's murder and writing that I forgot about the third level Anna refused to show me. I strolled up and down the corridor from one end to the other. No sign of another stairwell anywhere or any other way to reach the third floor.

What was the point of having a third level if no one could access it? Since there seemed to be a shortage of guests, it was just as well.

Although I wanted to ask Anna about both, she'd only give me another vague answer. If she'd run Thistlewood for as long as she said, she had to know the truth. The whole truth.

If Bebe's killer was after Thistlewood, chances were I could be in danger.

Chapter Eleven

"*We have to get out of here.*" A child-like voice woke me from a restless sleep.

My head snapped off my keyboard and I banged my knee on the desk. My eyes burned, dry from staring at the computer screen. I'd fallen asleep hunched over my laptop after writing for hours and my entire body was stiff. I glanced at the time to reorient myself. It was only nine o'clock.

I saved my work before closing my laptop. Mabel needed down time as much as I did. I blew out a breath, pulled on pajamas, then reached for my toiletries bag. Careful to close my door behind me, I strolled down the hallway to perform my nightly routine and take my medication.

My head spun from the events of the past few days. There were so many things I needed to tell Roxie and my mom but had avoided returning their calls. I had no idea where to start.

I was nearly back to my room when I heard voices in the foyer. Anna was talking to a man. Foster? Or Sal? He was so soft spoken it was hard to tell.

"Why should I keep my voice down?" Anna asked in a harsh whisper. "She knows about Bebe. It's not my fault she doesn't remember anything."

Curiosity piqued, I crept closer to the opening above the foyer hoping to catch a glimpse. A wave of nausea hit me as I reached the railing. My fear of heights won.

I closed my eyes until the man murmured something about a will.

"That's common knowledge." Anna huffed as the door opened. "You need to keep an eye on things. The last thing we need is someone nosing around."

My heartbeat whooshed in my ears so loud I was afraid I'd miss something.

"She's only his daughter in name," the man said.

When the door closed, I shuddered. What did that mean? I took a couple deep breaths to stop shaking while car tires kicked up loose gravel on the driveway. The mystery man left me even more confused.

I returned to my room to gather my dishes from earlier. With one hand on the rail, and the other clutching the cup and plate, I crept down the stairs. No one lingered in the large kitchen.

"Break time?" Anna asked from near the front door.

I jumped, dropping the plate. It shattered on the floor. "Oh, no. I'm so sorry. Yes. I...um... I need a drink."

"You and me both. Don't worry. I'll grab the broom." She grimaced. "Are you a wine drinker or do you prefer beer?"

"Wine," I admitted. "But I meant water. I'm tired."

"Jetlag finally caught up to you, huh? I made a pot of herbal tea. I was about to bring you some before I went to watch a movie. I'll pour you a cup."

"That's okay. I'll get it." I rinsed my cup then refilled it with chamomile tea. "I thought I heard a man here."

"Owen was on his way out," she said quickly.

"This late? I didn't realize he had a car."

"Uber." Anna poured a cup of tea and added sugar. "How's your book?"

I yawned. "Good, but something Owen said earlier bothers me. He mentioned that I used to live here. That I left in a black car with my mom and my sister when I was little."

Anna stopped stirring and seemed to hold her breath. Finally, she cleared her throat. "Owen's a storyteller, Alison. I'm glad he's comfortable enough to share his stories with you."

It was plausible, but I didn't buy it for a heartbeat. "You're right. He is a good storyteller. I'll take my tea upstairs then turn in. It's been a long day."

"Did you want a couple of cookies?" she asked.

"I'm good thanks. I don't want to sacrifice any more plates."

As I carried my tea to my room, music flowed down the hall. I froze. The music came from the suite at the end of the hall where the fire started. Someone had torn the caution tape, which dangled free on either side of the door.

"I don't believe in ghosts." I tried to remind myself of my own convictions. "I don't believe in ghosts. This is just a sick joke."

I set my cup on the desk before tiptoeing down the hallway. Halfway there, I remembered the key in my bag. I turned the doorknob anyway. The door that should've been locked swung open, which scared me more than any threat of ghosts. The music grew louder.

The once beautiful suite was a charred mess. All of the bedding and draperies were now mere ash. Scorched and broken furniture, including the small table where the statue of a horse and rider once stood, littered the room. The statue must've been buried in the rubble.

It looked as though someone had searched the room, then tried to hide the evidence. Soot and ash covered every surface. Except one. In the center of the room, half-buried in a mound of burned debris and ash, sat an old tape recorder. The source of the music that sent shivers up my spine. All Bebe had was her old record player.

I reached for a piece of singed fabric and used it to push the stop button. Whoever left it wouldn't get a second chance to scare me. I wrapped it in fabric. There had to be fingerprints all over it. I needed to find a bag to transport it to the police station.

Was someone attempting to gaslight me? I'd read about gaslighting before. Making someone think they were crazy was a tradition throughout the ages. All I'd ever done was show up in Cedar Grove at Bebe's request.

And inherit Thistlewood Manor.

I blew out a deep breath. If someone wanted Thistlewood more than I did, what lengths were they willing to go to? My next conversation with Sharpe should come sooner rather than later.

"You shouldn't be in here," Owen said.

I covered my mouth as I spun to face him.

He hovered in the doorway rubbing his arms like he had a chill.

"What are you doing here?" Anna had lied; Owen was home. I didn't bother to hide the tape recorder from him with the hope he'd recognize it.

"There are ghosts here," he whispered. "Did you hear them?"

I held up the recorder. "If you mean Bebe's music, someone set up a tape recorder. They left it on top of the burned stuff."

"I'd get out of there if I were you." He took a couple steps back. "It's not safe here, Ali. Don't you remember...?"

As his words trailed off, I met his frightened gaze. "Remember what?"

"Oh no. Oh no. You have to remember before something else bad happens."

When he turned and ran down the hall, my first impulse was to chase him. I wanted to shake him until he told me but resisted. The last thing he needed was me interrogating him.

Surely any other clues in the master suite were gone. Just as Sharpe said, someone wanted to cause damage but wanted Thistlewood intact.

Apparently, Owen and I shared a secret that I couldn't remember. What happened that only we knew about?

I returned to my room, placed the tape recorder on my desk, then froze. I'd closed my laptop, yet the monitor was open and the screen lit. My skin crawled as I unplugged Mabel and placed her in my bag. Was someone trying to get a sneak peek of my next novel, or were they looking for information? Luckily, they hadn't got past the password page I'd added to keep anyone from snooping.

The only other sign of someone trespassing was a single flap sticking up on a box of Bebe's belongings. All I'd packed in that box were writing books. I fixed the flap before taking the top two boxes off the stack and opening the bottom one. I tucked both the tape recorder and the glass shards inside, then restacked the boxes. Just in case of an encore visit. If someone wanted the evidence that badly, I'd make them work for it until I took it to Sergeant Sharpe in the morning.

I locked the door then pulled on my flannel pants and long-sleeved, waffle weave shirt. Digging out the envelope from Foster, I realized I'd have to find a good hiding place for the will. I sat with my legs curled beneath me on the bed and shuffled through the papers for several minutes but couldn't focus on a single word. Unable to relax, I put them in my laptop bag, then took a book from Bebe's stash to unwind.

I'd barely made it through one chapter before something clattered against the window. I lowered the book to listen, but the sound stopped. "Weird."

As I read the next sentence, the sound of small stones hitting glass, came again. I threw back the blankets, climbed out of bed, then pulled the curtain aside to peer out. Mac stood in a patch of light streaming from the kitchen.

I debated opening the window to ask what he wanted. Instead, I closed the curtain and padded away. Before I'd even reached the bed, more pebbles hit the glass.

"That man's crazy," I muttered. Shaking my head, I opened the window and whispered, "What do you want?"

"I need to tell you something."

I shivered as night air swirled around me. "Talk fast. It's cold."

He groaned as the kitchen light turned off. "Come down."

"No way. I'm going to bed."

"It's important," he said.

"It'll still be important in the morning." I shut the window, then shuffled back to the bed, going so far as turning out the lights, closing my eyes, and pretending to go to sleep. As if he could see me. Maybe I was the crazy one.

The night grew silent. No more clatters. No more music. Just my breathing and my rapid-fire thoughts.

"What's so important he'd stand in the cold throwing rocks at my window?"

Unable to stand the suspense, I pulled on my coat as I snuck downstairs. I grabbed my boots, then crept out the patio door, not sure where to look first.

"What took you so long?" Mac sat on the railing ten feet away.

"I was asleep."

"No, you weren't. Your light was on."

"Maybe I'm scared of the dark. Did you ever think of that?" I folded my arms as best I could in my parka.

"That would surprise me. I doubt you're afraid of much." He grinned. "Well, except maybe commitment."

My mouth dropped open. "Oh really? And what about you, Mr. Big, Bad Firefighter? Aren't you afraid of anything?"

His eyes widened just enough for me to notice in the dim light before he looked away. "Just crazy women who run into buildings while I'm on a scene."

"You're afraid of me?"

"Absolutely. Let's go for a walk." He hooked his arm around mine and steered me toward the water.

The lull of the water calmed me as we stepped over the same driftwood and puddles as I had the night before. Islands dotted the strait. Was Perry on one?

My breath swirled around my face when I asked, "What did you want to talk to me about?"

"Are you still looking for Bebe's killer?" He stooped to pick something up.

"She brought me here for a reason. I just wish she'd told me what it was before..." I closed my eyes. "I kept her personal papers and things aside, hoping to find a clue and tonight someone was snooping in my room."

Mac raised his eyebrows. "Did you catch them?"

"No. I heard music down the hallway. Someone had set up an old tape recorder in Jack and Bebe's room. I went to put it in a box for the police, which is when I saw someone had opened one of the boxes and my laptop was open. Good thing I have it password protected."

One corner of Mac's mouth twitched as he threw a rock into the water. "You're a romance novelist who sells candy. What are you afraid they'd find?"

Did I tell him I'd worked in a candy store? Bebe must've mentioned it.

"You've been doing research, haven't you?" he asked. "I'll bet you know everything about everyone in town and have a long suspect list."

"Ha. Ha." I faked amusement, but not well. "I told you I've been trying to find Perry and learn more about Bebe. Do you think he would've killed her?"

"Not a chance." Mac bent down for another rock.

"How do you know for certain?"

"He's not that kind of guy."

"I guess you'd know," I grumbled, picking up my own rock. "Will you still help me track him down?"

"I'm working on it," he said. "Why wouldn't I want to help?"

"Because no one else around here seems all that helpful." I stuck my hands in my pockets as a chill went over me. "Do you know where he is now? He's not dead, is he?"

Mac threw his rock. "Yes, I know where he is and he's very much alive. He's a bitter man who lives in the middle of nowhere and, to be honest, I don't think he'll want to see you."

"Why not?"

"Because he doesn't want to see anyone. He wants to be left alone."

Heaviness settled like a smothering blanket across my shoulders. "All I need are a few answers, then I'll leave him alone."

He threw another rock into the water before he met my gaze. "Why did you leave Cedar Grove?"

"Why does everyone ask me that? I swear I don't remember being here before."

"You saw Bebe's pictures," Mac said. "Those are proof you lived here. You and your sister had swings on the big tree in the backyard.

I'd come over to play with you guys while my dad helped build this place."

I turned and yelled, "Then you already know more than I do. Why can't I remember?"

Mac took a slow breath before he led me over the rustic beach to a log. We huddled against the wind and spray of water.

"Go through Bebe's photos, Ali," he said. "Your whole family is in them. Everyone you loved before you were taken away."

"You make it sound like I was kidnapped."

He shrugged. "Maybe that's how it seemed."

"I've gone through everything, Mac. Nothing's jogged my memory." I wiped my tears away. "Why would my mom take us away from our family and why can't I remember? You'd think something so traumatic would stand out."

Mac shrugged. "Because for some reason you blocked it out. You were just a kid. Did your mom have family in Toronto?"

"Just my aunt. For a long time, I thought Stephen was my real dad. My sister never got along with him, so she'd tell me stories about a make-believe dad who flew planes and fought fires. I thought she'd made him up. He was a hero, not someone who rolled from job to job, drank, and yelled at us. Mom told us our real dad died, but all I had were her stories and my scars."

Mac's head snapped back. "The ones on your hands?"

"I have a lot of them all over. Mom said my dad and I were in a bad accident."

"Have you remembered anything since you got here?" he asked.

"Nothing. I don't have any memories of being here at all. None of those pictures helped. Why won't anyone tell me the truth?"

Mac placed his hand on my thigh. "I wish I could. My grandpa died so I was in Michigan with my mom when the accident happened. I never saw you after that. Maybe Perry can fill us both in."

I covered his fingers with my hand with the intention of removing it. His warmth stopped me. "Why would you do that for me after I risked your life?"

"The fact you're an heiress to the Beyer family fortune helps."

"That better be a joke."

He leaned against me and chuckled. "I assure you, I'm no gold-digger."

"Are you flirting with me?"

Mac gave a dramatic groan. "Honey, you can't be much of a romance novelist if you have to ask when someone's flirting with you."

"Maybe you're not as good at flirting as you think."

He flipped his hand over and gave my hand a squeeze. "You should've worn gloves, Sweets, you're freezing."

"I was in a bit of a hurry. Besides, I was warm and cozy before you showed up."

"Let's get you back to the house. I guess I should've just texted you to meet at the diner for breakfast in the morning."

"Why didn't you?" I asked.

He flashed a sheepish grin. "I missed seeing your smile. That and I don't have your number."

"Even after I tried to kill us both?" I teased, searching my pockets for a pen. My entire body was suddenly much warmer.

"Yeah. Call me crazy, but I like a challenge."

"What?" My sexy hero used the same line in my book. Mac actually had read my notes. "Am I a challenge?"

"You need some sleep. Obviously, you're not thinking clearly."

"You're right. I'm not." I wrote my number on the palm of his hand.

He put his arm across my back as we walked back to Thistlewood. "I'm waiting for a call. With any luck, you'll meet Perry soon. Maybe he'll give you the answers you need."

"Really? Oh, Mac, thank you." I hugged him. "I'll keep my fingers crossed. Once they thaw."

All my rational thoughts of any sort were long gone. I'd finally get to meet my father. The warmth of Mac's body against mine and the furtive glances he threw my way rattled me even more. He walked me to the patio, then brushed a stray hair off my cheek.

"For now, you'd better get inside before you catch a chill. It'll be hard to question anyone if you lose your voice."

"Was that your plan all along?" I met his gaze, my voice tired and heavy.

"Absolutely." Mac kissed my forehead. "Don't worry, Ali. We'll both get some answers soon. One way or another."

By the time I entered my room, I no longer felt a chill. My entire body tingled, especially the spot on my forehead Mac's lips had touched. I forgot how warming yet unnerving that could be. More fodder for my novel. Once my heart stopped racing and I could curl my fingers, I reached for a pen and paper to finish the scene I'd struggled with.

Chapter Twelve

"Any new suspects in your investigation?" Emily asked when we connected over Skype at six o'clock the next morning. Between the time difference, the murder, and my book, I'd been pre-occupied. I'd nearly forgotten about the emails from the library about my workshop Monday.

I yawned as I cuddled beneath the blankets with my laptop. Coffee made the top of my wish list. "Same ones I had before. Owen told me I used to live here before moving to Toronto, although I swear I've never been here."

She sat in the boardroom at her office sipping from her favorite ceramic mug. "Are you positive? No sense of déjà vu when you're in certain places?"

"Which places?"

"Your bedroom. The kitchen. The bathroom. I don't know." She sounded frustrated as she rubbed her eyes with one hand.

I sighed. "I miss you."

Emily waved her cup in front of the camera. "I miss you, too. You need a coffeemaker in your room. Great Christmas idea, don't you think?"

"A coffeemaker sounds like a great idea. Not sure I'll be here for Christmas though. Chatting with you in the evening would be better.

Maybe after work? Around six or seven. That's about three or four here."

She laughed. "I'll think about it. Boss needs the room. I have to go. Keep me in the loop."

"I'll send you the notes about my suspects and the victim. Maybe you can see a connection I'm missing."

Emily's eyes lit up. "Ooh, speaking of connections. I want to hear more about that hot firefighter. I'll bet he's making your new romance novel a snap to write."

"Yeah, romance. My characters, my storyline, and my book. Not the firefighter."

"You're such a bad liar." Emily laughed. She knew me too well.

Getting to know Mac and trying to find Bebe's killer left little room or energy for my hero and heroine. I pulled up the file I'd labeled "Y." Short for "Why was Bebe murdered?"

"I'll send you everything I've found so far." I typed a short email, then attached the spreadsheet. I'd just hit send when someone pounded on my door.

"Why do you have company this early in the day?" Emily asked. "The sun isn't even up yet, is it?"

"Barely. Hang on." I set my laptop on the desk, expecting to see Anna or Owen. When I opened the door, I sputtered. "What are you doing here?"

"Good morning would be a nicer way to greet guests, Sweets," Mac said.

"I'll be right there, Em."

He'd brought two cups of coffee in a paper tray. "Although I assume you don't get many of those here. Guests in your bedroom, I mean."

"Turn the screen a little more," Emily shouted, then added. "One sec, I'm almost done my meeting."

"Who's that?" Mac peered around me.

"My roommate." I avoided his gaze as his face reddened. "Look, I have work to do, so you need to—"

Mac pushed past me then set the tray on the desk as he leaned over up my laptop. "Hey, roommate. What's your name?"

"Emily," she squeaked.

"Nice to meet you, Emily. I'm Mac," he said. "Sorry to interrupt your call, but Sweets and I have some business to discuss."

I nudged him away from my laptop. "I'll call you later, Em."

She raised both thumbs and flashed a huge grin. "You're right. He's cute."

"Bye, Em." My face burned as I ended the call and closed my laptop. "What do you want, Mac?"

"You told her I'm cute?" he asked.

"Get out." I stuck my laptop in the bag, then folded my arms across my chest.

"You need to come with me." He picked up the tray.

"Why?"

My phone pinged. It was Emily. *"SWEETS??? We SO need to talk!"*

Mac held out a paper take out cup from the diner. The scent of coffee wafted toward me. "I'm dropping off some things for Perry. You want to come?"

"You're going to see my father right now?" I glanced down at my pajamas.

"As soon as you get dressed," he said. "Unless you'd rather go in your jammies."

I took the cup, took a deep whiff, and moaned. "Give me five minutes."

"I'll wait downstairs. I don't want to make Anna suspicious."

Thank heavens for ponytails. I was ready to go in less than two minutes. Rather than taking my purse, I grabbed my anxiety meds, my debit card, and my driver's license and tucked them into my pocket. For added measure, I grabbed my pineapple rock, then pulled a coat on over my hoodie in case it was still windy.

"I should bring Mabel," I said aloud, then reconsidered and tucked her into the bag and stuck it inside my suitcase.

Before we left Thistlewood, I texted Roxie. She'd be thrilled to hear I was going to see Perry. I didn't bother to text my mom. She would start drinking way too early in the day.

I hopped into Mac's blue Jeep, then replied to Emily who hadn't stopped texting since I hung up on her. "Where are we going?"

"To the airport," he said "There's a small airport ten minutes away. That's where I keep my plane."

My mouth dropped open. "You own an airplane?"

Mac pulled up in front of a low white hangar and waved for me to follow him inside, scents of fuel and grease accosted me. Tools lay in a cart near the wall to my left. The metal building housed several planes, one of which was white with a wide blue stripe down each side. "This is Molly. She's a Cessna Skylane with two hundred and thirty horsepower and room for two."

"Molly?" I asked, trying not to smirk. "You named your plane?"

"You named your laptop."

I gazed out the hangar door at the dark clouds rolling in and backed away. "Fair enough. I have a better idea. You tell me where we're going, and I'll start walking."

"You can't walk. There are no bridges to the islands," Mac said. "You go by boat, or you fly."

"Then find me a boat and I'll start paddling." My breath came in small gasps.

"How did you get here from Toronto?"

"In a real plane. With lots of seats and attendants and pilots."

"Chicken." Mac ignored my next three steps back while he prepared the plane. A couple minutes later, he flagged down another man to give him a hand.

"Uh-uh." I stood my ground inside the hangar. "No way this is going to happen."

"It is if you want to meet your father."

My stomach sank. He was right.

Mac and his fellow pilot pushed Molly out of the hangar before they checked it over from end to end. When they were done, Mac asked, "Are you waiting here?"

"For what?"

"I have to file a flight plan." He walked toward a single-story, stone-faced building.

Not sure what else to do, I ran after him. He chatted with two men inside as he handed them some papers.

"Where are you off to today?" one man asked.

"To see Perry," he said.

"Perry Beyer?" A tall man with a thick moustache chuckled. "Hope you packed a suit of armor."

"Funny." Mac rolled his eyes as a couple other men in the room cracked jokes. It seemed Perry wasn't the most popular man around.

Moustache man scowled. "There's a squall coming in. You'd be best to go wide and avoid it or wait an hour or two."

"We'll be fine," Mac growled.

I held my tongue until we were halfway back to his plane. "What did they mean by that? Don't they like Perry?"

"They were being jerks. Get in the plane," he snapped.

My heart raced. "Not a chance. You heard the man. There's a squall."

He opened the passenger door. "Get in."

"No. Way." My hand covered the pocket where I'd put my anxiety medication.

Mac bowed his head. "Do you want to talk to your father, or not?"

I gazed at the tin box he expected me to climb into. I'd flown before, but never in something so small that I'd be squished right up against the man at the controls. Not that I minded that part.

If I were one of my characters, I'd be excited for the new adventure. Instead, I took slow, even breaths and tried not to vomit. "Fine. Just let me text Emily and Roxie goodbye."

Mac laughed as he got in the other side then leaned close to help me fasten my seatbelt. He smelled of lemongrass and cinnamon. Both were comforting.

Emily would've fanned her face. I was too surprised to move.

I tried to focus on our mission while I rubbed the pineapple stone in my pocket. My entire body shook as I gazed at the hangar then back to the slate gray sky. "Those clouds look ominous. Are you sure we should go?"

"Relax, Sweets, it's a short hop. We'll stay below the clouds. Where's your sense of adventure?"

"Cowering in my suitcase," I muttered.

He raised his eyebrows. "Are you sure?"

A surge of heat shot through me as he started the engine. If I didn't keep my mouth shut around this guy, I'd spontaneously combust. Maybe then I'd be grateful for the rain on the horizon.

"Maybe we should go when the sky doesn't look so scary."

"Relax, we have a big enough window to get there." Mac gave my hand a fast squeeze before the radio crackled with instructions. He taxied the plane down the runway. "Too late now. You want to see Perry. If we wait, we could miss him."

"What do you mean miss him?" I asked over the roar of the engine. "It's not like he'll fly away before we get there. He's retired. If we turn back, I can call and arrange—"

"I hope your seatbelt's snug." he asked. "This could be a bumpy ride."

My words were lost to a startled gasp as Mac pulled back the controls. The plane lifted off the ground and soared over the cresting white caps of the Strait of Georgia. I clung to the first thing within my reach.

Mac cleared his throat. "Not that I don't like you, but could you ease your grip on my thigh? You're making it hard to focus."

My fingers were stark white against his denim-covered thigh. I released my grip and sat back to take several deep breaths. "I should have stayed home. I never should've listened to you."

"Check out the view," he said.

"Not a chance." I closed my eyes. "I hate heights."

As we crept higher, my stomach sank lower. When the sun burst with one last hurrah, I snuck a quick glance out the window. The water below became a glittering blanket. The amazing shades of blues of the water tempered by the rusts and grays of the rocks and trees.

"Oh, wow. It's beautiful," I whispered.

"That's the number one reason I fly. The scenery's spectacular."

I couldn't help but agree, even as my nails bit into my palms. "What's the second reason?"

"Girls love a fly boy." He grinned.

I tried not to look at the dials. Those were scarier than the view. "Do you really want to date a pilot groupie? You should set your sights higher."

He chuckled. "That was a bad pun. Do you mean like wanna-be writers who work in candy stores and have daddy issues?"

"Even you deserve better than that."

"Then you obviously don't know me that well," he said. "Why do you think I'm still single?"

"You're not a great salesman, are you?"

"That's why I'm a firefighter. Did I tell you about the first time Perry took me up in his plane?"

"No. You're lucky."

"That I was as green as you and puked?"

I gazed at the islands below then closed my eyes, which only made me more nauseous. "Because you knew him. You got to fly with him. As much as I want to meet him... I'm scared."

"You're afraid of the unknown. That's natural," he said as the plane bounced. He pointed the nose higher, but the cloud-cover didn't seem to end. After several minutes, he levelled out the plane once more before he blew out a breath that unnerved me.

"We should go back," I whispered.

"You don't think I can fly in this?" He grinned, but his knuckles grew as white as mine. "I've flown in worse weather for dumber reasons."

"For girls or a cheap thrill?" I asked, gripping the sides of my seat.

"Both."

Another pocket of turbulence rocked us from side to side. My stomach churned making me glad I hadn't eaten yet. I hated rollercoasters on a calm, sunny day. This was quickly becoming one wild ride. In a similar sized seat.

"The storm's getting worse." I closed my eyes as we bounced. For a split second, I pictured the plane skimming like a rock across the water.

"Don't puke in my plane," he warned, "or I'll make you clean it when we land."

"I won't."

Mac tightened his grip on the controls. "I was talking to me. It's a short flight. We'll be there soon."

"Perry's going to be surprised to see me. I hope it's a good surprise." I flinched as the first splatters of rain hit the windshield.

"You, yes," he said. "I'll get a lecture for endangering your life."

"I'm the one who wanted to find him. You've been good enough to help. Well, until we got into the sky. I'm not taking credit for being up here."

The crack of a clap of thunder rocked the plane from behind us in the tail section. As the plane shuddered hard, so did I.

Mac tapped one of the gauges. "Do you know how to swim?"

"That's not funny." My chest and throat tightened. I had such a tight grip on the sides of my seat that my fingers hurt.

"If we get hit by lightning and go down, I have no idea where we'll land." His voice stayed calm while he searched the clouds below and checked his instruments to get our exact bearing. Finally, he radioed the airport.

I shrieked as the plane bounced again. "We're gonna die."

"We won't." Mac managed to level us off several feet lower as the radio crackled.

"But we could." Hysteria threatened to take total control.

Mac growled. "Alison, knock it off. We need to be positive here."

I began to hyperventilate. "I am. I'm positive we're gonna crash."

"That's a start, Sweets."

"Can you not call me Sweets?" I yelled. "You're getting on my nerves."

He shook his head. "You're scared. You'll get over it."

"Yeah, as soon as we crash." I wanted to tuck my head between my knees like they tell you on real planes but was paralyzed.

Our altitude dropped one heart-stopping plunge at a time until we fell below the clouds. A wave of nausea washed over me when the white caps came into view.

Tears filled my eyes. "Now we're going to die."

"I won't let that happen." Mac stared straight ahead with his jaw tight.

Not surprised by his determination, I was comforted by his focus. He was a firefighter. A hero. I took a deep breath. "I believe you."

"At least one of us does." He flashed a small grin as he eased the plane in the direction of the nearest island. "There's a runway on the other side of those trees. It's a private field. Hopefully, he'll be in a good mood."

"Because you didn't bring a suit of armor?"

"Exactly."

As if we didn't have enough to worry about. "What if he's not in a good mood?"

"Then he'll shoot us."

"You're just full of good news today, aren't you?"

"Hang on tight, Sweets."

Mac flew us toward the shoreline above tree height and focused on setting the plane down on the island runway. The engine hummed while we inched toward land against the buffeting wind.

Suddenly the air sparked with electricity. An ear-splitting bang rattled the windows and shook the entire aircraft so hard my head hit the side window.

Mac swore. "Did you see it? That was close,"

Ripples of static rippled along my scalp as my head throbbed. "Lightning hit the plane, didn't it?"

"Something like that." He kept his attention on the runway as smoke seeped into the front of the plane.

"That's not normal, is it?" I held my breath while the aircraft shuddered and leaned to one side.

"Nope."

Bolts hit the back of the seats as a chunk of plane tore off. Debris and gear hit the water below as smoke swirled around us. I sucked in a sharp breath waiting for the rest of the plane to burst into flames.

Mac struggled to keep the remains from spiraling. I barely had time to take a deep breath before the plane nosedived and submerged below the choppy Pacific Ocean. Everything became dark and muffled. For a brief second, I was sure I'd died. My fear of heights and fire was nothing compared to my fear of drowning.

I sat stunned for an eternity constricted by my seatbelt while water gushed into the cockpit from where the tail used to be. I grabbed one last breath as the water passed my chin.

Even in the murky depths, Mac moved fast. He pulled out a knife to cut his seatbelt. Seconds later, he'd cut mine. Kicking open his door, he grabbed my hand and pulled me out.

We pushed away from the wreckage and struggled upward through about six feet of rough, dirty water amid bits of plane, electrical parts, and plastic boxes. As we bobbed to the surface, I expelled a rush of stale breath only to suck in a gust of wind and salt water.

While I coughed and sputtered, Mac towed me ashore by the back of my coat and asked, "You okay?"

"Great," I croaked. "You?"

My lungs ached and I couldn't feel my fingers or my toes. In fact, my entire body felt like a block of ice.

"So far so good." He helped me ashore then half-dragged me to a large rock. I took several slow, deep breaths while he checked my pupils then ran his hands over my arms and legs. "No pain? Is anything broken?"

"I don't think so."

"Stay here. I'll be right back." Mac started to walk away.

My eyes grew wide as I shrieked, "Where are you going?"

"To get a few things we need." He waded into the choppy water and pulled piece after piece of wreckage from the water before carrying a couple of brightly colored bins ashore.

When he dove beneath the water, I stood with the intention of helping. Little pinpricks of light flashed in front of my eyes. I ignored them as well as the impending sense that I was about to faint. Only once I was knee deep in the icy water did my vision clear.

"What are you doing?" Mac yelled as he tugged on a piece of his plane that looked suspiciously like a wing.

"Helping."

He didn't look impressed but said, "Grab the other end."

While he pulled, I grabbed the cold metal and lifted. Although I had the narrower end, I struggled to get my footing on the rocks as the rain splashed into my eyes.

"What are we doing?"

"Building a wind break to keep us sheltered." Mac directed me to lean the wing against a couple of boulders.

I frowned. "Why don't we just go find Perry? Are we on the wrong island?"

"I just got blown up. I don't wanna get shot at just yet." He stared at me for a long moment then winced as if he was in pain. "Wait here."

Blown up? Was he serious?

After a few long, shivery minutes, Mac returned with one of the sealed plastic bins and sat next to me near the wing.

"What's in there?" I leaned forward while he opened the lid.

"A few things we need to survive in case Perry's not actually here and we're stranded," he said. "I'll drag a couple more pieces up to build a shelter if the rain doesn't let up."

"I thought you told him we were coming?"

Mac averted his gaze then continued to rummage. "Not exactly."

"Then what was the phone call you were waiting for?" I checked my pocket for my stone then pressed it against my leg. My anxiety heightened another notch. At least I had my anxiety medication in my pocket, even if I'd forgotten my regular medication, but nothing to wash it down with. "I don't suppose you have a bottle of water or some dry clothes in there, do you?"

He pulled a small package from the bin. When he tried to open it, his hands shook as much as mine.

"Here. Let me get it." I tore off the plastic before unfolding a thin, reflective blanket.

Mac draped it across my head and shoulders. "This will help keep in some body heat, so you don't get hyperthermia."

"Are you okay?" I became more concerned when that pained expression returned to his face. When he nodded, I tugged the metallic material around me. "Not exactly thick and fluffy, are they?"

"They'll ward off the rain and keep in your body heat." Mac took another one out of the bin, then handed me the package to open while he put the lid back on. He wrapped the second blanket around his torso. "Give me a couple minutes to catch my breath, then we'll go look for Perry."

"If he's here." My eyes teared up as small bits of his plane floated on the choppy waves of the Pacific. Rain stung my face. "How will we get back to Cedar Grove?"

Mac snorted. "Are you a strong swimmer?"

"Not really."

"Then we'll have to borrow his plane or build a raft." He leaned against me.

My heart thumped against my ribs as I studied him. "You're not funny."

Mac's face was a couple of inches from mine. Our breaths mingled in the cold. "I wasn't trying to be, or I would've said something totally absurd."

"You taking my plane sounds pretty absurd to me," said a voice behind us.

We leaped to our feet and spun around in one motion. When the rocks beneath my feet shifted, he caught me, then winced again.

A middle-aged man with a two-day growth of beard and torn jeans held a shotgun trained on us as the rain grew heavier.

"Sorry to drop in like this, Captain," Mac said. "I thought my landing would be more graceful. We got hit by lightning."

"Lightning? That's a rookie move."

I stared. "Who is this guy?"

The man frowned. "What are you doing here, Mac?"

"We're looking for Perry Beyer." I told him.

The man flared his nostrils. "What do you want with him?"

"Ali." Mac warned.

I walked up the wet rocks hoping he wouldn't shoot me. "He's my father."

His eyes narrowed to slits. "Who are you?"

"Alison Cadell." Mac placed a hand on the small of my back. "Meet Perry Beyer."

The man lowered his gun. "A.J.?"

"Dad?"

It certainly wasn't the reunion I'd hoped for. This man looked older and more crippled than I'd seen online. He ran a hand through his dripping hair. After a long moment, he motioned for us to follow him. When I held back, Mac gave me a nudge.

Perry led us up a muddy, narrow trail through the trees to an open field. The narrow air strip Mac wanted to land on. A log cabin reminiscent of Thistlewood sat tucked into the tree line. It was made from smaller cedar logs but with fewer windows.

Mac and I shook off the reflective blankets and tucked them beneath a rock on the front porch. Perry let us inside before ordering us to wait on the coco matting by the door. He didn't say another word until throwing us thick towels.

"What the hell were you thinking? You two could have been killed. Who allowed you to take off?"

Before Mac could reply, Perry stormed out of the open-concept main room of the cabin. We were left alone with our towels and a fire crackling in the stone hearth across the room.

"I made a bad call," he said softly.

My eyes welled with tears as I faced the door. "We should leave."

"And go where? In case you forgot, my plane's in pieces. We're stuck here."

"He's not happy to see me," I whispered.

"It'll be fine, Sweets. Give him a chance." He gave me a quick hug.

Perry returned to the room wearing dry jeans and a blue Buffalo plaid flannel shirt with a pale blue t-shirt beneath it. He strode into the kitchen and poured a cup of coffee without looking at us.

"I'm sorry, Captain." Mac stared at the floor.

I couldn't stand the suspense any longer. "Can we at least come in?"

"It's not like I can stop you." Perry waved toward his kitchen table. "Then you can tell me what you want and why you're on my island."

I hugged my damp towel tighter around me before I glanced at Mac, who peeled off his soaked hiking boots and socks.

"Coffee?" Perry asked.

"Yes, please." Mac placed his towel on the seat of a wooden chair, then sat near the grizzled man. "I'm sorry about Bebe. It was a shock for all of us."

While Mac made himself comfortable, I stood mute by the door staring at my father. I had no idea what to do or where to start.

Perry poured two more cups of coffee. "Neither of you shouldn't be here. Mac, you know better. You could lose your license."

"It's my fault. I wanted to meet you." I blinked back hot tears as my chin quivered.

"Why now?" he asked, handing Mac a mug.

It was an odd question, but I blurted out the first thing that came to mind. "Roxie's getting married in May. She wanted me to find you."

"You came all the way here and nearly died in a plane crash to invite me to your sister's wedding?" Perry asked.

I sniffled and stared in stunned silence as my hands shook.

"I don't do weddings."

"Not even for your daughter?" I hugged the towel around me tighter.

"Cream or sugar?" he asked.

When I didn't reply, Perry shrugged, then turned his attention to Mac. "What happened to your plane? You went down awfully fast."

"Lightning, I think. There was a bang, then we lost power. Everything failed. I did my best not to nosedive."

"We all saw how well that worked," he said. "I'll radio the airport to let them know you two clowns are safe."

My chest tightened as my eyes filled with tears. I felt like I was six again and my mom had admonished me for breaking her vase before filling another glass with wine. "Seriously? You haven't seen me in twenty years and you're practically ignoring me."

"What would you like me to say?"

"Come sit down, Alison." Mac wrapped his arms around me, then led me to the table. "You're in shock. Have some coffee. You can dry off and get warmed up while we wait out the storm."

"I came to get answers," I told Perry as I began to hyperventilate. "The grandmother I never knew existed is dead. Possibly murdered. My sister and I inherited half of Thistlewood, and the father I thought died when I was little inherited the other half. I don't know what to say or do, or even where to start."

"You thought I was dead?" Perry asked, then frowned as he stared at me.

"Breathe, Sweets." Mac helped me take off my shoes and socks, then led me to a chair before he took my face in his cool hands. "We were in a plane crash, you're in shock, and we're stuck here. There's time for answers while we wait out the storm."

Perry stood. "I'll make lunch. You settle her down. Sugar in her coffee will help."

"Settle me down? The plane crashed. People will think we're dead."

"Breathe, baby girl," Mac whispered.

A flicker of sympathy crossed Perry's face. "I'll grab some dry clothes and put on soup and grilled cheese after I radio the airport. They'll get in touch with the Coast Guard."

I shook my head, unable to grasp what he said.

Mac took my chin between his thumb and index finger as Perry left the room. "You need to calm down, Sweets. Take a slow breath."

"I can't breathe," I whispered, my chest heaving.

"Here's some dry clothes," Perry said as he set a stack of sweatpants, socks, and sweaters on the round table. "Probably nothing her size though."

"Clothes?" The thought of clothes and food seemed preposterous considering our predicament. I was marooned on an island in the middle of nowhere with no way home. Stuck with Mac and my biological father who wasn't happy to see me. I began to laugh hysterically.

"Yup, she's in shock." Perry opened the fridge.

Mac reached for a thick, green sweater. The second he moved toward me, I jumped to my feet and lunged at Perry.

"I came all the way from Toronto to ask why I never even knew you were alive. Now that I'm here, you're doing everything you can to ignore me."

Perry's mouth hung open. "A.J.—"

"Don't A.J. me," I shouted. "What kind of father falls off the face of the earth and never bothers to get in touch with his kids?"

Mac reached for me. "Alison, don't—"

"I wish Mom never told me you existed in the first place." I raked my fingers through my hair. "Or that Bebe never brought me to Thistlewood. Why couldn't everyone just leave me alone? At least I was happy and…"

"Are you done?" Perry asked.

Far beyond rational, I had nothing more to say. With no idea what else to do, I shoved Mac out of my way then bolted out the front door in bare feet. My vision was blurred by tears and the sheets of rain that pelted me like hail stones. I turned left at the airstrip and ran down the trail toward the shore.

Rocks tore at my soles as I stubbed every one of my toes. As I started down the slope, I slid through a patch of muck. Tree branches grabbed my heavy, wet clothes, tugging me back. I snapped them off using brute force before I fell forward into a bush.

Emerging from the tree line, I tripped over a rock. My palms took the brunt as searing pain shot through my wrists and into my forearms.

Wet gravel bit into my skin and sprayed my face. I squeezed my eyes shut. Something hard dug into my hip. My so-called lucky stone. I wanted to toss it into the bay but couldn't move.

Out of breath, I panted as I lay sprawled face down on the rocks. I needed my anxiety medication but couldn't find my pockets. My entire body shook as my tears mingled with the rain to the saturated ground beneath me.

My mother's revelation. Bebe. My father. Thistlewood. The plane crash.

My senses overloaded.

I couldn't take anymore.

A heartbeat later, everything went black.

Chapter Thirteen

T he last thing I remembered was Mac's plane hitting the water. Gradually, images of the previous day came back to me. Mac pulling me through murky water from the wreckage. Heavy rain. Perry holding a gun on us...

Then I had a temper tantrum and lay on the cold, rocky shore in tears. Wet, shivering, and defeated after meeting my father who hardly looked at me, let alone talked to me.

I had no idea how long I slept. I was warm and dry, but my palms and knees stung. Something pressed against my right shoulder. A fire crackled nearby, and I opened my eyes expecting...

The expectation darted away before I could grasp it. Across the room, my clothes hung across a black fireplace screen along with Mac's blue jeans, sweater, and t-shirt.

The pressure on my shoulder shifted. Mac moved his head as he slept soundly against me. His sweaty hair stuck to my cheek as we huddled on the couch beneath a layer of blankets.

I yawned, stretching my legs, and groaning as pain shot through me.

"Good morning, sleepy head," a low voice said from the kitchen table.

Perry sat with his elbows on the tabletop. He clutched a coffee cup in both hands and appeared contemplative as he met my gaze.

"Good morning." My voice came out as a croak. My throat hurt from my temper tantrum the night before. My head hammered and I felt like I'd been run over by a herd of stampeding reindeer.

"Coffee?"

"Yes, please." As I inched away from Mac's heat, I regretted leaving the comfort of the couch. Beneath the thick, soft blanket, I wore a man's flannel work shirt, sweatpants, and my damp underwear. At least I wasn't naked with two men I barely knew.

"Cream or sugar?" he asked.

"Both, please." A chill hugged me as I rose from the couch. I took a blanket off the top of the heap and wrapped it around me. The cold of the wooden floor stung the grated skin on my bare feet. Gathering a few more ounces of bravery, I turned slowly toward the kitchen.

Perry placed a steaming mug next to a small carton of cream, a bowl of sugar, and my anxiety medication. "Your clothes are probably dry if you want to change. If not, I can toss them in the dryer."

"This is fine. How long have I been asleep?" Inching toward the fire, I scrunched my shirt then my coat and hoodie, respectively. They were warm and dry. I flipped my jeans over to let the underside dry. My pants pockets were empty. As a courtesy, I turned Mac's clothes over.

"Off and on, about eighteen hours. Mac told me you've been through a lot lately. I guess you couldn't deal with things anymore yesterday."

"Not well, anyway," I admitted. "Did my phone survive?"

"Hope so. I stuck them both in a bucket of rice, which always works when I drown mine," Perry said with a smirk. "That was the last of my rice though. I'll have to do a little shopping when I drop you two off."

I sat across the table and hugged the steaming mug. "I'll pay for the rice. Sounds like a good thing to have on hand."

He held up my pineapple stone. "This fell out of your pocket along with the pill bottle."

My face burned. "I don't even know where that thing came from. A pineapple's a weird thing to carve into a stone, but I've had it as long as I can remember."

He studied the stone for so long I started to squirm. "At least I know you are who you say you are."

"What do you mean?"

"It's a thistle. One of my early attempts."

"You made this?" I sucked in such a sharp breath that I coughed.

When he spoke again, I had a hard time hearing him over the crackles and pops of the fire. "The last time I saw you, I put it in your hand and wrapped your tiny fingers around it. I held you as long as I could."

"Why don't I remember?" I whispered.

"I got better over the years." Perry placed my stone in front of me, then walked over to the fireplace. The rock he took from the mantle was the same size, but the thistle carved into it was smaller and more intricate. It certainly didn't look like a pineapple.

"You can keep that if you want," he said.

"Thank you. You carved that big rock in front of Thistlewood, didn't you?"

"It was a gift for my mom." He sat across from me once more. "I keep meaning to make one here but I can't decide on the right rock."

I cradled it in my hand. He must have carved the boulder after Jack's death. After my mom took us away. Only someone with a steady hand, not a raging alcoholic, could have created something so beautiful.

"Do you do a lot of carving?" I asked.

"A man needs to keep busy all winter in a place like this. Since there's no shortage of rocks, it seemed like the thing to do." Perry reached to the chair between us and handed me some wool socks and a thick blue sweater. "Put these on. The damp can seep into your bones out here."

My gaze fell to my steaming coffee cup, then to the bathroom twenty feet away. I needed relief and warmth more than I needed coffee. I grabbed my orange bottle and left the table. My hands shook and my brain felt foggy without my other medication. I hoped I'd be okay until I got back to Thistlewood.

The bathroom was more luxurious than the rest of the cabin. A jacuzzi tub took up one corner with a large stone-lined shower overlooking it. The sink was carved from a large chunk of granite that glittered with pyrite. Rustic yet elegant in its own way. I was in love with every inch of the space.

Once I'd pulled on the extra clothes and had taken anxiety pill, relishing the wool socks as a barrier against the cold floor, I returned to the kitchen. "That bathroom is amazing."

He chuckled. "When you've broken as many bones as I have, arthritis sets in. That tub helps keep this old body moving."

"I'm sorry I behaved so badly yesterday." I sat to fix my coffee. "We should've called before we dropped in. Literally. When Mac said he was waiting for a phone call, I thought he'd spoken to you."

"Yeah, we sorted that out," he said. "It's just as well I had no idea. I would've told you not to come."

"Then we might've died from hypothermia and Mom would say she told me so."

"Oh, yeah. I remember her lectures." He sipped his coffee. "You would've been fine. Mac was on my crew before I retired. He's well-trained in survival skills."

"Mac was a jumper?" I gazed at the man sleeping peacefully on the couch, hugging a cushion to his chest. "Is that why he calls you Captain?"

"It is."

"At least I can tell Roxie that I met you, which should get her off my back for a while. I'll explain that you don't do weddings."

"You'd do that?" he asked.

"It's the least I can do after we crashed your island."

He pointed a finger. "You're funny. That I know you got from me. Thank you for offering to run interference with your sister."

Perry refilled his cup, then added cream and sugar.

"We take our coffee the same way."

He raised his eyebrows. "You and I always were the most alike. As a kid, you were such a daredevil you drove your mother crazy."

"Me? I'm the biggest chicken you've ever met. I only came to Cedar Grove was because Roxie and my roommate talked me into it."

He seemed saddened by my revelation. "That's too bad. You were never a scaredy cat as a kid. You drove us all to exhaustion."

Tears filled my eyes. "I wish I could remember. I didn't even know you were alive until Roxie told Mom she wants to have kids and asked about your medical history. I tried to track you down but ran into dead ends."

"I'm not surprised you don't remember," he said. "You were pretty banged up. Is that why you're on medication?"

The memory of lying in a hospital bed with my stone in one hand flashed through my mind then vanished.

"These are for anxiety. I have some other ones, but I left them at the manor," I told him, then paused to gather courage. "Mom said we were in a car accident when I was a kid. What happened?"

Perry ran a hand through his unkempt gray hair. "She didn't tell you much of anything, did she?"

"I thought Stephen was my dad and that I was born and raised in Toronto. Owen said I lived at Thistlewood, but he runs off like a scared cat every time I try to talk to him. I've asked Mom about my scars, but—"

"She refused to tell you about me, let alone about what happened."

Across the room, Mac groaned. When he stretched, the blanket fell away from his shoulders to his lap. He wore a blue t-shirt that strained against his broad chest, gray sweatpants, and a fresh layer of goosebumps on his muscular arms.

"Good thing you stoked the fire. It's damp today."

"Only the best for my uninvited guests," Perry told him while winking at me. "Coffee?"

"Black as your soul, please." Mac wrapped a blanket around his shoulders before he approached the fire. He checked his sweater before he dropped the blanket on the couch and pulled the sweater over his head. "Is it still raining?"

"Spitting. The clouds should clear off in another hour or so. I'll fly you back to Cedar Grove when they do."

Mac sat on a stool near the counter. "I suppose Alison already picked your brain about her suspects?"

"Suspects for what?" He raised his eyebrows.

My cheeks burned as I cleared my throat. "Someone strangled Bebe."

Perry nodded. "The police will figure it out. Sharpe isn't completely incompetent. Or so I've heard."

Mac chuckled as if they shared a secret joke.

"Aren't you the least bit concerned? She was your mother." What was with all the bloody secrets in this family? My family.

His jaw tightened, but he didn't reply. "Why don't I make us some breakfast then we'll get ready to fly?"

"Sounds good to me," Mac said. "I'll see if I can get any reception. Assuming my phone still works."

"There's a radio in my office. Use that." Perry rummaged in the fridge.

I got the impression Mac and I had overstayed our welcome. Perry probably spent the night figuring out what to do with us.

When Mac headed to Perry's office, I recalled how I'd met Bebe in the first place. "I have something for you. Bebe came to Toronto before I knew who she was and asked me to sign a copy of one of my novels. She left a note that she wanted you to have it."

"One of your novels?" Perry glanced over his shoulder. "You're a writer?"

"Yes."

"You should have started with that line yesterday. We might've gotten off to a better start," he said, cracking two eggs into a bowl.

Stunned, I stared until he winked. We both burst out laughing. "Can I help you with anything?"

"Yes. Convince your sister I have no desire to go to Toronto." He must've caught my frown before he added, "For now, you can make a pot of coffee."

"I can handle the coffee. Roxie will be a tougher nut." Just doing that simple chore of refilling the coffee maker helped me relax. "What's for breakfast?"

"Pancakes. I don't have any fresh blueberries though. We'll have to use frozen."

My heart skipped a beat. "I love blueberries pancakes."

Perry poured some batter into a cast iron frying pan. "You sound surprised. I know that. You and I used to make pancakes and scrambled eggs for the whole household every Saturday morning. Then we'd grill some bacon and serve it all with fresh whipped cream and fruit. The smell always got everyone out of bed."

I breathed in the scent of warm batter as it cooked to golden brown. Suddenly, I was standing on a chair next to my dad who had darker hair. We laughed and sang as we cooked. Mom always worried I'd light my long, curly hair on fire.

It was the same fleeting memory I'd thought of while making pancakes at Thistlewood with Anna.

"Whatever you're making smells good." Mac came out of the office and glanced from me to Perry. "What's going on?"

"Blueberry pancakes," I told him with a smile.

"A.J.'s favorite," Perry added.

Mac strolled over to place his hands on my shoulders. "Perry makes amazing pancakes. For years, we used to charter a boat and go fishing around the islands. He'd do the cooking. Those pancakes woke me up every morning."

"Sounds like you were the son he never had," I mused.

"Don't kid yourself. You were quite the fisherman as a kid," Perry said. "I'd take you out while your mom took Roxie shopping. You hated being in stores, which drove her nuts. You preferred fishing with me and Owen any day."

"Really?" I asked. "Sounds like a pretty cool childhood."

Mac laughed. "Alison fishes? She collects rocks, too."

"He made them." I reached for both engraved rocks as he set the table. "He gave me this one when I was little. I've carried it around most of my life but never knew where it came from."

Mac pulled a similar sized stone from his pocket. "He made mine when I was ten. It's a fireman."

"I was much better by then," Perry said.

"That's pretty cool." My father was definitely an artist.

While we ate, I got to hear fire jumping stories and was glad we came–despite the crash and my initial tantrum. I was eager to help wash dishes and tidy up. It seemed like the least I could do to repay his forced hospitality.

"Time to go," Perry announced after a quick walk out to the wood-pile. "The skies are clear, and we have a six- to eight-hour gap before the next storm."

"I'll get the plane ready," Mac offered.

"If the weather turns bad, you can stay at Thistlewood. It is half yours, after all." I put the last of the dishes onto the drainboard to dry. Part of me was disappointed to leave so soon.

"For the record, A.J., if I wanted that cursed place, I would've flown back as soon as Foster told me about Bebe." Perry said.

I set down the dishcloth. "Foster called you? I thought he didn't know where you were."

His blue eyes crinkled in the corners. "Bribery goes a long way."

"Did you move here to hide from everyone, or just me and Roxie?"

He glanced toward the door, probably hoping Mac would rescue him. "Actually, your mother's lawyers. Since my family had money, they assumed I had money. They wanted me to sell my plane, my property, everything."

"She had to support us after you left, you know." My eyes watered. "We moved to Toronto with nothing and lived with Mom's aunt. Mom got a job with flexible hours, so she could be home for us after school."

His face hardened. "Actually, your mom packed you and Roxie up and left Cedar Grove while I was fighting fires in Northern Alberta. She emptied all our bank accounts except the one I shared with Bebe.

By the time I got home, she had taken nearly two hundred thousand dollars and left with some boyfriend."

My eyes grew wide. "What?"

"She didn't tell you that part, did she?"

"No, she didn't." I wiped my eyes with my sleeve, ready to bolt back to the beach where I'd ended up yesterday. "Did you look for us?"

"Several times," he said. "Each time, she got a restraining order saying that I was stalking her."

"Oh." My shoulders sagged.

"I'd track you down and send more letters before she'd move you again, or at least made me think she had. Most of the things I sent came back marked return to sender. I even searched hospitals since I knew you still needed care."

I focused my gaze on a knot in the wood floor. "She never would've told us if it wasn't for Roxie getting married."

Perry gave me an awkward hug. "I'm glad you came. This has helped me more than you know."

"I still have so many questions. Why was I in the hospital?"

When the front door opened, Mac peered inside. "Are you two ready? I need help with that beast you fly now. I can't believe you got a four-seater."

"Did you call the airport?" Perry asked.

"Just like you taught me, Captain." Mac grinned. "Oh, a salvage crew will pick up the wreckage later today."

"Perfect." He nodded. "I'll be back in time to give them a hand. Hopefully, we can minimize any environmental damage."

When Mac left, I frowned. "Does Mom know you own an island?"

"Nope, and I'd prefer if we kept it that way. For now, anyway."

"Only if I get to come back to visit sometime."

"Drop in anytime." Perry chuckled.

"I'll rent a boat. It's safer."

He leaned over to kiss my forehead, then flinched. While his forehead kiss seemed to catch us both off guard, it also seemed natural.

"Thanks." I gave him another hug before I gathered my things.

"We'd better get moving before Mac flies off without us." He locked the cabin door then strode across the airstrip toward a green barn.

I ran behind him like a five-year-old, only pausing to turn on my cell phone. Perry's rice trick worked. The screen glowed to life. Roxie would want proof I met our father.

Inside the open doorway of the barn, sat a white Cessna with four seats and a wide emerald stripe down each side. I took a few pictures while Perry and Mac went through their pre-flight check. Rubbing my upper arms, I hovered near the doorway in the sunshine. I wasn't in a hurry to get back into an airplane so soon after the crash. My hands shook at the thought.

"Are you okay?" Mac stood so close his body heat warmed my left arm.

"Great." My voice came out as a bird-like squawk. From the concern on his face, I probably looked terrified.

"Come on, A.J.," Perry called out. "The best way to get over that fear is to get back in the air. Help us push this baby out of the barn."

Mac gave me a one-armed hug. "Your dad's right. The only other way off this island is sitting on a log and paddling, which won't be as much fun as it sounds. You know how cold the water is."

"I remember." I looked past him to stare at the plane.

Perry and Mac walked to either side of the plane, grabbed the bars below the wings, then rolled the Cessna into the sunshine. I took a few pictures as her propeller emerged. The twin green stripes caught the light and sparkled. Mac opened the door, then climbed into the back seat leaving me to sit up front.

I lowered my phone and thought about demanding to hide in the back seat. Of course, I also thought about finding a solid log to paddle.

"Come on, kiddo," Perry patted the passenger seat. "Let's see if you still have that sense of adventure that drove your mother crazy."

"You, Sweets?" Mac asked.

I put my fists on my hips. "Yes, me."

He grinned. "Get in. Let's see what you're made of."

Perry was right. My mother would lose her mind, which was exactly why I needed to hop into the passenger's seat despite my pancakes threatening to make a reappearance.

Take off nearly made me lose my delicious breakfast. Not that it wasn't smooth, more because I envisioned the bang of lightning that hit Mac's plane. I closed my eyes and gripped my seat.

"Ladies and gentlemen, this is your captain speaking," Perry began. "Thank you for flying Air Beyer. We are flying today in a Cessna 172 Skyhawk. Our cruising altitude will be as low as I feel like flying. Any questions?"

"Is that why you call him Captain?" I asked over my shoulder.

Mac laughed. "He made that announcement every time we left the ground no matter what kind of plane we were in."

When Perry circled the plane around his island, I leaned back in my seat and held my breath, trying not to vomit. He remained low to take a better look at the beach where we'd crashed. The sight of the chunks of plane along the shoreline sent a chill over me. There were a lot of small pieces and a big chunk that was missing from the tail.

I ran out of air and gulped a breath.

"Are you sure you were hit by lightning, Mac? That's an awful lot of damage."

"There was a flash, then a bang that shook the whole plane."

I had a gut feeling there was something the two of them weren't saying aloud.

Perry nodded. "I'll take a closer look when the salvage boys get here. I'll let you know what we find."

"Sounds fair," Mac said.

We flew over several small islands, gliding around them like Perry knew every nook and cranny by heart. He told us about each island and who lived on them. I relaxed enough to snap pictures during our aerial tour.

"Time to get you two home," Perry said. "Anna will be worried sick."

Happily, we landed without incident. Aside from my fingernails digging fresh crescents into my palms. We taxied up to the same administration building where Mac filed our flight plan yesterday, which felt like a lifetime ago.

Once we climbed out of the Cessna, the two men had a quiet conversation on the far side of the plane. I caught snatches of things like Transport Canada and suspension.

Perry gave Mac a hug. "Good to see you again. Thanks for bringing my little girl to see me. Tell your folks I said hi."

"I'll do that." Mac walked around the nose of the plane and touched my elbow. "I'm going to run inside for a few minutes. I'll be right back."

"Wait." I hesitated then glanced at Perry. "Could you take a picture of us? If that's okay."

"Fine with me," Perry said.

When I stood next to him, my father put an arm across my shoulder and said, "fly" instead of "cheese." I couldn't help but laugh.

Once Mac handed my phone back and walked away, I had no idea what to say. There were so many things I wanted to know, but my time to ask was up for today.

"Thank you for everything." I backed away from the Cessna. "I appreciate your honesty. I still owe you a bag of rice."

"Consider it a gift." Perry held out a hand. Disappointed, I reached out to shake it. He pulled me into a tight hug. "I'm glad you came to see me and answered some of my questions."

When we parted, I told him, I was thinking about staying to run Thistlewood. "Roxie doesn't seem to be interested and neither are you. Someone has to make sure the place doesn't fall apart, right?"

"And here I thought I was the risk-taker in the family."

"Hey, I didn't come all this way for nothing."

"No, you came to find me." He placed his hands on my shoulders. "That was a huge risk."

He wasn't wrong.

"I also came to write. When Bebe invited me to be a Writer-in-Residence at the library, I had no idea who she was. Foster only told me after she died."

Perry flared his nostrils. "Be careful around Foster and Sal. Bebe complained about the two of them creeping around Thistlewood. She wanted me to move back to keep an eye on things. I refused, which is probably why she tracked you down. I guess she didn't get to tell you."

"Why didn't you help her?"

"There's too much history in Thistlewood that I'd have to live with." Perry grimaced. "Is that why you plan to stay there? To learn about our family?"

I glanced around. No sign of Mac yet. "Yeah. I don't remember any of it and I'd like to. Good or bad."

"I'd better go. I have a couple things to take care of before I head back. Like getting more rice," Perry said. "Tell your sister I'd consider the wedding, but only if she holds it at Thistlewood."

"That should go over well." My sister would laugh. My mom would become even more passive-aggressive than usual. "Roxie has a beautiful venue already picked out. Do you have an address where she can send you an invitation?"

"Care of Thistlewood." He took my phone and typed in his phone number. "You can let me know if I get mail."

"I'll send you Roxie's number. You can talk to her yourself." I paused to send him her information, then asked, "You sure you won't go to Toronto?"

He shook his head. "Not a chance."

"What about to Thistlewood?"

"A.J., if you're serious about running the place, I'll sign my half over to you and your sister," he said. "I might even stop by to say hello when I'm in town, but there is no way I will ever live there again."

"I am serious. This might be the opportunity I need to figure out my life. I'll need help though. I hope Sheila and Anna will stick around."

As Perry gave me a hug, he whispered, "Be careful what you wish for. You should know by now nothing is ever what it seems."

Chapter Fourteen

"My insurance agent already cringes when she sees me coming," Mac said as he bought us coffee at the diner. "This one will put her over the edge, especially with Transport Canada in the equation. Are you good to get back to Thistlewood on your own? I have calls to make before I talk to my parents."

"Yeah. I need some time to think." My current thoughts were a jumble of who to trust and what to believe. While I needed to call my mom and Roxie, I had no idea what to tell them.

He gave me a hug as Violet brought over our coffees to go. "I'll check up on you later, okay?"

"Thanks for taking me to see Perry. It wasn't what I expected, but I'm glad we went."

"Even if you'll have nightmares for weeks?" Mac walked me out of the diner, then hugged me and kissed my forehead. "Do like he said. Watch your back. Call if you need anything."

Too restless to sit let alone write, I took a stroll along the beach and ended up behind Thistlewood Manor. I sat on the log Mac and I discovered the other night. At first glance, the rocks looked as gray as my mood. Curious, I picked up a handful washed away their dullness in the water. Beneath the gray, I discovered an array of reds, rusts, granites with sparkles, and even rocks embedded with fossils. No wonder Perry had an awful time deciding which stones to etch.

That silly pineapple stone I'd treasured my entire life was a gift from my father. The father I'd forgotten.

Finding my family had rattled me. Bebe was sweet and joyful. Now she was gone. Perry seemed so nice. So genuine. Making pancakes had brought back a few memories, but not enough for a real a-ha moment. I still had no idea what had happened to me or those memories.

There were gaps I needed my mom to fill in.

The wind tossed my hair while I scanned through the pictures I took on Perry's Island. My mom wouldn't be happy. She'd kept Perry a secret for most of my life and had tried to talk me out of coming to Cedar Grove. Not that her opinion swayed my decision. With Roxie and Emily in my corner, and the promise of writing, she was outnumbered.

I still didn't remember ever being in Cedar Grove, let alone living in Thistlewood, dancing with Bebe, or fishing with Perry and Owen. Whoever Owen really was. The photos in Bebe's room should've brought back a surge of memories. Instead, all I had were more questions.

After a few more minutes of dread, I dialed my phone, then hung up and took a deep breath.

One sip of coffee later, I glanced around to make sure no one else was on the beach before I pressed my mom's name on speed dial and held my breath. Trying not to chicken out.

"Alison?" my mom asked. "What's wrong?"

Was everyone's mom a psychic or just mine? "Nothing."

"You never call unless you're in trouble. Do you need more medication or some money to come home? I told you not to go to that place. Why aren't you saying anything?"

"You haven't given me a chance."

She gave a dramatic sigh. "How is Cedar Grove?"

"Why don't I remember living here?" I blurted out the question before I could stop it, then braced for her answer.

There was such a long silence I thought she'd hung up until she finally said, "You were little when we left."

My pulse hammered in my ears. "I saw the pictures on Bebe's wall, but all I have is a weird feeling of déjà vu. No warm fuzzies. Not one of those pictures has helped me remember anything. Why is that?"

"You need to come home, honey," she said. "We can talk here."

"No. We can talk now. While I'm here." My hands shook more from nerves than the cold air. "What happened in Thistlewood, Mom?"

She didn't reply.

"Why did we leave Cedar Grove and why don't I remember my grandmother or my father?" This time, I didn't wait for an answer. Tears filled my eyes. "Owen said we lived in the manor."

"You met Owen?"

"Of course, I did. He lives here. Who is he?"

Rather than tell me the truth, my mom hung up. Disconnected as usual. Just like every other attempt at a mother-daughter conversation I'd ever made.

Wiping my eyes with the back of my hand, I realized I needed my medication before I had another meltdown. Why was she doing this?

"Are you okay, honey?" Sheila, the housekeeper, sat next to me on the log.

"I never should've accepted Bebe's offer. I've stirred up so much trouble. I keep bringing up things that make people want to run and hide. I'm just...confused. Why would my mother try to hide all this from me and my sister for so long?"

"That's to be expected. You've been a troublemaker since you were little."

"I have?" I caught my breath in surprise. "You're not the first to say that."

She touched my arm. "I agree. You deserve answers."

"Is it weird I don't remember living here?"

"No. That was a dark time." Sheila gazed out at the rippling water and seemed to choose her words carefully. "You were always curious and full of far more energy than some of us were able to handle. Your mom included. Owen was the only one who could keep up. He didn't like you when you were a baby, but you adored him. Once you started to walk, you followed him everywhere. That's when he took a shine to you. The two of you were inseparable."

That explained why Owen and I seemed to click. "Is that why he's mad at me?"

"He's frustrated and trying his best to give you time." She rummaged through her purse, then handed me a small packet of tissues.

While I dabbed at my eyes, she pulled out a picture. Despite the twenty years that had passed, there was no mistaking me and Owen. He had his arm around me while I cradled a crayfish the size of my face in both hands.

"How that boy kept you from running straight into the ocean every day, I'll never know," she said. "The rest of us could barely manage. The tide pools were fair game. You two would come home drenched but wearing the biggest grins I ever saw. We had to get a terrarium for all the critters you brought home."

I took a snapshot of her photo. "Owen told me he has memory problems after an accident. How did he get hurt?"

"You really don't remember?" she asked.

"Bits and pieces." I returned her photo. "But no one will fill in the blanks. Owen says I have to remember on my own, but he does slip me a clue now and then. I guess if I figure things out on my own, they're my memories, not someone else's."

Sheila patted my hand. "He has his reasons, honey. Anna may treat him like he's not that smart, but he's a good man. I wanted him to live on his own eventually, but he liked being at Thistlewood for Bebe. Her death has been hard on him but having you here helps."

"Oh, that's cool. I'm sure they're thrilled he writes, too. How do you know Owen so well?" I asked.

"Owen's my son. He and Teena are your cousins," she said.

"You're my aunt," I whispered. That explained her concern.

She gave my hand a squeeze. "Owen loves that his cousin is a famous writer."

"Hardly. But thanks."

A voice carried across the backyard as Anna called Sheila's name. Sheila's eyes glistened with tears. It seemed there were many things she wanted to say, but Anna waved from the back porch.

She gave me a quick hug. "There's so much you need to know, A.J."

The back of my neck prickled. "Perry called me that, too."

"You saw Perry?" When I nodded, she scurried back to the manor.

Just when I was on the verge of another answer, the person with the answers ran away. I itched to chase after her. Instead, I gazed out at the water, not ready to return to Thistlewood just yet. Meeting Perry was emotionally, not to mention physically, draining. I simply wasn't ready to deal with more, especially my newfound aunt and cousin. I was so rattled I hadn't I thought to ask about her husband. I had an uncle. I still needed to find out who he was.

Sheila mentioned Owen lived in Thistlewood to be close to Bebe. Why did Anna hover over him when I was around?

My gut said the only way I'd get any answers from Owen was to catch him somewhere away from Anna. We needed to talk one-on-one where she couldn't silence him with a look or send him to his room.

The Burlap Diner would be ideal. I just had to get him there.

Chapter Fifteen

When I returned to Thistlewood to warm up, Sheila gave me a nod. She waited until Anna left the room before telling me Owen went to the diner to write.

"Maybe I'll go do some writing, too," I said in case Anna walked in behind me. "I've been getting some good ideas at the diner."

I ran up to my room to take my medication first. I should've been elated about finding Perry. Roxie would be thrilled when I sent the pictures from the island. Instead, I held onto the information, not sure what I was waiting for. More answers? Another glimmer of memory?

Sure enough, Owen sat at the counter in the Burlap Diner hunched over his notebook with a white mug in front of him. For a grown man, I knew how mentally frail my cousin was.

I slid onto the stool beside him. "Are you working on your story?"

"Holy cow. Are you a ghost?" Owen covered his notebook with both hands as he gawked. "Anna said you were in Mac's plane when it crashed into the bay."

"The plane crashed, but I'm not a ghost," I told him. "We saw Perry."

"Whew. Did Perry rescue you and bring you back to Cedar Grove?" He poked my arm several times to make sure I was real.

"Yes, he did."

He blew out a sharp breath. "Did you remember anything else?"

"A few things. There's a lot he couldn't tell me. I hoped you could give me a few clues." I smiled when Violet placed a cup of coffee in front of me.

"How are you?" She touched my hand. "I hear you and Mac had a big adventure yesterday. You're both the talk of the town."

"I'll bet. First me running into the fire, now this."

Violet gave a nod to someone across the room. "I'll be back. Then you can fill me in."

Owen stared at his notebook, pressing his lips together so tight the lower half of his face paled. He took a sip from his mug.

"I met your mom on the beach earlier. She showed me a picture of you and me with a huge crayfish."

He twitched when I pulled up the photo and grinned. "My cousin was a daredevil. We climbed trees. We hiked a lot. We caught crayfish and frogs. Even though I was five years older, we were a lot the same."

"Sounds like you had fun." Just as he'd done, I tried to distance myself from the concept that I was his cousin. Like in a book.

He gazed toward the kitchen behind the diner counter before he doodled circles on his page. "I pretended she was my little sister, you know. I never minded looking after her while my aunt and my dad worked at the manor. My mom worked a lot, too. She helped Bebe decorate and cook."

"Where was her dad?" I asked, playing along.

"Fighting fires." A small smile lit his face as he drew. "My uncle was a hero. My cousin and I wanted to be just like him when we grew up."

I raised my eyebrows. "Is he dead?"

"Retired," Owen said. "Unless firefighters need a teacher. Although he says being retired is worse than being dead. He likes to keep busy."

"That I believe. Do you see him often?"

"Sometimes, but mostly that's what my dad told me." He asked Violet for a glass of water. "Whenever he came to visit Bebe, Anna said to stay away from Perry because he was trouble."

"Why is that?"

"She wouldn't tell me."

Violet set his water in front of him, then walked away with a carafe of coffee.

I needed to ask the burning question while I had him all to myself and he was opening up. "What happened to your cousin, Owen?"

"She fell from the sky. Then her mom took her far away and I never saw her again." He paused as he met my gaze. "Don't you remember yet, A.J.?"

Tears filled my eyes. "What do you mean she fell from the sky?"

He clapped a hand over his mouth.

I was losing him. My emotional couple of days caught up fast and my patience wore thin. "Owen, did you hurt Bebe? Maybe by accident? Did you want her to turn off the music or do something she didn't want to do?"

"No. No. No." He shook his head. "I stayed to help her. I loved her as much as I loved you. You just don't remember."

"I don't. I really wish I did." I reached for a napkin, then closed my eyes before any tears could fall.

"You will when you're ready," he whispered.

Owen slid off the stood, grabbed his notebook, then scurried out the front door leaving me to stare at his half full cup of hot chocolate.

I touched the odd lump and the jagged scars beneath my hair. When I was ten, I was convinced I had a brain tumor. I tried to shave my head and took pictures for a better look. Roxie knew she'd be punished for what I'd done, but she helped me take pictures.

How could I ask my mom about Owen's story without details? Maybe I was overreacting. Owen was known for making up stories. Even Sergeant Sharpe had read some of them.

In the end, I texted my mom three words, *"Who is Owen?"*

I doubted she'd answer, but it couldn't hurt to ask. Not from this far away. While I knew he was my cousin, what I wanted was her honesty.

"Are you okay, hon?" Violet waved the coffee pot as she reached for Owen's half-empty cup.

"Yeah." I slid my cup toward her. "I'm starting to think coming here was a bad idea. I've stirred up things no one wants to talk about."

"Like what?" she asked.

"I'm not sure." I added cream and sugar to my fresh coffee. "Owen started to tell me about my past, then took off before I could ask questions. That happens with everyone I talk to. I'm starting to feel like a pariah."

"Ah, the van's here." Violet gazed toward the door. "He probably left because his dad came to pick him up."

"His dad?"

"Ken Archer. From Georgia Shores. Didn't you meet him?"

I turned in my seat as I bit my lip. Ken from the bed and breakfast was my uncle. Suddenly, I had a zillion more questions.

She patted my hand. "I'll be back in a sec, hon."

My newly discovered family had grown by an aunt, an uncle, and a cousin in the span of an hour. Those pictures from Bebe's room suddenly took on more meaning. I needed to dig them out for a closer look.

What happens at Grandma's house stays at Grandma's house.

Violet slid a slice of lemon meringue pie in front of me. "How's your book coming along?"

"I've been so distracted with Bebe's death and meeting Perry that I haven't written much," I told her. "Plus, I need to check on my library schedule."

"Add in that plane crash and you've had a pretty rough visit so far. I'll bet you could use a lot of it in your book. Like meeting Mac, for example."

"Very funny. I thought I'd find more answers in Bebe's room. Instead, all I have are questions not even Perry could answer." I sipped my coffee. "What do you know about my family?"

She sighed. "Enough not to get involved. There was some bad blood after the accident and—"

"What accident?" Even Violet knew more than me.

"Can I get another cup of coffee over here?" A large man with a full beard and a dark blue baseball cap waved her over.

"At least the busy days go by fast," Violet said. "We'll talk later."

I cut the end piece off the pie with my fork. "Maybe we can meet when you get a day off and compare notes."

"Sounds like fun." She tore off a page from the small notepad she kept in her apron and wrote a phone number on it. "Texting me is usually best. Just be patient, half of the time I don't hear the darn thing."

"Miss Cadell, I hear you had a little excitement yesterday." Foster sat on the stool Owen had vacated.

I flinched, my back tensing. "I take it you talked to Mac."

Foster ordered a coffee and a BLT to go. "Actually, I spoke to your father."

"What did he want?"

He waited until Violet left before replying, "He signed his share of Thistlewood over to you, which I am not sure is a wise idea."

"To me and my sister, you mean."

Foster shook his head. "No, Miss Cadell, to you alone. I shall bring by a copy of the paperwork later. Once approved, you will own seventy-five percent of Thistlewood Manor."

I gagged then coughed so hard Violet rushed me a glass of water. Once I could breathe again, I stared at Foster and asked, "Why?"

Foster shrugged. "I suppose he was glad you came all this way, so he could shrug off the burden."

My thoughts became such a jumble the only coherent question I could form was, "What am I supposed to do with it?"

"Run it as Bebe wanted," he said. "That is likely why she brought you here in the first place."

The only things I missed in Toronto were Emily and Roxie. I'd left the candy store in dramatic fashion and wouldn't be welcomed back.

"I can draw up a Power of Attorney," he said. "You can assign someone to look after it once you return to Toronto. I would deposit a cheque to your account every month to reflect the profits, as well as the financial information."

Something about his offer made me uneasy. My need to call my sister suddenly seemed more urgent. "I need to talk to my sister."

"Understandable. This is a major life decision not to be made lightly."

I glanced over my left shoulder, surprised to see Anna and Sal seated near the window in an intense conversation. Since Perry warned me about Sal and Foster at the airport, I grew uneasy.

"How well do you know Anna and Sal?" I cut off more pie with my fork. "I mean, I'm sure you saw them at Thistlewood, but are you friends outside of that?"

"Why would you ask such a question?"

I shrugged. "I'm trying to figure out why anyone wanted to kill Bebe. I figured you'd be the guy to ask."

"Indeed." Foster gave a nod as Violet handed him a brown paper bag and a large coffee. Once he'd paid her cash and got a receipt, he faced me. "I would tread lightly if I were you, young lady. You are an outsider in Cedar Grove and few people take kindly to being thought of as murder suspects."

If that was a veiled threat, it was effective. My entire body tingled.

"You look like you're going to be sick." Violet returned from the cash register as he left and refilled my water glass.

"I asked Foster what he knew about Anna and Sal," I told her. "I think he just threatened me."

She topped off my coffee. "You want to hear something else weird? I overheard Anna and Sal talking about a break-in at Thistlewood last night."

My first thought was of Mabel. Had someone found her and the paperwork stashed in my suitcase? "Last night? Are you sure?"

"A hundred percent. It seems kind of odd that the one night you're gone there's an intruder. If I were you, I'd keep my eyes open. What were they after?"

"Maybe something that belonged to Bebe. Possibly a photo or some paperwork."

Violet met my gaze. "Do you have Bebe's will?"

It seemed like an odd question at first. I probably wasn't the only person with a copy. "Yes. And I'll bet whoever killed her is named in it. At least that's the way it works in the movies."

"Just be careful," she said. "You're asking a lot of questions. It's only a matter of time before the killer makes a move. If he hasn't already."

Especially now that I owned three quarters of Thistlewood Manor.

Was it possible the plane crash had nothing to do with the storm and everything to do with getting rid of me?

Chapter Sixteen

Thistlewood stood silent. Sal and Anna were at the diner. Owen was likely with Ken. While I would've loved to explore while no one else was around, the last thing I wanted was for anyone to walk in on my conversation unintentionally.

I ran up to my room and unlocked my door. The lid on the top box of Bebe's belongings was open. The one that held the books I took from her shelves. Why leave them open? If they'd closed them, I'd never know anyone had been there. Instilling fear seemed to be the biggest factor.

Before I took off my coat, I texted Roxie to make sure she could talk. My cell phone rang seconds later.

"This better be good. I'm having a dress fitting," my sister said. "My maid of honor should be here, but she took off to the other side of the country."

"You're the one who wanted me to find Perry. Is Mom there, too?" I asked.

"No, I took an early lunch to escape the people I work with."

"That sounds fun."

"What's going on?" she asked. "You sound weird."

I took a bracing breath then turned my back on the boxes. "I met Perry."

"What?" She told someone on the other end to let the hem down another inch then to give her a minute. "You met Dad in person?"

Dad. I couldn't bring myself to call Perry that. "I stayed at his place last night."

"And you didn't bother to call while you were there?"

I filled her in on the plane crash, our chat over breakfast, and how he'd signed over his half of Thistlewood. The whole time I talked, I pulled Mabel and the paperwork out of my laptop bag.

"I don't care about some musty old bed and breakfast. Is he coming to my wedding or not?"

I sat at my desk. "I gave him your phone number. You can send his invitation to Thistlewood, but the only way he'll attend is if you move the wedding here."

"Ali...," she paused, then sighed. "I need him to show up to get Mom off my back." she said, sounding on the verge of tears.

"What do you mean?"

My sister sobbed as a door slammed. She must've gone into a change room. "Mom wants him to come to Toronto. She's going to have him arrested for not paying child support."

All the crocodile tears at the airport had a hidden purpose. My mother had even come prepared with that envelope from Perry.

"Why doesn't she just sue him like everyone else on the planet?" I sat on the edge of the bed.

"Because she has to find him first. I have to go."

Foster and Bebe's sudden arrival in Toronto had worked in my mom's favor. Did she know Roxie and I would inherit Thistlewood? I doubt she expected to be named in the will and there was no way she'd hire someone to kill Bebe. Perry would've been her target.

I skimmed through the other names in the will but could only cross off Owen and Mac as suspects.

Then I came to Sunrise Shelter. Bebe had left them half a million dollars.

I pulled out the notebook where I'd written notes about Bebe and my suspects, then placed Mabel on the desk to search for information. Sunrise Shelter was a local homeless shelter that gave twenty people somewhere to stay each night.

Bebe had donated over a million dollars toward renovations and expansion. I'd have to ask Foster if Bebe made monthly or annual injections of money to the shelter. According to the website, she and Ken had purchased the building to house its residents just as Mac said when he showed me where it was.

On a hunch, I did more digging on the other people in the will. If I couldn't get answers in person, I'd see how I could do online.

There was little information about Sal. Jewels had more social media presence as a teenager than I did as an author. I'd have to hit her up for pointers. Sal's wife died in a car accident ten years earlier, leaving him to raise his daughter alone.

Anna Larkin's online presence was limited to events and advertising on the Thistlewood Manor website. She also volunteered at Sunrise Shelter. In every photo, she smiled. Even when Bebe took the limelight, although Anna's smile seemed tighter.

I found nothing about Owen. Absolutely nothing. It was eerie. Everyone had something about them somewhere in cyberspace these days, didn't they? Even Perry, hermit that he was, had an encyclopedia of information online thanks to his impressive career.

Typing in Mac McKittrick took me straight to a fire station website a few kilometers south of Cedar Grove. Beneath his photo was his full name, Trevor "Mac" McKittrick. Photos of him in full turnout gear, of him hanging Christmas lights around town, as well as racing in a fun run wearing a Sunrise Shelter T-shirt filled the town websites.

The biggest surprise was the photo of him wearing his short-sleeved, black dress uniform. I'd never been one to swoon over a man in uniform, but my heart raced as I zoomed in on the tattoos on his forearms. Flames and a dragon. I saved the image to send to Emily. At least that's what I told myself.

Mac couldn't have set the fire, killed Bebe, or searched the boxes. He was with me each time. At the diner, then stranded on Perry's island. Unless he'd had an accomplice. Violet crossed my mind, but she had nothing to gain.

Perry Beyer. I started to search, then stopped. I doubted I'd discover anything I hadn't already found. Since he didn't want anything to do with the manor, he had no plausible motive.

Nothing seemed to be missing from the boxes, not that I remembered every single thing inside. Was someone after a valuable book or were they simply trying to scare me?

The aroma of food caught my attention. My stomach growled. I'd been so absorbed in research and hadn't heard anyone return. I packed Mabel and my paperwork into the laptop bag. Rather than place it under the bed, I tucked it in the top of the closet beneath an extra blanket.

Anna cursed in the kitchen below, which wasn't what I expected to hear. I rushed down the stairs in time to see smoke wafting from the oven.

"Is everything okay?" I asked, keeping away from the staircase railing.

"I knew I shouldn't have left," she said. "Now I've burned the roast. All I went to do was get some fruit for dessert and stopped to chat with a lady from my bridge club."

Bridge club? I hadn't seen a deck of cards anywhere and already knew she was with Sal.

"I've done that so many times. Luckily, my roommate taught me how to make stew from the good parts."

"That's a good idea." Anna sliced the roast in half. While the thin outer layer was charred, the rest was practically raw. More like someone seared it on high heat rather than roasted it in a slow oven, which I would've smelled earlier.

"I'll get some veggies," I offered.

"And I'll cut this thing into chunks."

While Anna sliced the roast, I scrubbed carrots and potatoes and told her, "I haven't made dinner in a long time. My roommate does all the cooking. This time of year, I work longer shifts between Halloween and Christmas."

"Where did you work?" she asked.

It didn't escape me that she used the past tense. "In a candy store. Although after the way I left, I doubt I'll ever work there again."

"Left on bad terms, did you?"

"Oh, yeah."

"What will you do when you get back to Toronto?" She paused. "Or are you going back?"

As I chopped the carrots into thin coins, I wondered if Foster told her about Perry's visit. "What do you mean?"

"You own part of Thistlewood now," she said, washing her hands. "To be honest, it would be nice to have someone else help to run this place. You seem to like to cook, and you've adapted to Cedar Grove. I guess a small part of me hopes you'll stay."

True. I'd talked to Perry about running Thistlewood, but I hadn't made the decision to stay. It was a lot to take on and I hoped she'd stay to help. Maybe Foster would continue to look after the financial end of things. In a perfect world, I'd run the manor and still have time to write.

"I'll see what my sister wants to do with her share. I may need your help. I don't know the first thing about running a bed and breakfast."

Anna's smile didn't reach her eyes. "I imagine you'll want to keep Sheila on as housekeeper and Sal to do maintenance. Should I talk to them?"

"No. I still need to think things over." I leaned against the counter before scraping the carrots into a bowl.

"Good idea." Anna dumped the meat into a large pot along with onion and garlic that I hadn't seen her chop.

"What about Owen?" I asked, cutting a potato into cubes.

She froze. "What about Owen?"

"Does he work here, too?"

"Owen is like a mascot. He kept Bebe happy." Anna stirred the sizzling beef.

"A mascot?" Owen screeched from behind us. "Mascots have oversized heads and fake fur. I am not a mascot, young lady."

I spun around in time to see him grab a paring knife from the drawer.

"Put that down," Anna yelled.

Owen held out his hands. "I'm getting an apple. I'm hungry."

"Great." I tossed him an apple before he got any closer with the knife. "Now you've made me hungry. Do you want to help with the vegetables?"

"That's okay. I have things covered here," Anna said. "You have about an hour until dinner."

She was probably rethinking the whole idea of me working in the kitchen, especially with Owen around. I grabbed an apple and headed for the stairs. Before I reached the top, my cell phone rang. "Hey, Roxie."

"Thanks a lot, Alison," my sister growled.

"What's going on?" I darted into my room and closed the door.

"Thanks to you, Perry doesn't want anything to do with us."

Her accusation knocked the breath out of me. I leaned against my bedroom door. "What did he say?"

Roxie growled. "He knew exactly why I wanted him at my wedding. He refused to attend unless I move it to Thistlewood."

"I told you that. How did he know about Mom wanting to have him arrested?"

"Didn't you tell him?"

"I didn't know." I set my apple on a tissue on the desk. "I'd be upset, too. Look, Roxie, we need to talk about Thistlewood. You should come see it, so we can talk. We have to decide what to do with it."

There was a long silence, but at least she didn't hang up. Yet.

"Alison, I'm getting married in May and moving to a big, beautiful condo in downtown Toronto." She enunciated each word like I was three. "What in my history leads you to believe I'd fly across the country to some run-down shack?"

"It's not rundown and the scenery is spectacular. You could take photos for weeks. Just come see it."

My sister huffed. "Forget it, Ali. I'm done. I was done with him when he never came to find us. He never even sent money to support us."

"That's not what he told me."

The phone hummed in my ear.

If there was ever a time when I needed a voice of reason, this was it. My hands shook as I finished my apple and called Emily in my contact list. She texted back that she was on a date and would call me later.

After dinner, and before we'd dug into the apple cobbler Anna whipped up, I tapped my fork on my water glass to get everyone's attention. Everyone being Owen, Anna, and Sal. Jewels never ate with us.

"I wanted to let you all know I'm planning to stay here to run Thistlewood." I cleared my throat. "I'll need help to keep this place going, so nothing will change right away."

They all lowered their gazes and finished eating.

Owen glanced up. "Can we have dessert now?"

Sal and Anna exchanged glances.

"Thanks for dinner. Goodnight." Sal shot out the utility room door before I could say another word.

It would be easy for him to slip in and out of Thistlewood Manor unnoticed. No one but me would think twice about him being inside.

Owen dropped his fork and stared at me over the ruins of his dinner.

"What's wrong?" I asked.

"Does that mean you'll move into Bebe's old room?" he asked. "You know, the big one she lived in before—"

Anna shook her head. "Owen, no one is moving into the master suite."

"I'm happy with the room I'm in now," I assured him. "If we fix up the old room, we could use it for a bridal suite. I'll bet Bebe would love that. She seemed like a real romantic."

He frowned. "I'd rather you live in it than some stranger." He hesitated, then added, "I could help you fix it up. It's my favorite room in the whole house."

"I said no, Owen," Anna snapped.

As she began to clear the table, he took his plate and cutlery to the kitchen before running up the stairs two at a time.

"That room is where the fire started," Anna said, holding a knife in one hand. "It needs a lot more work than you think."

"I'm sorry for bringing it up. I'll go talk to him."

She stopped me with something that sounded like a guttural growl. "You've upset him enough. He needs to be alone."

Considering how riled up talking about the master suite made her, I didn't ask about the other rental rooms. If there were any. I was starting to wonder.

Remembering the tape recorder, I excused myself. I needed to get out of the house before I caused more trouble. I dug out Sharpe's card and arranged to meet him at the station. I grabbed the tape recorder and the shards of glass from my room and stuck them in my laptop bag before I headed to the RCMP station a couple blocks past the diner. Directly across from the Sunrise Shelter.

While I should have brought them to the RCMP days ago, I'd been distracted after meeting Perry.

"You found this where?" he asked, looking from the tape recorder back to me.

"The glass was in Bebe's wastebasket. The tape recorder was in the room where the fire started. It was on a pile of debris." I leaned forward on my tiptoes to look but didn't dare touch it again. "Someone played the same song Bebe used to listen to. I think they're trying to scare me off."

"Who would want to do that?" he asked.

"Whoever wants me to go back to Toronto and take over the manor. I hoped you might have an idea." I hesitated. "How did Jack Beyer die?"

He sat back. "You don't know?"

I shook my head. "I've heard bits from Owen and Mac, but it's sketchy. Owen sees it like a test. If I don't figure things out on my own, he won't believe it's really me. I hoped you had a police report I could read to speed things up."

Sharpe flashed a small grin. "You're really not a crime writer, are you?"

"Nope. Still a romance novelist."

"If you were, you'd know the police aren't in the habit of handing out private information to just anyone." He shuffled some papers.

"Wouldn't it be a matter of public record by now?"

"Not necessarily."

I blinked back tears. "Oh, come on. I'm not just anyone. I know you've checked me out. Jack Beyer was my grandfather and I think his death, plus the fact I don't remember ever being in Cedar Grove, might be related."

He pulled a folder off a stack and tapped one edge against his desk. "And what do you intend to do with the information, Miss Cadell? Write a book with me as the bumbling detective?"

"What? No." My mouth dropped open as I sat across from him. "Look, I've had strange nightmares for as long as I can remember, and I need to know what happened here. This is for my sanity. Maybe even for my sister if she'll listen."

He leaned forward to reach for his coffee at the same time as he handed me the folder. "That's too bad. I'm curious how you'd portray me in a book."

I took the folder. "I'll have to figure that out."

"I'd make a great hero," Sharpe said. "Keep that. It's a copy. I figured you'd nose around here sooner or later."

"Maybe I will have to try my hand at a mystery novel after this."

He grinned. "I'd buy a copy."

On my walk back to Thistlewood, I tried to focus on my novel, but the lack of straightforward answers was starting to get to me. I needed a clue. Something to spark my memory. The folder seemed the most likely place to start.

Anna was in the kitchen making tea.

I headed straight up to my room to avoid her. Left to my own devices, I sat down with the folder.

All I had left to do now was write a book and teach a few workshops at the library—and solve a murder.

Chapter Seventeen

"*L et's get out of here," a boy's voice crackled with fear and ado-lescence. "Hurry, A.J.! Climb out the window to the balcony or we'll get burned."*

"We have to go downstairs," a younger child said. Me, yet not me. "He needs help, or he'll die."

Owen grabbed my shoulders. "The stairs are on fire. We have to get out now."

Flames licked the void below as they rose toward us. Suddenly, there was a loud crack. I dropped like someone pushed me from a plane. The rush of air and smoke in my face took my breath away as the ground grew closer...

I awoke with a start and clutched my chest as I struggled to catch my breath. The room was dark. No flames. No smoke. Only darkness.

Papers were strewn all over my bed. I'd fallen asleep while reading the reports about Jack's death. He was bludgeoned but died of smoke inhalation. Murdered, just like Bebe. The majority of clues in the case went up in flames with no witnesses. As far as I'd read, anyway. I couldn't stomach more photos or details.

Shaking, I let the pillows hug me while I caught my breath. I needed to write the dream in my journal. I wanted to ask Emily what she thought it meant. As I gathered the papers, then reached for my journal, I froze.

Light poured through the narrow gap beneath my door. A shadow moved past before another door closed. I was the only person staying in this wing of the manor. If Anna hadn't rented Bebe's room, who was poking around?

It was five o'clock according to my phone. I wiped my palms on the top sheet as I sat up. Had I missed something when I removed Bebe's belongings from her room?

When the light went out, I flinched. Fabric rustled as footsteps faded into the distance. Shoving the papers under my pillow and throwing back the blankets, I shuddered as the air hugged my sweaty skin. I ran to open the door as quickly, yet quietly, as possible. The person in the hallway went down the stairs, boots clicking on the wood with each step. Then silence until a door closed on the lower level. The garage?

Barefoot, I trotted down the stairs, then paused at the bottom. The utility room door was closest. I turned the doorknob slowly and slithered a hand inside to feel for the light switch. I wasn't one of those people in the movies who walked into a dark room to search for a killer.

Killer? I gulped.

Intruder?

Trespasser sounded less frightening.

Leave it to a writer to struggle for the right word at the worst possible time.

All I found inside the utility room were the washer and dryer as well as brooms, mops, cleaning products, and more boxes. No dark, lurking figures wielding weapons. Beyond everything stood another door I assumed led to the garage.

I eased the second door open and wiggled my hand along the wall inside until I found a line of switches. Fluorescent bulbs buzzed to life. Three cars awaited in a neat line. A tidy work bench stood near the door. Garage doors lined the wall to my right. Two smaller doors, one at the far end and the one to my left, which led to the backyard and to Sal's cottage.

When it occurred to me the trespasser could be hiding behind the cars or in the backyard, my bravery diminished. No way was I going outside in the cold wearing only my pajamas to chase anyone.

Just like out on the back porch, the lightbulb in the utility room dimmed then brightened. This time, I took it as a sign to run. I locked every door before flicking off the lights and scampering up to the bathroom.

Breathless from fear, I flicked on the lights and locked the door behind me. My face was pale. My hands shook. I splashed warm water on my cheeks and rubbed my forehead, then peered out the bathroom door.

The hallway was quiet.

My bedroom door stood ajar.

I must've left it open in my haste to see who was in the hallway? Either that or Thistlewood really was haunted.

As I reached for the light switch in my room, I realized I'd make a lousy police officer. I was as brave as a chipmunk. No one was in my room. I checked my closet before locking my door.

Bebe's boxes appeared to be undisturbed. Mabel was still in my suitcase. The police report about Jack...

Was still under my pillow.

Releasing a deep breath, I tucked the police report into my bag and returned it to the suitcase. Just in case. Thankful my bed was still warm, I tugged the blankets to my chin and reached for my anxiety pills.

Whoever left through the garage entrance must have come in the same way, but who'd want to break into Thistlewood?

Owen would be tucked in bed. I was too afraid to get up and check on him or Anna. Earlier in the day, Violet overheard Sal and Anna discussing a break-in when I was on Perry's island.

Would Foster, who appeared to be somewhere in his seventies, or beyond, still capable of moving that fast? One thing was for certain, when I got up in the morning, I'd scrub every inch of Bebe's room by hand in case I'd missed anything. Like a hidden compartment or a safe.

I awoke around ten with a throbbing headache. I'd slept right through Emily's morning call and string of texts and hadn't taken my medication yet. After dressing in clothes I didn't mind getting dirty, I roamed down to the kitchen for breakfast.

"Rough night?" Anna asked.

I poured a cup of coffee. "Yup."

"Were you ill? I heard you get up a couple times last night," she said.

My hands shook. I leaned against the counter to steady myself. "Just once."

Anna tilted her head when she glanced at me, then cracked eggs into a bowl. "Really? I heard someone around five o'clock. I thought it was you getting some fresh air. I'm not sure what time it was before that, but there were definitely thumps on the stairs."

"Maybe Owen was up early."

"Not a chance." She beat the eggs. "Owen's afraid of the dark. Besides, he takes sleeping pills."

Sleeping pills? My stomach sank as I recalled the bottle I'd found in the drawer. I sipped my coffee and stared at the frying pan as she poured in the eggs.

"Sal could've had something he needed to fix," she said.

"In the middle of the night?"

Her gaze met mine as she chuckled. "You're right. It's hard enough to get that man to work during the day."

"I was thinking of cleaning Bebe's room today, so we can have guests stay there. I'm sure the fire and Bebe's death have both put a damper on rentals for a while, but it's good to prepare, right?"

The eggs sizzled and crackled while she stared at me. "Really?"

"I need something to take my mind off my book. I'm stuck on a scene and need something mindless to do."

"Is that what they call writer's block?" Anna asked. "Works for me. Cleaning supplies are in the utility room."

"Yeah, I..." I paused. "You told me when I got here."

"Go ahead and use what you need," she said, stirring the eggs.

After a surplus of coffee, scrambled eggs, and bacon, I went to Bebe's room with a bucket and cleaning supplies. Figuring out who killed her was making me anxious. As I cleared away thin strings of cobwebs, scrubbed marks off walls, and washed the windows, my thoughts bounced from Bebe to my novel, then back.

I hadn't seen Mac since Perry brought us back to Cedar Grove. That was for the best. He was a distraction. I couldn't seem to write a romantic scene without picturing those hypnotizing green eyes and muscular legs. Not to mention those napkins he'd found and read. Waking up next to him at Perry's hadn't helped.

Thankfully, I'd crossed Mac off my suspect list already, since I'd need his knowledge of the people involved. The problem was, he was about as forthcoming as everyone else in town.

"Hey," someone said.

I jumped with a shriek.

"That was funny." Owen grinned as he stood in the doorway, note-book clenched in one hand. He hadn't run a comb through his hair. A clump stuck up on one side.

"I'm sure it was." I rinsed my cloth in the bucket of water. "What's up?"

"Why are you doing Sheila's job?" he asked.

I gazed at the water rippling in the bucket. "I wanted to freshen it up before anyone stays here."

He winced. "But it smells like Bebe. If you clean it, then it won't."

The room did smell like Bebe. I closed my eyes and remembered dancing with her in the hallway. The scent of the flowers surrounding us as I stood on her bare feet in the grass as we sang that song...

I opened my eyes with a start. Grass? What on earth?

"Alison?" Owen peered into my face. "What happened?"

I was sitting on the bed with my strength sapped like I'd fallen asleep and just awoke. I certainly hadn't stood on Bebe's feet when we'd danced in the hallway, and there was definitely no grass. Had I finally remembered something?

"Should I get Anna?"

I grabbed his arm. "Owen, no. I'm okay. Don't worry Anna."

Sal cleared his throat from the doorway. "What are you two doing in here?"

"Cleaning." I coughed and rubbed my forehead as a dull ache set in.

"You'd better do a good job," he said. "We'll have guests soon. City folks are fussy about clean rooms."

I rushed past Owen and asked, "Hey, Sal, were you up here last night?"

"Are you accusing me of something else now?"

"No." I took a step back. "Someone was in Bebe's room last night. I followed them downstairs, but they disappeared before I saw who it was."

"Did you ask Anna?" Sal asked.

"She had no idea."

"Disappeared?" Owen's eyes grew wide. "You mean like a magic trick?"

I shook my head. "No. They left through the garage door."

Sal scowled. "You followed an intruder downstairs, but were too chicken to follow them outside? Are you serious?"

"It was cold. Plus, I was in my pajamas with bare feet."

"You would've got sick," Owen said.

"Exactly."

Sal folded his arms across his chest. "I wasn't in the house. I wasn't in Bebe's room. Nor did I sneak down the stairs in the middle of the night. Anything else?"

Owen took a menacing step toward him and asked, "Are you a magician?"

"Certainly not."

"Did you kill Bebe?"

"Owen!" I warned.

When Sal snorted, my cousin ducked to cower behind me.

"Is that what you two are up to?" Sal asked. "You think I killed Bebe?"

My heart raced. "You had the opportunity and the ability."

Sal stood so close to me his breath hit my face like a hot wind. He smelled of coffee. "My daughter and I were at our cottage near Buttle Lake that day. Besides that, Bebe gave me a job when no one else in Cedar Grove would give me a second look. She let me live in the cottage, so I'd have a place to raise Jewels. She bought me a truck to get around Thistlewood and got me landscape jobs on the side, so I could make a living. What possible motive could I have for killing someone my daughter and I owe our lives to?"

I crossed him off my suspect list. "None. I met Jewels. She's a great kid."

Sal softened, but just a teensy bit. "Thanks. Bebe helped her learn to read. She borrowed books all the time."

I reached out a hand. "Friends?"

"Don't push it."

Owen peered over my shoulder. "Be nice and shake her hand."

"It's okay, Owen. I had it coming." I retreated into Bebe's room. Was it Jewels looking for books that I heard? She had access to Sal's keys which unlocked every room in Thistlewood. Including mine.

When Sal headed down the hall to the master suite I peered around the corner. I wanted to follow him but was afraid of making him angrier. What was he up to? He didn't have tools or anything to make repairs or clean up debris.

"Is he looking for the tape recorder?" Owen whispered in my ear.

"Maybe," I whispered back. "Why don't you go see?"

"Because I'm scared of him."

"Me too, but at least he likes you."

Owen reached for a dry rag and a bottle of cleaner. "I'd rather help you and stay out of Anna's hair. She's mad at me today since I wouldn't take my medicine last night. You're the only person who isn't mad at me."

"Thanks for having my back."

He raised his thumb. "Anytime, cuz. Us writers have to stick together."

"You got that right."

Sal passed the doorway about ten minutes later. He paused and met my gaze with a grunt.

Owen abandoned his rag five minutes after that and took off with his notebook.

Once more, I was left alone with my thoughts. While my suspect list was shorter, my novel still had a gaping plot hole I needed to fix. I washed the insides of the dresser drawers, the closet, and every other surface I could find. When I reached for the waste basket to wash it out thoroughly, I frowned.

It looked like it had been replaced rather than washed. Was that why someone broke in last night? I hoped the shards and the tape recorder provided the police with new evidence.

When my stomach growled, I ignored it. I was nearly done with Bebe's room and still hadn't figured out how to fix my story. Lunch could wait.

"I figured you might be hungry by now. I hope you like turkey, cranberry, and Havarti." Sheila stood in the doorway holding a plate and a bottle of water. "The room looks great. You're good at this."

"Thanks." My thoughts leaped from my book into reality. "I'm not trying to take your job. I just needed to..." I waved a hand as a wave of emotion swept over me.

"Understandable." She handed me the plate. "I'm sorry for the way you found out. I wish she'd told you the day she found you in Toronto like she wanted."

My throat tightened. "You knew?"

"She told us what she was up to before she left," Sheila said. "I wasn't happy about it at first."

"And now?"

"I'm glad you're here."

I sat cross-legged on the floor before I took a bite. "This is good."

"Thanks. I've had practice." Sheila started to sit in the chair then reconsidered and sat next to me. "How are you enjoying Cedar Grove? Aside from the obvious. Are you getting any writing done?"

"It's been interesting," I admitted. "I've written some, but Bebe's death, then meeting Perry, distracted me. I need to touch base with the library today and make sure I have my schedule."

"You saw Perry?" she asked.

I filled her in on our adventures on Perry's island, then asked, "How long have you known Ken? You guys seemed pretty relaxed when we were all staying there."

Sheila frowned. "It's weird to think you don't remember a lot of things. Ken and I have been married for twenty-eight years."

I set down my plate. "He's Bebe's other son. My uncle. Owen said I used to live here."

"You all did," she said.

Tears filled my eyes again. "Why did we leave?"

"That you'll have to ask your mom."

"She won't talk about it, except to blame Perry," I whispered. "Can you tell me something?"

"What's that, honey?" She met my gaze.

"What happened to Owen? How did he fall?"

Owen stormed into the room. "Don't tell her! She has to remember on her own. It's important."

His mom stood to hold him back. "She has a right to know, Owen."

"You can't tell her," he bellowed. "She needs to remember."

I closed my eyes. "Owen, I've started to remember a few things. Like my dad's blueberry pancakes."

"What made you think of those?" Sheila asked.

"I helped him make some on the island. The smell reminded me."

Owen crouched in front of me. He placed a hand on my shoulder. "Think hard, Ali. You have to try."

A tear rolled down my cheek. "I could use some help. Why won't you help me?"

His chin quivered. "Because you're not her anymore."

"I'm not who?" I asked.

"That silly little girl I used to have fun with," Owen said. "You left and grew up and I hoped you'd remember everything we did. Climbing trees, playing in the water, hiking around Cedar Grove… When you remember, you'll know what I mean."

When he left Sheila and I alone, we stared at each other in silence before she handed me a napkin. "I need to check on him."

"He said Anna was mad at him for not taking his medication last night."

"That'll do it. Why don't you go for a walk and clear your head? Just stay out of the water. It's too cold for swimming today."

"Thanks."

I finished the rest of my sandwich before bringing the plate to the kitchen. Once I'd put away the cleaning supplies, I made sure my laptop bag was secure in the closet before I locked my door. Then I roamed across the hallway for a long, hot shower and a good cry.

While I understood why Owen was so adamant that I remember on my own, a few clues would be helpful. I hadn't discovered anything new in Bebe's room. I did have time to think, and Bebe's room was spotless. Maybe I'd take that walk and go to the diner. I could chat with Violet and have a milkshake and fries before checking in at the library.

When I returned to my room, I gasped. Mabel sat on top of my desk with the password screen lit. One of the boxes filled with Bebe's writing books was open. I sank onto the bed as I struggled to catch my breath.

Whoever broke into my room had a key, had found my laptop, and hadn't bothered to hide the fact they'd been in my room.

Sheila had a key. Her voice carried down the hall from Owen's room.

I returned Mabel to the laptop bag and decided I needed to take the bag, the will, and everything wherever I went. Shaken, I pulled on my coat and hat and had nearly reached the front door when Anna called me.

"Oh, hey, I thought you were out." I glanced over my shoulder.

"I bought some fish for dinner," she said. "When I came back, there was a package for you."

"For me?" I frowned. Had my mom finally decided to give me the rest of the letters Perry sent? No, she'd probably kept any money and destroyed them.

When I followed her to the kitchen, she handed me a brown paper wrapped box the size of a shoe box. No return address, simply a black "Cedar Grove" stamp on the right corner over some crooked postage stamps. Someone had mailed it locally.

If it was mailed at all.

My curiosity amped up a hundred-fold.

Chapter Eighteen

After I snapped a picture of the package, I sent it to Emily, Roxie, and my mom in the off chance one of them sent it. I took the package to the one place I felt safe—The Burlap Diner.

"Can I borrow something to cut this open?" I asked Violet as she scurried past.

She did a double-take. "Of course, honey. I'll be back in a jiff."

A jiff turned out to be less than twenty seconds.

I cut the tape and opened the flaps. Beneath a handful of wadded paper, lay dozens of photographs. Some black and white and some color. A few were duplicates of ones I'd cleaned out of Bebe's room. Most I'd never seen before. It was like snooping in someone else's life. As I sifted through photos of life at Thistlewood Manor when I was a kid, I forgot all about sharing with anyone.

"Are those what I think they are?" Violet asked as she sat across from me.

"This is me and my sister," I told her. "I look about three. I'm amazed I was so filthy. My mom can't stand the sight of dirt."

"This is Jack." She pulled another photo from the box. "I used to take my kids trick-or-treating at Thistlewood. Mostly because Jack and Bebe went all out with decorations, not to mention the candy. Full size chocolate bars, bags of chips, and a toothbrush."

"A toothbrush?" I asked. "That's funny."

One picture brought tears to my eyes. Perry, Roxie, me, and my mom. "My family looked so happy."

"Aww! Look at those cheeks," Violet gushed, pinching my cheek.

Most of the photos were of me and Owen. We were usually dirty, wet, or both as we played at the beach with turtles, fish, and other critters. Some made me laugh while others brought tears to my eyes. Thankfully, someone took the time to write names and dates on the backs. I hoped they'd trigger some memories.

Teena stopped next to the table. "Where'd you get the old pictures?"

"Oh cool." Jewels snapped her gum.

I showed them the brown paper wrapping as Violet got up to grab the coffeepot. "Someone mailed them, but there's no return address. I think it was someone local. I doubt there's enough postage to get it far."

"Weird," Jewels said as she sat across from me.

Teena slid onto the bench next to her. "Ooh, your very own mystery."

"You want anything, girls?" Violet asked.

"A job, so I don't have to work with my family anymore." Teena sighed. "But I'll settle for a strawberry milkshake."

Jewels flashed a smile. "Chocolate milkshake for me, please."

"Just water for me," I told her. "I'm not sure I can handle anything stronger."

Violet patted my shoulder. "I'll bring you some tea."

"Hey, is that my dad?" Jewels took the photo from my hand. "He helped plant all those trees in the backyard at Thistlewood. They're a lot bigger now."

When she turned it so I could see, I recognized the spot immediately. "Wow. Those are the cedar trees between the main house and the cottage."

She took a second look. "That makes sense. My dad told me a dozen times how they planted them in Jack's memory after the fire."

"What fire?" I recalled the papers from Sharpe and put the two together before either of the girls could reply. The date on the back of the photo was August. It was taken twenty years ago. The year my mom moved us to Toronto.

"The one when you and Owen got hurt and Grandpa Jack died," Teena said.

I struggled to catch my breath. "Owen and I were there when Jack died?"

She shrugged. "That's what Owen said. I wasn't born yet."

"One chocolate milkshake and one strawberry milkshake." Violet set silver cups in front of the girls and a mug near me. "Chamomile tea. Guaranteed to help calm frayed nerves. Did you girls hear Alison and Mac were in a plane crash?"

Jewels stared. "That was you guys?"

"My dad said the plane pretty much fell apart," Teena said. "Was it really hit by lightning?"

I sat back to pour my tea. "We think so. We shouldn't have flown that day, but Mac took me to see Perry."

"Perry Beyer?" Jewels asked. "Why?"

"He's my father." I picked out a photo of me and Roxie with Perry.

"I didn't know that," Jewels whispered.

"Neither did I until my sister was planning her wedding. Then Bebe hired a private detective who found me. In turn, Mac helped me find Perry. It's awful that I didn't know who Bebe was until..."

I blinked back a surge of tears.

Violet placed a hand on my shoulder. "It's okay, hon. Bebe must've brought you here to help. I'll bet she sent you those pictures."

"Help what?" I wiped away a tear with the back of my hand.

She pointed to the photo in my hand. Me, Perry, and Roxie mugged for the camera. "To fix that. Your mom might not want anything to do with Thistlewood, but it belongs to you three. You need to decide what to do with it."

"Kind of like Camelot," Teena said. "King Perry and his princess-es."

I squeezed my eyes shut and exhaled. "Yeah. Only King Perry doesn't want anything to do with his princesses or his castle."

Silence fell over the table while the restaurant hummed around us.

"I shouldn't have brought this here," I whispered at the photo in my hand.

Jewels sipped her milkshake. "I'm glad you did. Owen used to tell us stories about you and your sister."

Teena nodded. "You guys did some pretty neat stuff. I've never seen these pictures before."

"Me neither." Jewels agreed. "Not even when I spent so much time at my dad's or hung out in Bebe's room."

Which confirmed Sal didn't send the photos. Neither did Sheila or Owen.

Violet peered into the box. "I don't see many pictures of your mom in here. She's only in that one of the four of you."

She was right. The rest were of me and my sister with various family members. Even a few of Sal and a much younger Anna. There were also photos of Owen and Sheila with Ken Archer.

What had happened between Bebe and her son Ken? "Teena, did your dad and Bebe get along?"

"I think this is where I need to interrupt." Sharpe stood near the table.

"Good timing," Violet said. "I'll grab you a coffee."

"I'd better go get my homework done." Teena's cheeks reddened.

"Nice seeing you, Alison," Jewels said. "Maybe we can hang out again sometime. I'd love to hear about your books."

Once they were gone, the sergeant sat across from me and chuckled. "If you ever want to clear a room, get yourself a badge."

"I don't need a badge. I just have to open my mouth."

"Looks like you've had a rough day."

"Try a rough week."

"What's all this?" he asked.

"Someone sent me a gift." I pointed to the brown paper wrapper. "Violet thinks it was Bebe."

He grimaced. "I suppose you got fingerprints all over them."

"Yeah. Sorry. I hadn't thought about that." I'd only hoped to stir up some dusty memories locked in my head.

Sharpe pointed to a young man in the background of one of the photos. "Hey, that's me. Before I became a law man, I worked as a carpenter's assistant and helped Jack build the kitchen cupboards. I even put my initials in the top of one."

I sipped my tea. "Did you know my whole family?"

He flipped from one photo to the next then stopped at the one of both my parents with me and Roxie. When Violet slid him a coffee, he said, "I met your mom through Perry. She seemed nice and loved you girls to pieces."

"But."

"Ingrid loved the romantic notion of being the wife of a hero, but she had no idea how to handle the times he was out in the field not knowing if or when he'd be back. No one knows how stressful that kind of life can be until you live it."

"In the end, she settled down with a guy who can't hold a job," I told him, struggling to find a silver lining. "At least her husband can cook."

He continued to shuffle through the photos then stopped at one of me with Owen and Ken Archer. "Do you think Ken or Sheila sent these? After all, they are your godparents."

"My godparents?"

Sharpe groaned. "No one has laid out the family tree for you. Are you serious? I thought they'd fall all over themselves as soon as you arrived."

"Owen told me I had to remember things for myself. I've tried, but it's like pulling eggshells out of egg white. Sometimes it works and sometimes you just deal with the crunch."

"Can't tell you're a writer," he said with a grin. "May I suggest you talk to your uncle in person? He's the guy I should've sent you to in the first place."

"My uncle." One photo was stuck beneath a small piece of cardboard at the bottom of the box. A small child wrapped in bandages lying on a hospital bed. Wires and tubes ran from machines into every part of the child's body. Bandages covered the child's head.

I tapped the image. "Is this Owen?"

Sharpe took the photo and cradled it in his hand. He read the back before he showed it to me. "This is you, Alison."

"Me?" My eyes and mouth opened so wide I probably looked like one of those goofy selfie photos minus the rabbit ears. For a long moment, I could barely breathe. "What happened to me?"

"Did you read the file I gave you?"

"Most of it. I fell asleep and it gave me nightmares."

He placed the pictures in the box, then asked Violet for a bag and pushed the brown paper wrapping inside using the end of a spoon. "I'll look after this. Go talk to Ken Archer. He'll give you a straight answer. Whether you want it or not."

Far more confused than ever, I closed the box. I'd hoped to find some answers, but all I had was more questions.

The biggest one was who had sent the photos and why?

Chapter Nineteen

Sharpe convinced me that talking to my uncle face to face was best. If Ken Archer had answers, I needed to hear them, not read them on some faceless website I hadn't discovered yet.

Violet waved off my attempt to pay for my tea as she gave me a hug. "I'm glad you're finding out more about your family. Hopefully, it'll help catch whoever did that to Bebe."

I clutched the shoebox to my chest. "I hope so. It's ironic that I stayed at his house after the fire and didn't know who he was. Why didn't they say anything?"

She gave me a hug. "I guess they left it to you to make the first move. I hope you get your answers, hon."

Dread swept over me as I walked toward Georgia Shores Cottages. The cold didn't bother me nearly as much as the task ahead. I'd run into so many dead ends because no one wanted to be the person to tell me the truth. But why?

Bebe's son Ken used a different last name and wasn't named in her will, yet Sheila worked at Thistlewood, and Owen lived there. None of it made sense. To own the bed and breakfast, Ken must have a tidy fortune of his own.

Sal's old blue Chevy rolled out of the driveway heading toward Thistlewood. Had Teena and Jewels told him about my photos?

I stopped at the end of the laneway to study my uncle's bed and breakfast. The main building was a simpler version of Thistlewood. Two-story without the elaborate lobby. It also had fewer windows to clean. The entrance was a heavy wooden door identical to the one at Thistlewood.

As I raised my hand, the door opened before I could knock.

"Alison, I heard you were coming," Ken said with a relaxed smile.

"You did?" I asked, clutching the box closer despite the fact he seemed genuinely happy to see me.

He opened the door wider to reveal a rustic, welcoming foyer. "Teena just got home. She said you received an interesting package."

My phone chimed. "I did. Do you have time to chat?"

"For you? Of course." My uncle waved me toward a cozy office to my left. "Have a seat while I grab us some coffee. Days like this, that wind goes right through you. What do you take?"

Numb from going through photos, I hadn't even noticed the wind. "Cream and sugar, please."

"You got it."

I took a deep breath as I wandered into the tidy, well-organized office. Tall bookshelves lined the wall behind a cedar desk and high-backed office chair. The large window with cream roller blinds overlooked the front entrance.

Still hugging the box of photos, I sat near the desk in a low-backed, brown leather chair. I had no idea where to start. There was so much I wanted—needed—to know.

"Here we are." Ken returned with a tray he set on a coffee table behind me. He wore a burgundy sweater and blue jeans and seemed far more relaxed than me. "Why don't we take a seat over here? It's more comfortable."

I was so wrapped up in my thoughts, I hadn't noticed the leather sofa and chair. With a nod, I sat at one end of the couch still unable to put my thoughts into words.

Ken poured two cups of coffee from a silver carafe before he set one in front of me. "Sheila made the cookies this morning. Chocolate chip and walnut."

"They sound good." I placed the box beside me as I fixed my coffee. While I sure didn't need the caffeine, the warmth would help me shake off the chill.

He waited until I sipped my coffee before he said, "Sheila told me you have questions, but can't get any straight answers."

Hugging the coffee mug, I sighed. "Am I breaching some kind of protocol by asking? All I've asked for is the truth, then I got these. Now I have even more questions."

"There's no protocol breach that I know of," he said, then indicated the box. "May I?"

I opened it to let him examine the photos. "Why didn't you tell me who you were the night of the fire?"

"When Bebe came up with this crazy plan to get you here, I didn't want to go along with it. I tried to contact Ingrid, but she refused to speak to me. Perry brushed me off saying you'd never come."

"Did you give Bebe your approval?" I asked, reaching for a cookie.

"Nope." He chuckled. "Mom was one headstrong woman who wasn't one to take no for an answer. She did it anyway."

"That explains why Foster was perturbed."

"Foster's always perturbed," he said with a chuckle. "My dad built Thistlewood to give her a place to host guests. He would've been happier with something smaller."

The cookie was amazing. I'd have to ask Sheila for her recipe. "Did they plan to run a bed and breakfast when they built it?"

Ken sipped his coffee. "Your Grandpa Jack built it so Bebe could have what she wanted most. The whole family under one roof. Kids, grandkids, everyone could be one big happy family."

While he sifted through the photos, he told stories about us kids playing in the water, tinkering in the garage with Perry, and climbing trees while everyone else built Thistlewood.

"I was here while it was being built?" I asked.

"This little tomboy is you. Owen and Roxie taught you how to walk out in the backyard."

"This is the first time I've ever seen baby pictures of me," I told him. "Mom said she'd lost them. If everything was so good and happy, why did you move to your own place and change your last name?"

My question caught him off guard. He held the photo of Perry, my mom, my sister, and me then met my gaze. "Our big, happy family fell apart."

"How come?"

Ken handed me the photo of me in the hospital bed. "We all had meetings and appointments that day. Jack stayed home to watch you and Owen. We have no idea how the fire broke out or what happened, but the three of you were the only ones home."

"Then there was a fire." The girl in the photo held a pink teddy bear. Owen's story about half-priced chocolate and a pink teddy bear came back in a rush. Didn't Sharpe say Owen's stories mirrored the truth?

"We guessed Jack was hit by falling timbers and died instantly. You and Owen ended up in medically induced comas. You were five. He was ten. You both had multiple broken bones, severe burns, and severe head injuries and withdrew into your own worlds. We pieced together what we could."

Ken frowned. "Your mom snuck you out of the hospital while Perry was at work. She grabbed a few of your things and left without a word."

"In a big black car." More of Owen's words came back to haunt me.

"Exactly." He crossed the room and returned with a framed photo.

Owen and I lay on a hospital bed with our arms around each other. Both bald. Our skin rippled from burns. My weird scars and bumps looked far worse in the photo than they did now. My left arm was in a full cast from shoulder to fingertips. Bandages peeked out around the neckline of my hospital gown.

"That was the first time you saw each other after the fire," he whispered. His voice crackled with emotion.

"I don't remember." I touched the glass that protected my cousin and me from the rest of the world.

"It was my fault you left," Ken said. "After the accident, Perry became even more reckless. He went to Alberta to escape. I told your mom we needed to have an intervention. That you and Owen needed a safe, stable environment."

I closed my eyes. "Rather than getting help, she cleaned out their bank accounts and took us to Toronto."

"I told her she needed to make a better life for you girls." Ken rubbed his jaw. "I didn't want her to run away with you, just to find a way to help support you all instead of..." He paused and met my gaze. "Not being there."

"Was she drinking then?" I asked.

"She was trying to cope."

"Why did you change your name? Were you ashamed of my father's behavior?"

He placed the photos, including the framed one of Owen and me, back in the box before he reached for another cookie. "Alison, I'm ten years older than Perry. We only lived together for a few years before I moved out. I didn't really take an interest in him until he graduated from high school and became a firefighter."

"Why was that?" I took another cookie as well. The blend of chocolate and walnut was comforting, which was one thing I sorely needed.

"By then, I'd become a carpenter as well as a volunteer firefighter," Ken told me. He took out his wallet to show me another photo. He and Perry dressed in full turnout gear with one arm across each other's shoulders. "We finally had something in common. Then we had families."

"Why did you change your name from Beyer to Archer?" I went to sip my coffee but realized it was already cold.

Ken frowned. "Perry was always the apple of Jack's eye. Even when we were kids, Dad and I fought. He reminded me every chance he got that everything I had was because of him."

"Kind of sounds like my mom. She's so proud of Roxie but hates that I remind her of Perry."

"I get that," he said. "Things got worse when your dad became a fire jumper and a pilot with a gorgeous wife and two precious little girls. Perry was living Jack's dream. Ingrid wanted a place of her own. So did Sheila and I."

"That must have upset Bebe."

Ken nodded. "She wanted everyone to get along, but I couldn't stand living there. The day I moved out, Jack disowned me. Sheila and Owen were always welcome. It made Christmas kind of awkward."

I bowed my head and let it all sink in. "Wow. I'll bet."

"Bebe forced Jack to divide their estate, so Perry and I would stay close. This bed and breakfast is my inheritance. Your dad kept you guys at Thistlewood because of his job. By then, he'd earned his pilot's license and flew charter flights when he wasn't fighting fires."

"Where did the name Archer come from?"

"It's my mom's maiden name," Ken said.

As we went through the photos in the box one more time, Ken told me even more stories about growing up in Cedar Grove. Christmases and Easters as well as camping trips.

Finally, I stared at that framed photo of us in the hospital once more. "Mac took me to see Perry."

"Yeah, I heard about the plane crash. I'm glad you're both okay. I'd be a mess if we'd lost you a second time."

"Thanks." I started to feel at ease enough to say, "Perry said he's signing his share of Thistlewood over to me and Roxie. He doesn't want anything to do with the place. Frankly, neither does Roxie."

"Plus, he hopes you'll stick around to make Jack and Bebe proud. That's something neither of us could do."

I bit my lip. "I hope I'm doing the right thing."

"A.J., whatever you chose to do will be the right thing. If you return to Toronto, we'll make arrangements to look after Thistlewood."

"That's what Foster said." I hugged my arms around my belly. "Speaking of arrangements. What about Bebe's funeral?"

He rubbed his jaw. "That's a sore spot right now. She wanted to be cremated and scattered with Jack. Perry wants to wait until Roxie can join us, but the town wants some kind of memorial before then. I'll let you know."

"If I decide to stay, I..."

This time Ken's smile seemed to light up the room. "Then I will personally teach you everything I know and will help any way I can. Owen will be thrilled to have his cousin back and I..." His eyes watered. "I've missed you, kiddo. There was never a dull moment with you around. I actually missed finding snakes and turtles in the bathtub after you left."

"Thank you." I couldn't stop the tears.

My uncle handed me a napkin, then pulled me into a bone-crushing hug. "I wish I could help figure out what happened to the three of you that day. All we could do was guess. There are things you need to discover, so you can heal."

I dabbed at my eyes. "I'd be grateful for your help. There's no way I can do everything by myself. I might even ask my friend Emily to come help for a while."

"You're family, A.J.," he said as he kissed the top of my head. "Just ask."

After I had a good cry and nearly soaked his sweater, Ken directed me to the washroom. I splashed my face with cold water and caught my breath before I returned to his office.

"Sheila and Teena read both your books after Bebe gushed about you coming," Ken said as he walked me to the door. "I hear she wanted to pick your brain about working on her memoirs."

"Sheila did?"

"Bebe."

"Her memoirs? That's interesting." I pulled on my gloves. "I didn't find any notes in her room."

He chuckled. "I'm surprised Anna let you set foot in Bebe's room let alone go through her things."

"She had no choice. Since I'm one of her heirs, I decided to take care of her things. I have most of them in boxes, except clothes. I figured someone might need those. At the time, I didn't know who to talk to."

"Fair enough," he said. "Just don't forget you have family."

"I won't. Thank you. I'm grateful for that, even if I don't remember any of you."

Ken handed me a business card. "If you need anything, here's my cell number. Call me. And if you want to find out more about your injuries, stop by the hospital. Maybe they can give you copies of any records before they shipped you both to Victoria. You might want to call the hospital in Victoria too while you're at it."

"That's a good idea. Thanks."

"Would you like a ride?" he asked. "Teena can keep an eye on things while I take you back to Thistlewood."

"That's okay. I need to walk." I braced myself against the cold and set out down the driveway.

Even the writer in me could never have imagined the weird family dynamic that had emerged since I'd arrived. Jack disinherited Ken, but why wasn't he named in Bebe's will? If he discovered she left him out, did he kill his own mother? He didn't seem like the kind.

I hugged the box to my chest. As far as figuring out what happened to me and Owen, I was a small step closer. I also had a new reason to search through Bebe's paperwork. Any notes she'd made for a memoir might give me more clues.

Was that why someone kept searching my room?

The front door of Thistlewood was locked. Anna didn't seem to be home. Neither did Owen. That gave me an opportunity to test the second key in the door down the hall. I was on full alert while I crept up the stairs. Anna seemed overly protective of that room, or at least something inside of it. Her concern could be sentimental, but what if she knew about Bebe's rumored manuscript? Would it be reason enough to want her dead?

I dug into my bag for the keys, then grabbed my phone. I tried the first key while my heart raced. Wrong one. I took a deep breath and glanced over my shoulder, then slid in the second key. The lock gave a soft click. I swallowed hard and opened the door.

The stifling scent of stale smoke hit me. Whatever Sal was doing in there, he hadn't cleaned up.

Ash still covered the floors and furniture. Soot darkened the walls, yet there seemed to be no damage aside from the furniture. As Sharpe said, it was like someone didn't want to cause structural damage.

I skirted around the mound of burned items in the middle of the room and searched all the obvious places first. The few dresser drawers still in place; night tables, and closets were all fair game. Nothing.

When I was a kid, I had a diary that Roxie would search for just to see what I was hiding. It became a game. I'd hide my diary. She'd find it. Eventually, I discovered three great hiding spots that she never discovered.

One was under the loose carpet near my closet door. Bebe and Jack's suite had hardwood flooring. While I could search for a loose board, I went with my second idea first. I walked around the room and tried to jiggle all the air vents, hoping to find a loose one. Most were screwed into the floor securely.

I stared out the window near the bed and turned to check for a loose ceiling panel. The bed was far enough from the wall that I saw an air-intake vent at mattress height.

A blackened dime lay on the floor. I used it as a makeshift screwdriver to take out the screws, then gently pulled off the vent cover.

Jackpot.

Chapter Twenty

A journal hid inside the vent. Unfortunately, it was blank except for the names Alison, Roxanna, and Madeline. Nothing but a dead end and a new suspect. Who was Madeline?

With no other leads, I took my uncle's advice. I grabbed my laptop bag and took a walk to the hospital a half hour walk away. The woman at the information desk was helpful enough to tell me that I needed to contact the medical records department, which closed at four. With a request in writing.

"Here's a form," she said. "Come back tomorrow."

Helpful, but I doubted they'd do a rush job.

In need of a break from all the chaos of my real life, I returned to Thistlewood and brought my coat to my room. I locked my bedroom door and headed down to the great room to write in front of the fireplace. I brought Bebe's journal with me while I tried to figure out who to ask about Madeline.

A book lay open on one chair. A thriller. Anna's, I guessed.

I curled up on one of the wing-backed chairs. In need of a distraction, I pulled out my notebook, then closed my eyes to think. I'd left my characters in limbo in an awkward situation. The hero was trying to rescue the heroine after the villain tied her to the outside of a balcony railing fifteen floors up. My stubborn heroine insisted on getting herself out of the bad situation without his help.

Boy, did that sound familiar.

I had to call Roxie to fill her in on everything I'd discovered. My mom had answers she didn't seem to be in a hurry to share. I needed to fix that.

So much for focusing on my book. I pulled out Bebe's journal and released a deep sigh.

"Sounds like someone's got writer's block." Mac said, making me gasp as I jumped. He held two paper cups in front of him. "I have just the cure."

"I didn't hear you come in."

"I followed Anna home. She's making dinner," he said. "Thought you could use hot chocolate with whipped cream, that may or may not be melted into oblivion."

"Thank you. What have you been up to all day?" I asked, taking one of the cups.

He moved Anna's book to the chess board and sat. "Work. Sleep. Explaining to two dozen people who hold my career in their hands why I took off in a small plane when a storm was imminent and endangered both me and my passenger. What about you?"

My mouth fell open. "Back up. They said you endangered both you and your passenger's lives? Interesting. You do realize that you put me at far greater risk than I put you in."

"I suppose that's true."

"Does this mean we're even?"

He bowed his head and groaned, before he met my gaze. "Fine. Let's call it even. Would you like me to leave?"

"No, I need to fill you in on the latest." My chat with Sheila, receiving the photos, and meeting my uncle officially.

"Perry and I should have told you the truth." Mac met my gaze. "Did Ken give you the answers you wanted?"

"No, but apparently Bebe mentioned writing her memoirs. I searched her boxes again but haven't found anything."

"That's too bad," Mac said. "I'm sure any notes she had would help. I could ask my grandma. If anyone would know, it would be her."

The journal. I held it out to him and asked, "Would she also happen to know who Madeline is? Bebe wrote her name as well as me and Roxie's in this journal. They're the only things she wrote though."

He flipped through the book before he met my gaze. "My grandma's name is Madeline. She and Bebe were best friends for most of their lives."

I tapped my fingers on my notebook. "If I want to know more about Bebe, I guess she'd be the one to talk to. Ken told me Owen and I were injured the day Jack died. He doesn't know the whole story. Owen never told him, and I couldn't speak. Then my mom took us to Toronto."

"Did any of the pictures jog your memory?" he asked.

"No, but this was in the box." I handed him the photo of me in the hospital with the pink teddy bear that I'd stuck in my bag.

"Is that you?" he asked.

My eyes welled with tears. "Yeah."

"Oh, Sweets, you were in bad shape. Looks like second- or third-degree burns. Broken arm and collar bone. Possibly a bad concussion. You must've had a few plastic surgeries."

I met his gaze. "I'm going to the records department at the hospital tomorrow. Does it make sense that I don't remember the accident or having surgery?"

"If you had a brain injury, you could have amnesia. The brain does work in mysterious ways." Mac reached over to take my hand. "Were you sick as a kid?"

I gazed into the fire while he stroked a scar on the back of my hand with his thumb. "I had a couple of bad sunburns when I was little and ended up in the hospital. My skin was sore and raw, but other than that..."

"Maybe that's when you had plastic surgery."

"I would've remembered that."

"Not if you remember it as bad sunburns," he said.

"What are you doing here?" Owen asked behind us.

Mac and I both jumped. I pulled my hand away from his out of reflex.

"Enjoying the fire," I told Owen. "I got a chill earlier."

Mac shook his head. "Not you. Me."

"You? Why?" When I faced Owen, he was pale. "Are you okay?"

He frowned as he took a deep breath. "Mac was here the night Bebe died."

"Of course, he was here. He's a firefighter," I reminded him. "He was here to keep stupid people from running inside."

Owen shook his head. "Before that. After the power went out."

"He wasn't here. He was at the diner talking to Violet when I got there," I insisted. "Before that, he was hanging Christmas lights."

"She's right," Mac said. "You can ask Violet, Sal, and anyone else who helped, including the guys on my shift that night. They picked me up on the way."

"But I saw you." He insisted. "I even yelled your name. You stopped but didn't look at me."

Mac and I exchanged glances before he asked, "What was I wearing?"

"I saw you from the back. You left the garage and headed into the woods wearing a dark coat, a hat, and gloves."

I flinched. "He left the garage?"

"And went to the trail that goes into town." Owen was close to tears as he sat on the couch. "I saw you. I know it was you."

I sat beside him. "Maybe you saw someone who looked like Mac. It was cold that night. Everyone was bundled up."

Mac ran a hand through his hair. "You know I loved Bebe like my own grandma. I'd never hurt her."

I took my cousin's hand. "Mac carried Bebe out of the building. Why would he try to kill her, then rescue her?"

Owen flared his nostrils. "To look like a hero. He wouldn't have bothered if you didn't go get your computer."

"Good point," I told him. "But he couldn't be in two places at the same time."

Looking troubled, Mac cleared his throat. We needed to give my cousin some space. "Owen, do you want to play chess? Alison can work on her book down here while you and I hang out."

My cousin met my gaze before he gave a slow nod. "Okay."

Grabbing my notebook, laptop bag, and hot chocolate, I curled up on the end of the couch and tucked my feet beneath me.

While I made a brief outline of the next chapter I intended to write, I tuned out all talk of fishing. My eyes burned and fatigue caught up. I closed them until something Owen said caught my attention.

"Really? I didn't know you wanted to be a firefighter," Mac said, speaking my groggy thoughts. "I could help you."

"No." His voice rose an octave. "I used to. After the accident, I was afraid."

"What are you afraid of?"

"Fire," Owen whispered.

"Fire's a scary beast." Mac kept his voice low. "Sometimes I get scared, too."

"Alison wasn't afraid."

My breath stuck in my chest as my eyes welled with tears. I should never have run into Thistlewood that day.

"Afraid of what?" Mac cleared his throat. "You mean because she came all the way out here by herself?"

"No," Owen replied. "I mean the day Grandpa Jack died."

While I wanted to jump up and ask more questions, I didn't want to scare him. A tear rolled down my cheek as I listened, but my cousin had already clammed up after giving all the clues he was willing to share.

What was it he refused to speak out loud?

Chapter
Twenty-One

"*D*id you see that?" I was little, around five. My eyes wide. My heart pounded over the screams of the smoke alarms and the whoosh of the flames. No one would ever believe me.

"The house is on fire," Owen said, his voice already raspy from the smoke. "We need to get to the garden. Everyone will be looking for us."

I yanked my arm from his clutch. "He needs help."

"Who?"

"Grandpa Jack." I pointed to the prone figure on the floor near the kitchen. "He's hurt. We have to help."

My cousin peered over the railing then glanced behind us. "The stairs are on fire. Let's go out the window and get help."

"Daddy jumps out of planes into fires," I shouted. "If he can do it, so can I. We have to get Grandpa Jack outside."

I pulled myself to the top of the railing and stood on the six-inch wide beam like a gymnast. My pulse sped up as I wobbled. If I landed on the flowered couch, it would break my fall.

Owen peered over the railing. "It's too high. You'll die."

"Not if I bounce on the couch like a trampoline," I told him. "Are you coming?"

"Are you crazy?" His eyes were wild, and his breath came in gasps.

"We have to help Grandpa Jack."

As I reached down to him, there was a loud crack.

The entire earth seemed to give way. I plunged toward the burning foyer, trying to aim for the couch. Instead, I inhaled a lungful of thick smoke. The heat of flames singed my hair an instant before I heard a loud crunch. My tiny body was racked with searing pain. Everything went black.

I sat up, gasping for breath as I knocked my notebook off my legs and flailing my arms like I'd run into a spider web. My rocks skittered across the floor when my bag fell over.

Owen peered over the back of his chair with his eyes wide.

Mac leaped to his feet. "Alison, what's wrong?"

"I remembered," I whispered as my hands shook.

"What are you talking about?" Mac asked.

"Remembered what?" Owen scurried toward me.

"I saw them. Us." I let Mac help me back onto the couch. "Your stories. The ones you gave the sergeant to read. They're not just stories, are they? They happened to Grandpa Jack and Bebe, and us."

"Are you okay?" Mac placed a hand on my shoulder.

"Owen told me I used to live here and that something bad happened before we moved to Toronto."

Owen picked up my rocks and examined them. "And now you remember?"

"What you said about being afraid of fire." My entire body shook so hard my voice trembled. "I've been afraid of heights my whole life. Now I know why."

Mac led me to the chair he'd vacated near the crackling fire and helped me to sit. "I'll get you a drink, then you can tell us."

"She has hot chocolate." Owen rubbed my rocks with his thumbs.

"Something stronger than that," Mac said, as I hugged my arms around my trembling body.

He nodded. "Apple juice helps me."

"I was thinking alcohol."

"Ew. No, thank you." My cousin knelt in front of me to gaze into my face. "What did you remember?"

"The balcony railing broke. That's how we got hurt." My chin quivered. "We were playing on the third level when we heard arguing downstairs."

"Do you remember what was up there?" Owen asked.

"All I saw was the foyer below us."

"Drink up." Mac handed me a glass.

Just a whiff of the amber liquid nearly set my nostrils on fire. I coughed then took a sip. My mouth burned from the whiskey, making me gasp then gag.

"Told you apple juice was better," Owen said.

Mac rolled his eyes, then asked, "What did you remember?"

I closed my eyes and took a couple slow breaths. "Jack argued with a man in a long coat and a fedora. The man was mad. He hit Grandpa Jack over the head, and I saw him lying on the floor when the man lit the fire."

"That's it!" Owen shrieked, then covered his mouth.

We all glanced toward the kitchen hoping Anna hadn't heard that I was close to the truth, but I still only knew fragments.

Who was the man and why was he yelling at Grandpa Jack?

I took another small sip of whiskey. The burn in my throat was oddly comforting even if it made my eyes water.

"What else did you remember?" Mac crouched in front of me, placing his hand on mine.

I leaned back in the chair. "I didn't see the other man's face, but the way he moved seemed...familiar."

Owen blew out a breath. "I didn't see his face either. I just saw him take a lighter out of his pocket and set things on fire."

"Then he ran out the door," I added.

The corners of Owen's mouth drooped as if he were about to cry. "Whoever killed Grandpa Jack did the same to Bebe."

"And if somebody wants Thistlewood that badly, Perry and I might be next." Tears swarmed my eyes.

"It's not me," Mac said, shaking his head. "I hate cleaning."

Owen handed me the rocks. "Me, too."

"I need to figure out where the box of pictures came from." I started to get up, then paused. "Neither of my parents sent it. Anna has had access to all Bebe's photos. She also has a key to my room, Bebe's room, and the master suite."

"And my room," Owen whispered.

I touched his hand. If I was in danger, he was as well. "Bebe could've sent them before she died, but why bother when I was staying across the hall?"

"Unless she was drugged," Mac said. "But how could she be sure you'd be here to get them?"

"The tape recorder," Owen whispered.

Mac raised his eyebrows. "What tape recorder?"

I shifted in my chair. "Someone set an old tape recorder in the master suite to play Bebe's song. It scared me half to death one night. Owen and I thought her ghost came to haunt us."

"What did Sharpe say?" Mac asked.

"That he'd dust it for prints. Same with the shards I found in Bebe's garbage can buried in ash." I paused to make sure Anna wasn't in the room, then lowered my voice. "The first night I was here, Anna brought Bebe a nightcap. A glass of brandy, I think, but she told me it was tea. She also reminded Bebe to take her medication."

Mac grimaced. "That's not a good combination."

"Bebe didn't take medicine," Owen insisted. "Neither do I."

I met my cousin's gaze. He had no reason to lie, did he? "But there's a bottle of pills with Bebe's name on them in the kitchen, and Anna told me you've taken sleeping pills since the accident."

Owen flared his nostrils. "Never. I hate pills. They make me..."

"Looney as a ferret?" I asked.

He grinned. "Yeah."

Mac shot me a confused look, then blew out a breath. "It's possible Anna drugged Bebe before she started a fire in the garbage basket to get rid of her fingerprints."

"No, way. She wouldn't," Owen insisted.

"From what I hear, Bebe was scrappy," I told them. "If she caught on and threw the glass and the drugged brandy in the garbage, Anna would have to figure out how to stop her from telling anyone. I'll bet she burned the glass to get rid of evidence, then set the fire in the master suite and left. It would be easy to make it would look like there was an intruder."

Mac ran a hand through his hair. "Bebe had bruises around her neck. Do you think Anna did that?"

"Owen, Sergeant Sharpe said you gave him stories you wrote that sounded similar to what happened," I said, as I met my cousin's stunned gaze. "Can you tell us about the night Bebe died?"

He clamped his lips together, shook his head, and returned to their chess game.

I pushed past Mac then pinned Owen's shoulders to the brown leather chair with my face scant inches from his before I whispered, "Don't you care who killed Jack and Bebe?"

His chin quivered.

"Come on, Owen," Mac said. "You owe Bebe that much."

Owen wiped his eyes with the back of one hand. "The day Grandpa Jack died, the man with the hat came to the house with papers to sign. Me and Alison went up to the playroom, so they could talk."

"Papers?" I sucked in a sharp breath. "Was it Foster?"

While Owen wouldn't confirm my suspicion, his eye twitched. "Ali wanted to play fireman. We had a big box Bebe let us paint to look like a firetruck."

My eyes filled with tears. I'd wanted to be just like Perry. Was that why my mom was always so hard on me? "We painted it red and attached a short garden hose we used to fight pretend fires in Roxie's dollhouse. Then what?"

"The guy in the hat started yelling at Grandpa Jack. You went to look over the railing," he said.

Suddenly, I knew exactly what he'd say next. "The man hit Grandpa Jack with the horse statue from the table."

Owen's eyes grew wide. "Yeah. I never saw it after that."

A wave of dizziness hit me. "It was in the master suite when Anna showed me the day I arrived. I knew I'd seen it before. When I found the tape recorder, the statue was gone."

"Alison? Could you give me a hand in the kitchen?" Anna called.

We all jumped. Mac placed a protective hand on my lower back.

"I'll be right there," I replied as my hands started to shake again, then whispered, "Do you think she knows what we were talking about?"

Owen grabbed my hand. "Don't go, Ali. What if she's trying to get rid of us like she got rid of Bebe?"

"She'll be fine," Mac said as he removed his hand from my back. "All she has to do is scream."

"This will give me a good excuse to see if there's anything I missed." I patted Owen's shoulder, then met Mac's gaze.

"We should call Sergeant Sharpe," Owen said. "In case we need back up."

Mac grinned as he pulled out his phone. "Good idea."

While I was glad I'd remembered more about the night Jack died, I couldn't see Anna strangling Bebe. Or setting fire to Thistlewood after years of dedication.

Unless she thought she'd inherit the place since Roxie and I were gone and Perry didn't want it.

As I walked into the foyer, my breath escaped in a gush. On the table stood the horse statue. It wasn't there when I'd walked by earlier.

Suddenly, I wanted to vomit. What was going on?

My legs weakened as I rounded the corner into the kitchen.

Anna stood at the far counter with her back to me. Even though she was shorter than Mac, she had roughly the same build. Wearing a heavy parka on a gloomy day, she could've passed for him at a distance.

"What would you like me to do?" I asked, my voice crackling.

She glanced over her shoulder. "Oh, dear. You sound like you're getting sick. Who won the chess game?"

A pot of potatoes boiled over and hissed on the hot stove. I jumped and clutched my chest.

Anna turned to face me. "You need to cut back on coffee. You're awfully jumpy. I made some herbal tea. Let me pour you a cup."

Herbal tea wasn't going to help. The sight of the horse sculpture shook me. If she made a sudden move, I'd run like a wild stallion and wouldn't stop until I reached the RCMP station. Or Victoria airport.

"That horse statue." I hesitated. "Where did it come from?"

"It was covered in soot from the fire, so I had someone clean it," she said, pouring me a cup of tea. "They dropped it off earlier."

I stirred the potatoes then eased the heat a couple notches lower before I followed her back to the far counter. In front of her stood stacks of glittering white invitation cards. Exactly like the one I received from Foster on Bebe's behalf. Most were in boxes the same size and shape as the one I'd received the photos in.

Ignoring my own intuition, I sipped the tea. Sweet, as usual, but this time I welcomed the flavor as my anxiety heightened. Maybe my presence here wasn't Bebe's idea. What if someone convinced her to invite me?

"What are you doing?" I took another sip as I peered past her.

"Addressing the invitations for the McKittrick Christmas Ball," Anna said. "I've volunteered to send them the past three years ever since Mac's grandma had a stroke. We'll have a full house with guests from all over the country. This year will be extra special."

"Why's that?" I reached for an invitation.

Anna snatched it from my hand. "Could you check the chicken? It must be nearly ready."

"Sure." A little more relaxed, I took another sip of tea as I turned to the stove.

There was a wooden stamp behind the invitations.

She used it on the envelopes she'd addressed before setting it back in place. The base of the stamp was about two inches around with a three-inch long thick wooden handle. The plastic label around the edge of the base read, "Cedar Grove."

"You sent me the photos," I whispered, placing my cup on the counter.

"What?" Her entire body stiffened.

"That stamp. The same imprint was on the box of photos." If I still had the wrapper, I could confirm my suspicion, but it was police evidence.

"That stamp came from McKittrick house along with the invitations. Mac brought them over just now." She avoided my gaze as she scurried to turn off the oven and the stove burner. "The organizers insisted I use the vintage stamp."

"When did Mac bring everything here?" I took a step back and bumped into the counter with the invitations and the stamp. Was he playing me the whole time?

"A few minutes ago," she said. "That's why I asked for your help. I need to get things organized to mail out the invitations tomorrow."

My vision blurred as I gazed around the kitchen. The bottle of pills I thought I'd seen days ago sat next to the pot of herbal tea on the counter. "Was that Bebe's medication?"

Anna growled as she faced me. Her nostrils flared like an angry grizzly bear's. "You were supposed to leave after Bebe died. I was going to take over Thistlewood and get what I deserved. Instead, Perry signed the place over to you, not me. You're just as nosy as he always was."

Drugs in the tea. No wonder it was always so sweet. She'd been trying to kill me since I got here.

"You drugged Bebe, didn't you?" Reaching behind me, I felt around the cupboard for the stamp. Envelopes fell to the floor as I began to panic. "Foster finished the job and started the fire. It was him Owen saw leaving that day."

"You're half right. I didn't need Foster for that one, but no one will ever believe you." Anna wrapped her hands around my throat.

That one?

She was stronger than I expected. I couldn't even whisper let alone scream for help. I gurgled as her fingers dug into my flesh. Why didn't Mac come to check on me? Was he in on it too?

The front door opened as I fumbled with the wooden stamp. I prayed it was Sharpe's shoes that clicked across the foyer.

"Alison?" Mac called out from the great room.

"Help!" I croaked as my fingers found the handle. I wrapped my fingers around it and swung.

The rubber-coated end of the stamp connected with her temple. A black smudge colored the side of her face. Her grip loosened enough for me to shove her away and stumble toward the great room before I collided with a solid object.

Foster blocked my path. He held something raised above his head. Still no sign of Mac or Owen.

"You never should've accepted that offer," he said. His voice sounded exactly as I remembered from the day Grandpa Jack died. Low and threatening.

"You killed Grandpa Jack," I shouted. "I saw you."

His eyes narrowed. "You were a kid. What do you know?"

"I know you hit him with that statue and set fire to Thistlewood."

Before I could move, Anna grabbed me from behind as another set of hands wrenched the statue from Foster. When he spun around, someone punched him across the face. His head snapped to one side before he collided with me and Anna. We all tumbled to the ground in a heap.

"You okay, kiddo?"

I looked up at Perry before Anna shoved me off her. Wriggling out from beneath Foster, I started to get to my feet. Anna knocked me into the cupboards then dodged past us toward the front door.

"Stop her," I yelled. "She's Foster's accomplice."

Mac set the horse statue down before catching her in a bear hug. They wrestled in front of the door until he finally got her on the floor to kneel on her back. "Settle down. You're not going anywhere, lady."

"What are you doing here?" I asked, as Perry helped me to my feet. I closed my eyes against a wave of dizziness.

"Saving you from a couple of murderers." My father grabbed the collar of Foster's coat. "Sorry it took so long to put two and two together, especially after they blew up Mac's plane. Are you okay?"

"I think she drugged me with the tea in the pot. I only drank a little, but it was enough to make me groggy."

Before he could take a look, the front door flew open, and Sharpe walked in waving a piece of paper. Everything and everyone seemed to stop at once.

"Huh." He stared. "It would appear I'm right on time."

Perry walked Foster toward the officers who came in behind Sharpe. "I hope you have enough room to give these two a lift."

Sharpe grinned. "I also have some cheap accommodation for them. I tried to call earlier, Alison. Anna's fingerprints were all over that wrapper you gave me."

Anna snorted. "Of course they were. I handed it to her when she came downstairs."

"On the inside," he said. "I know for a fact you were nowhere near her between the time she opened the package to when I took the wrapping to the station."

Foster huffed. "I'm a lawyer. I'll be out on bail before you close the cell door."

Anna flashed a grin. "And since he's my lawyer, I'll be out with him."

"Funny you should say that." Sharpe waved the paper. "This is a search warrant for Thistlewood Manor. We've executed similar ones at both your office and your home, Mr. Foster. Is there anything else you'd like to say, or would you like to make an attempt at remaining silent?"

"What are you searching for?" Foster asked.

"Documents, medications, you name it."

Foster scowled at me. "I told Bebe bringing the girl here was a bad idea. If only you'd left like you were supposed to."

"After you murdered her, you mean." Sharpe, wearing gloves, reached for the horse statue.

I went to the kitchen for the stamp, careful to pick it up with a towel. "The statue was used to kill Jack Beyer. The rubber stamp is the one Anna used on that package. I hit her in the face with it when she attacked me."

"That explains the black smudge." Sharpe grinned, then asked, "Were those for the McKittrick invitations?"

"How did you know?"

"Looks like you have one more job to do. Make sure those get sent this week."

"Me?" I asked.

Mac chuckled. "Don't worry. I'll help."

"Where's Owen?" I asked. "I need to thank him for unlocking those last few memories." I glanced down the hallway wondering why he hadn't joined us after all the commotion.

Mac shrugged. "He was still by the chessboard when I came out here."

Perry stepped aside as Sharpe and his men handcuffed both Foster and Anna, then walked with them out to the squad car.

Mac and I watched from the doorway to make sure they were both secured.

"I hope dinner's ready," Owen said behind us. "I'm starving."

Chapter Twenty-Two

We didn't let the chicken and trimmings go to waste. Sharpe took dinner to go so he could process his suspects. The rest of us ate with the promise we'd give our statements later.

After dinner, Owen and Mac laughed while they did dishes.

I stared at my father over the chess set while we sat by the fire. "What are you doing here? I thought you were never coming back to Cedar Grove."

"Violet texted to warn me you were asking questions," he said. "She had a hunch about Foster when she saw him follow you a couple times. We were worried you might be in serious trouble."

"Who me?" I squirmed in the wing-backed chair.

"I know. What were we thinking?" He chuckled. "When I took a close look at the wreckage of Mac's plane, the first thing I thought was that it looked like a bomb went off. The salvage crew and I found proof that someone tried to kill you. It was an explosion from the inside that blew out the fuselage and took off a wing. They were after you. Mac would've been collateral damage."

I grew light-headed. "But no one knew we were going to see you. I had no idea until right before we left Thistlewood."

Perry nodded. "Did you mention anything to Anna?"

"No, but she was constantly eavesdropping." I closed my eyes. "Maybe she paid someone at the airport."

"That was when I asked Violet and Sal to keep an eye on you."

"Sal? But you told me to watch out for him."

"I know. Bad move. After we spoke, I found out he had a solid alibi and I didn't want anything to happen until I got back here." He reached for my hand. "I sent Sharpe pictures of the wreckage and the feds packaged up the fragments we found of the bomb."

I raised my eyebrows. "Wow. Sounds like you're in the wrong line of work, Detective Beyer."

"Who knows? Maybe I'll try my hand at mystery writing," he said. "It would be a nice change of pace from carving rocks."

"Speaking of." I ran upstairs to my room and returned with the signed copy of my novel. "Bebe wanted you to have this."

Perry studied the cover then my autograph inside. He flipped the pages until he reached my photo on the back "You really wrote this?"

"Yes." My heart raced as I winced.

He scratched the stubble on his cheek. "And you expect me to read a romance novel."

My face burned. "What you do with it is up to you. Bebe wanted you to have a copy. She even tracked me down in Toronto to sign it."

"You do know a part of me wished she hadn't found you," Perry said as he met my gaze. "I could've sold this place, then everyone would've left me in peace. You could've lived happily ever after without knowing anything about Thistlewood or the fire, or Jack's death."

I stared at my book cover. "True, but Jack and Bebe's killers would be free, and your life might've been in danger. If it wasn't for me, they could've swindled Thistlewood from Bebe, and no one would ever know."

"True." Perry nodded.

"And I never would've met you." My eyes filled with tears as my throat tightened. "We could still sell the place. I could get a job with Violet at the diner and find somewhere else to live."

"It doesn't matter what I want. You and Roxie own Thistlewood, not me." He fell silent for nearly a full minute. "You still want to stay in Cedar Grove after everything that's happened?"

"I like it here. It's a great place to think and write. Besides, with Anna going to jail, someone has to take care of the manor. I called my friend Emily to see if she'd like to take a sabbatical from work to help. She's an amazing cook."

He frowned. "What about your sister? Will she ever come here?"

"Funny you should ask," I told him. "Roxie had a long talk with Mom and her fiancé. She's coming with Emily. She wants to check things out and maybe stick around for the McKittrick party. You'll finally get to see her again."

"I'd like that. I haven't had Christmas with my girls in twenty years." He paused, then smirked. "Do you still play with dolls?"

"No." I laughed.

Perry flipped through the pages of my novel again and asked, "How many books have you written?"

"I've published two. That's my first and I'm working on the third."

"Impressive." He tapped the front of the book, then stood. "Guess I need to get home and get started."

"On what?" I tilted my head.

"Reading." Perry waved the book. My book. "Something tells me there are a lot more stories coming, and I need to keep up. Just like the old days."

I got up to give him a hug. "Maybe I'll host a book launch at Thistlewood when it releases. Would you come?"

"Anything's possible," he said. "Send me an invitation. Any chance you might write a mystery?"

"Anything's possible."

Just like that, one of the loopholes in my life was sorted out. I had my father back in my life.

Now if I could only figure out how to fix the plot holes in my novel.

Want to know what happens to Alison next and learn about upcoming books?

Sign up for my newsletter at: https://substack.com/@dianebator

About the Author

Diane Bator began writing as a kid when she fell in love with story-telling. After ten years with various traditional publishers, she's created her own company, Escape With a Writer Publishing to relaunch her previous work plus many new titles. She is also a member of Sisters in Crime, Crime Writers of Canada, The Writers Union of Canada, and International Thriller Writers.

A proud mom of three, Diane is also a Reiki Master, a blue belt in goju-ryu karate, and an artist who loves stopping at odd places on road trips.

She is represented by Creative Edge Publicity. Her website is https://dianebator.ca/ Join her newsletter and Escape With a Writer!

Manufactured by Amazon.ca
Bolton, ON